Second Chance Succubus

Capitol of Second Chances, Book 1

Siobhan Muir

ISBN: 1-947221-05-1
ISBN-13: 978-1-947221-05-5

DEDICATION

Dedicated to the ladies in the Las Vegas Romance Writers of America, specifically Shannan Albright, Natascha Jaffa, CR Moss, Kristina Mull, Jessica Cline, and Anita Boyer. If it weren't for you, I'd never have gotten this one started..

ACKNOWLEDGMENTS

Writing a book is never really a one person job. Keeping track of details is so much easier when you have help. Not only does it take a great deal of hard work, editing, and research on the part of the author to get things correct, but without my compatriots, there'd be a lot more mistakes. Great thanks go to Silver James who made sure the typo bugs weren't too big and my police procedures made sense. Any mistakes made are all my own. Thanks to Tom Keller for fixing some of the logistical issues with dead body placement, and Shannan Albright for long term knowledge of Las Vegas. Thanks to Lissa Matthews for making me study the whys behind each of the characters' needs. Thank you to Kallypso Masters and Ekatarina Sayanova, and all the folks in the Master's Playroom group for their knowledge and expertise of the BDSM lifestyle, and their willingness to answer my questions. Y'all have taught me so much. Thanks to E. Drew for catching my copy and line edits, and to Cara Michaels and Kris Norris for designing the cover art.

CHAPTER ONE

Drip, drip, drip.

The soft patter of liquid against a hard surface echoed in the silent room. A muted glow from recessed lighting barely touched the growing pool on the floor below the hanging silhouette. The soft hum filtered through the quiet space as the air conditioning units clicked on and the silent form swayed gently, twisting until the light illuminated the face.

Eyes wide and glassy, horror marked the slack features stretched around a ball gag. The arms had been bound behind the back, pressing the torso forward against the bands of the confining cage in which the body hung. Wicked slash marks strafed the exposed portions of skin on the legs between the cage bands in jagged cuts. The genitals remained untouched and slack against the great, crimson swath painting the inner thighs down to the ankles.

The soft pattering continued, each scarlet drop from the heels increasing the spreading stain.

Another body lay against the base of one concrete wall, the ribs rising and falling with life. Dressed in black leather thigh-high boots with stiletto heels and a brocade corset, the woman rested face down like an abandoned ragdoll.

The tools of her trade lay strewn about the room as if someone had swept them off their perch in a toddler's tantrum. Paddles of different sizes sat scattered over a flogger and a metal chain with small, rubber clamps on the ends. Several other ball gags decorated the floor as if a juggler had dropped his toys in haste.

The cage holding the body slowly turned in the morbid light and the subtle dripping continued with brutal repetition.

****

Nik Wolffe smelled her long before he saw her. The human woman wore enough perfume to make up the entire perfume counter at Macy's, and he held his breath, praying to anyone listening that she'd pass his office on another errand. His hopes crashed and burned as a feminine silhouette paused before the clouded glass then the handle swept toward the floor and the door opened.

The woman looked to be in her early forties with a few silver strands in her mousy brown hair gathered in a neat ponytail at the base of her neck. Her faded blue eyes darted around the room as she courteously closed the door behind her with a soft click. When she saw Nik she grimaced and rubbed the gold cross at her throat as if to gather her courage.

"May I help you?"

"Are you Nik Wolffe, Private Investigator?" Her voice held worry and fatigue.

"Yes, ma'am."

"Your ad on Google said you could find anyone in Las Vegas."

Nik nodded. "Yes, ma'am."

She bit her bottom lip and settled herself gingerly in the chair across from his desk. He wished he'd thought to turn the ceiling fan off before she came in. Her *Eau de Macy's* wafted in repeated swaths across his senses with each pass of the faux wooden blades.

When she didn't say more, Nik leaned his elbows on his desk and tried to smile through the stench.

"Why don't we start with your name?"

"Why don't we start with whether or not you can find who I'm looking for?"

The strength of her response surprised him and he cracked a grin. "Yes, ma'am. Who are you looking for?"

"My husband."

Nik raised his eyebrows. "Okay. What is your husband's name?"

"Richard Johnson." As he took a breath to say something, she added tersely, "Yes, I know it's a common name. But he was here with the Nebraska Tractor Consortium conference at the Desert Oasis Casino and he should have been home three days ago. No one has seen or heard from him since Thursday evening."

Nik's gaze rested on the little wooden desk calendar, five rotating blocks carved with the day, month, and date. Monday, February 10th. He glanced back at the determined woman.

"That seems a bit quick for you to be here, Mrs. Johnson. It takes twenty-four hours to file a missing person."

"Yes, and it has been *three days*, Mr. Wolffe."

"Why didn't you go to the police first?"

"I did. They told me I had to wait." She raised her chin in challenge. "I came to find my husband when he wouldn't answer my texts or calls. He *never* goes this long without contacting me. Something is wrong. I can only assume it's this cesspool of sin." She wrapped her hand around her gold cross and squeezed until her knuckles turned white.

Nik kept his voice level. "So you thought you should come here to look for him?"

"I want to be here when he's found."

What if he doesn't want to be found? Guys often came to Vegas to escape life at home. *He's probably here for his mistress.*

"Where was he when you last heard from Mr. Johnson?" Nik pulled out his tablet and light pen to take notes.

"At his hotel. He said he was going out that night, but he'd be back in time to catch his flight out early the next morning." Nik heard genuine concern in her voice. "He never made his flight."

"And he's staying at the Desert Oasis?"

"Yes."

Nik wrote notes directly into his tablet with his stylus. "Did he have any friends or associates he saw regularly that might have been with him either at the conference or wherever he went that night?"

"He knew a lot of them. They were on his sales team." She frowned and rubbed her hands together. "He was closest with Paul Hemmings, my brother. He was here at the conference with Richard."

"Have you heard from Mr. Hemmings since the end of the trip?"

"Yes. My sister-in-law said he returned home as scheduled."

"Did he say anything about your husband's whereabouts?"

"No. They had different flights."

Nik wondered if Mr. Johnson had a gambling habit and went off the grid to hide it from his wife. "Did your husband gamble?"

"Oh no, never." She shook her head emphatically. "He was never interested in that. He never visited any of the casinos here or at home."

"How often did he come here?"

"Twice a year. This was his first of this year. It's their annual convention and they always come here." She grimaced and glanced down at her hands. "He comes a second time to meet face to face with his Nevada clients. He's very hands-on."

Might have mistress or gambling problem. Check contacts in the casinos, Nik wrote.

"What about a mistress?" When Mrs. Johnson drew back like he'd slapped her, he added, "I'm just trying to be thorough, ma'am. Is there a possibility he had another woman?"

"No." Her lips compressed so tightly the skin around them turned white. "Richard was happy and we never had any...sexual problems."

Nik nodded, but her scent conveyed her doubt. *Poor woman. The bastard probably was playing on the side if he kept coming back twice a year.*

"Okay. Here's how this works. The price is two thousand for time and expenses simply to locate and snap a few pictures." Nik pulled out a standard contract. "If at such time as I find him, you want more intensive surveillance, we'll renegotiate for costs. Does that a sound fair?"

Mrs. Johnson heaved a sigh. "Yes, Mr. Wolffe."

"Good. Initial here and here, and sign and date at the bottom."

The scratch of the pen seemed loud in the silent room, but the woman's scent pulled back a little from fear and tension. *She must think finding her husband is a done deal with the signature.* That hadn't been his experience, but he wouldn't rush to judgment just yet.

"Thank you, Mrs. Johnson." Nik separated the copies for her to keep. "How would you like to pay? Cash or credit card?"

The woman grimaced, but fished out her wallet. "I'd like this to be a cash transaction."

Nik nodded. That was often the case in his business. Most folks didn't want a record of their visit. "Would you like a receipt?"

"No, the contract is sufficient."

After Nik took the cash, he took down all the information she had on her husband's trip. Hotel, known associates, friends, favorite locations around Las Vegas. Richard Johnson seemed like a fairly ordinary guy. *According to his wife.* He held back a grimace. Most of the men he trailed hid everything they could from their wives.

"Well, Mrs. Johnson, I truly hope this two grand is a waste of your money."

"What do you mean by that, Mr. Wolffe?"

"I hope we find your husband doing nothing more than getting lost on a binge in some casino or stumbling in drunk to his hotel instead of something more sinister."

Her expression hardened. "For his sake, I do, too, Mr. Wolffe."

Aw hell. Maybe he did come here for relief from this woman.

Mrs. Johnson retreated out his door and Nik surveyed his notes, wondering where this story would go. *Hopefully, this guy just got a little lost and he'll be home soon.* But something about the case made Nik's gut tighten and his nose twitch.

Time to make some phone calls and start tracking the guy down. *Goddess, I hope he's not still in bed with his mistress.*

CHAPTER TWO

Las Vegas had the nickname of the Capitol of Second Chances, but this guy wouldn't get one tonight.

"No doubt it's a murder."

Detective Chayse Wolffe looked up from his notes at the owner of the voice and tried to shove away his disgust. *What was your first clue, genius?* The uniformed cop grimaced at the dead body and crossed himself.

"We'll know after we study the forensic evidence." Chayse turned back to his work.

The body of the middle aged man sat slumped against the dirty alley wall just outside the Hump & Bump strip club. At first glance, he looked like he'd fallen asleep after too much alcohol during a strip tease. But upon closer inspection, Chayse noted ligature marks on his wrists below his shirt cuffs and an odd set of bruises on either side of his mouth. *Looks like you've been gagged, my dead friend.*

"What've we got, Wolffe?" Chayse's boss, Maxine Peterson, tossed her fiery red mane over one shoulder as she stopped beside him.

"One dead white male, I'd say mid-forties, and smells like he took a bath in coconut suntan oil."

"Name?"

"Richard William Johnson, according to his Nebraska driver's license. And all his money and credit cards were in his wallet. Homeless guy took it off him, but surrendered it as soon as we arrived."

"So, not a robbery, then." Peterson tilted her head to get a better look at the victim's face. "Are those bruises on his mouth?"

"Looks like."

She crouched and lifted a cuff with her gloved finger, exposing the marks on one wrist. "Looks like Mr. Johnson got himself all tied up with nowhere to go."

"Yes, it does." Chayse tipped the man's head to the side. "The marks go all the way around his cheeks. I'd guess he was gagged at one point."

"Tortured?"

Chayse frowned as he scanned the pale body. *All the blood is gone from this guy.* "I don't know. Hard to tell. We'll have to give him to the Medical Examiner to find out. But here's what's weird. He's got these marks on him and he looks like he's lost a lot of blood, but his clothes are clean and there's no blood here."

"So he was killed somewhere else and dumped here." Maxine sighed and shot a look at the lurid neon flashing in the entry to the alley. "Tourists. I still can't figure out why they would come to this kind of place for a good time. Takes all kinds, I guess."

Chayse nodded, but caught sight of something sticking out of the jacket pocket. He pulled it free with his gloved hand. The glow of the neon lights highlighted a paper napkin with the silhouette of a woman hidden behind two large fig leaves posed beneath the words "Eve's Paradise."

"I think we might be farther afield than we thought, Lieutenant." He held up the napkin. "Mr. Johnson may have been visiting a couple of different places tonight."

Maxine groaned. "Great. I'll get Michaels and Patterson

to check out the Hump & Bump. You and Jamison go visit Eve's Paradise, and we'll see who gets lucky tonight."

"Will do. I'll finish up here at the scene and head over there." Chayse threw his head back and inhaled. The scents of urine, stale alcohol, and vomit perfumed the air of the alley, but no blood. *So not brought from somewhere close.*

"What are you doing, Wolffe?" Maxine raised her eyebrows. He'd forgotten she didn't often come out to the crime scenes anymore.

"Taking in the scents of the scene. Do you see or smell any blood?"

She spun slowly in a circle. "No. But we knew he was dumped here."

"Yeah, but he doesn't even smell like alcohol, just the usual rot. Bet he's been here about three days or so given the stench and bloating. The ME will have to confirm, but I suspect this guy was sober when he was killed." Chayse looked at the pallid skin on the corpse's neck. *No bite marks so not vampires this time. Thank the Goddess.* Covering up Elder Race murders was a pain in the ass. "There's no visible exit wound for his blood loss, but maybe the autopsy will give us a clue about it." He rose and scanned the napkin in his hand. "I'm done here. I'll head over to Eve's Paradise and see what kinds of things I can sniff out."

Maxine nodded. "All right." She waved to the ME patiently waiting to collect the body while the other crime scene techs gathered up the evidence bags and headed for the truck. "I'll go back with the evidence and get the team started. God, I hate being out here in the trenches." She wrinkled her nose and shuddered. "I prefer the lab and the evidence on a clean table."

Chayse chuckled. "Yeah, I remember that feeling when I switched over from CSI tech to detective. It ain't pretty out here, boss."

"No. Humans are disgusting."

He laughed. *You have no idea.* "Yes they are."

"Who found the body?"

"Homeless guy going through the trash. With the days warming up, no one noticed the extra flies buzzing around."

Maxine turned a little green. "Dear God. All right, has anyone talked to him?"

"Yeah, Jamison took his statement. He protested up one side and down the other he didn't kill the poor bastard, though he had gone through his pockets searching for money. That's how we got the wallet."

She shrugged. "Other than the ID, the dead guy isn't gonna use the cash." Maxine had a rare pragmatic streak when it came to the dead.

"Yep. I figure the cash might go missing before it reaches the evidence locker tonight."

"How much was there?"

"Seventy-five dollars."

"Yeah, I can see how that might be misplaced." She also had a soft spot for the disenfranchised, having been a runaway back in the day. "You know what? Why don't you let me take care of the cash."

"Yes, ma'am."

"Good. Let me know how it goes with the Eve's Paradise proprietor. She's smart and wily, but usually pretty fair."

"You've met her?" Chayse raised an eyebrow.

Maxine shook her head. "No, just her assistant. But she helped with the breakup of that underground reverse sex ring with the infamous Madame LeBeau. Lady Aislynn gave us tips on where to find the LeBeau's underlings around the Strip."

That had been a huge operation for the LVMPD and the undercover cop who'd brought a victim out alive. A Navy SEAL as he recalled. It was before Chayse's time with Metro, but they were still talking about it. The cop had since retired and moved away.

"Right. I'll keep that in mind."

"Good. See you back at the lab when you're done."

"Yes, ma'am." He watched Maxine saunter away from the corner of his eye as he took an extra picture of the dead man with his phone. *Don't worry, Mr. Johnson, we'll find your killer and remind him that what happens in Vegas follows you everywhere.* And didn't Chayse just know it.

He shoved the unsettling thoughts away as he waved to his partner. Solving murders helped him focus on the now rather than the past, and the past was better left alone. But something in his gut warned him he might be facing it sooner than he'd hoped.

CHAPTER THREE

It didn't take long for Nik to find out from the concierge of the Desert Oasis Hotel and Casino which haunts Mr. Johnson frequented most. The Desert Oasis always hosted the NMC conference bi-annually and Johnson was a favorite of the staff. He apparently tipped well and always strove to be flexible and relaxed when visiting.

"He was a big fan of visiting Eve's Paradise Strip Club, which I told the police when they came looking for him." The older woman behind the counter gave Nik a saucy wink. "Went there every night he stayed in Vegas."

Guess they finally took Mrs. Johnson's advice to look into her husband's location.

Nik nodded. "And did he ever check out of the hotel?"

"Let me check." She tapped the keys on the console. "Yes. Someone checked him out on Friday and made sure the bill was paid. There were some items left in his room when housekeeping came through that afternoon, but Mr. Johnson wasn't there."

"What did you do with these items?"

"They're currently being stored in the hotel's lost & found. Why?"

"Can you please hold them for a Mrs. Louise Johnson? I'll contact her to collect them."

"Oh, of course." She wrote a note and tapped at the computer. "There, all done. Is there anything else I can do for you today, Mr. Wolffe?" She smiled a coy smile and dipped her chin playfully. "If you're headed to Eve's, maybe I could meet you there after my shift ends."

Nik raised his eyebrows and gave a non-committal smile. "Nope, that's all I need. And thanks for the offer, but when I'm on the clock, it's an all or nothing sort of thing. I appreciate the information, though." He patted the counter and headed for the doors.

"The offer still stands."

He waved as he sailed out of sight and shook his head. He doubted she'd like the kind of sex he went for, and he really didn't have an interest in starting anything romantic at the moment. *Too many memories of the last real relationship gone to hell.* Nik turned his mind to Eve's Paradise and his gut clenched. The strip club was a legal front to the Underground, a club catering to the more alternative types of love. He should know. He was a card-carrying member.

He tried to think if he'd ever seen the man Mrs. Johnson described come in, but he rarely stayed up in the public strip club while visiting. His attention always centered on the playrooms downstairs. Nik frowned as he climbed into his truck and pulled out of the parking garage. Had he seen Johnson down there? Could the man also be a member of the Underground?

Nothing came to mind as he drove the backstreets of Vegas toward Eve's. February in Vegas often sustained high winds, but this evening sat still and cool. He drove with his windows cracked and inhaled the cool night air. A heavy wetness flavored the city atmosphere, and the possibility of rain made him smile. All Vegas residents rejoiced when the sky opened up.

Nik parked his Chevy pickup outside of Eve's Paradise, one of the premier gentleman's clubs, and grimaced. The place was crawling with cops, which didn't bode well for his investigation. Personally, more than professionally. Not only was Eve's Paradise a cover for the Underground, the clandestine BDSM club, but if the cops had arrived, most likely so had his twin brother.

Fuck.

They hadn't spoken since Chayse severed their ties over a woman. Nik's rage had ebbed, but it simmered below the surface, and he didn't want it erupting during an investigation. He grabbed his tablet and keys, and locked the truck. *I'm following leads, that's why I'm here. No one else needs to know my familiarity with the place.* Especially not his brother.

He zipped up his leather jacket against the cool February night and headed for the entrance. He passed the flashing lights of three cop cars and scanned the officers. *All this for a traffic stop?* The guy seated in the back argued about the legality of his actions.

"Hey, Wolffe, what're you doing here?"

Nik paused and gave a one-shouldered shrug. "Investigating a lead. What you got there, Hendricks?"

"Sex bust. Guy claims he didn't know she was under-aged or that Vegas doesn't allow prostitution within Clark County." The uniform shook his head. "That damn 'what happens in Vegas' line again."

Nik grimaced. "Yeah, they think it won't matter here. Good luck."

"Yeah, you too. Detective Wolffe is inside. You on the same case again?"

Nik shrugged again as his gut sank. "Dunno. I guess I'll find out. Thanks, Hendricks."

The cop waved and went back to his partner while Nik headed for the entrance to the Eve's. He had the keys to the kingdom, but he hesitated to enter while his brother shared the space.

Ah, let it go. It's been five years. Get over it already.

He swung the door open and stepped inside, allowing the odd calm to settle over him. The proprietor, Lady Aislynn, had some sort of sound machine working in the club to make the attendees feel at ease as soon as they entered. His superior hearing caught it every time he walked in, but he never pinpointed the source.

The energy had shifted tonight with the presence of his brother and his partner Jamison talking to the proprietor's assistant, Felicia. Tension sang along with ripples of sexual interest and the even the dancers on stage seemed nervous. Nik shrugged it away and scanned the room for any other cops, but only the two investigators were visible. Felicia gestured toward a door at the end of the bar, and Nik took a step in their direction before something else caught his attention.

Scent of blood?

Nik swung his gaze back toward the dancers, but the blood scent faded. Damn the air conditioning. The current in the room made pinpointing the smell difficult. He'd smelled blood in the Underground, but not up here in the main portion of the strip club. *Did Felicia over-imbibe?* Though the lovely woman's main source of sustenance came from the human patrons, she'd never smelled like blood so strongly before.

Nik strode toward his brother and the other cop, but when the scent of blood hit his nose again, he diverted to chase after it. A few other patrons nodded toward him as he moved through, the minute dip of a chin to acknowledge his presence. He was known to a select few as Master Canin in the Underground, but tonight he had to keep that persona under wraps.

Waiting until the cops had disappeared through the door to the upstairs office, Nik tried to ferret out why there'd be so much blood scent in the air up here in the club. He knew some folks really enjoyed the impact and knife play in the playrooms downstairs, but the scent had never been so pronounced. All his instincts screamed a warning as he slipped through the Underground door and down the steps.

Fuck, how much blood did one of the Masters spill tonight?

No one else appeared in the hallways as the lights on motion detectors lit his way. He worked his way toward the more extreme playrooms. The blood scent disappeared abruptly and the sting of a strong cleanser burned his nose. Nik coughed and paused, his eyes watering with the strength of the cleaning solution.

Holy shit, what the hell is going on?

The solvent didn't come from the playrooms where he expected to find it and he continued through the hallways aligned like the fingers of a Buddha's Hand fruit. *Too bad it doesn't smell like one. I could really go for some lemon zest right now.* Nik wiped his eyes as he closed in on one of the dungeon-like rooms where some clients preferred to be bound or whipped. Even when the Masters broke skin with their toys, they didn't need so much solvent to clean up afterward.

The overpowering stench of astringent wafted out of a dungeon with authentic looking hewn stone walls. An Iron Maiden cage hung from the ceiling and a thick wooden table crouched against one wall. Everything reeked of cleanser, but the strongest concentration sat in the middle of the floor below the cage.

Nik scanned the bars in the dim light from recessed bulbs, but it showed no sanguinary discoloration. Despite the cleanliness of the room, Nik grimaced. Someone had bled a lot in this room. Enough to probably die from it. *Shit, has there been a murder in the Underground?*

He bet no one had told Metro, but if his brother was smart, he'd catch the scent of blood and solvent. Nik backed out of the room and firmly closed the door before wiping the handle down with a bandana. The last thing he needed was his brother figuring out he'd been there. Chayse used his nose as well as his training to see more than the average detective and he'd scent Nik.

Which means he's gonna know my proclivities real quick.

Nik retraced his steps toward the gentleman's club as quickly as he could. He needed to speak to Felicia and find out what had happened. He suspected he wouldn't like the news. And if his brother was here, it would get complicated real fast.

CHAPTER FOUR

She's lying.

Chayse met the serene gaze of the vampire in front of him and tried not to choke on the stench of her deception. They'd tracked Richard William Johnson to Eve's Paradise through the concierge of his hotel and the scent of blood permeated the whole room. It was subtle close to the door, but increased in intensity as Felicia Amberhall met them at the bar.

His partner Jamison didn't seem to notice, but he was human and wouldn't have any idea the woman speaking to them used his species for sustenance.

Felicia must have sensed Chayse's disbelief because she raised her chin and smiled. "As I said before, Detectives, I can confirm Mr. Johnson was here with a friend from seven-thirty to nine-thirty, but after that I have no knowledge of where he went or what happened to him."

The fetid untruth made him want to wrinkle his nose, but Chayse had no way to get her to say differently with his human partner standing so close.

"What happened at nine-thirty?" Jamison didn't sound convinced, either.

"I had my mistress to attend to. She was feeling

poorly."

That rang true and Chayse briefly wondered what had afflicted the owner of the club. "We'd like to speak with Lady Aislynn as soon as it's convenient."

"Of course. I will be sure to give her your message." That at least was the truth.

Chayse dug out one of his cards just before the scent of his twin brother hit his nose. His gaze swung around the lavish club, a mixture of anger, fear, and guilt suffusing his chest. *It's been five years and I did it to protect him. Let it go.* But the ache for what he'd lost still burned his heart.

Nik's darker visage appeared at the end of the bar, moving their way. Though they shared nearly the same face, Nik stood two inches taller and had dark hair to Chayse's blond. He was also fifteen minutes older, but those minutes meant little now that they'd reached their late forties.

"Hey, Wolffe, isn't that your brother?" Jamison nudged Chayse's shoulder.

"Yeah, it is."

Felicia inhaled as she turned to note Nik's approach then shot a look at Chayse, one elegant eyebrow lifting. *Thanks a lot, Jamison.*

"Detective Wolffe." Nik's voice held wariness. "Detective Jamison."

"Nik."

Jamison nodded and raised an eyebrow at Chayse's less than enthusiastic greeting. Nik didn't bat an eye, but his scent shifted toward irritation. *Right back atcha, buddy.*

"What are you doing here, Nik?" Chayse didn't need his brother sticking his nose into police business, especially in a place like this.

"I'm here on a case, but I need to talk to you about it after I speak with Felicia. You got some time?"

Chayse didn't want to give his brother time, not when it would likely bring up all the old hurts. But with two other people standing there and listening, he'd look like an asshole if he blew Nik off.

"Yeah, I got some time. How's tomorrow morning?" He glanced down at his watch. "Or rather, later this morning? I got nothing on my schedule until the afternoon."

Nik nodded, some of the tension leaving his body. "Sounds good. I'll send you a text to nail down a time."

"Right." Chayse focused back on the vampire. "Thank you for your cooperation, Ms. Amberhall. Please have Lady Aislynn contact me as soon as possible."

"Of course, Detective." Felicia gave him a blank smile that said precisely nothing, but her gaze slanted to Nik and one delicate eyebrow twitched.

Chayse closed his notebook and nodded as he and Jamison headed out of the strip club. Goddess, he hated the energy in the place. *It's because of her.* He wouldn't name the demon in the room, but he'd keep an eye on things. And he'd do what he could to save Nik from it. Again.

****

"What the hell happened, Felicia?" Nik followed the vampire across the club floor to the offices behind the bar.

"To what are you referring, Master Canin?"

The use of his Underground club name didn't faze Nik in the least as he crossed his arms over his chest. He'd often used his size and mass to intimidate people into telling him what he wanted to know, but this time it was defensive. Felicia was a Domme in her own right, and men didn't frighten her.

"I mean the stench of blood and strong cleaner in the Underground and the presence of the police in Eve's."

Felicia put on her stoic mask, one she'd perfected over the centuries, he suspected, and removed her robe. Under it she wore a small red lacy baby doll that hid very little and disguised nothing.

Nik didn't allow his gaze to drop even while his dick screamed, *But it's red lingerie, right there, where you can touch it.* Women had used the tactic on men for millennia and he wasn't falling for it.

"There has been an incident in the Underground. It's been taken care of, and Lady Aislynn is aware. The police are merely following up." Felicia dipped her head and raised an eyebrow. "What's your interest in it, Master Canin?"

"This wouldn't have to do with the disappearance of Richard Johnson from Nebraska, would it?"

Both eyebrows went up. "What do you know of him?"

"Only that he came to Eve's a couple of nights ago and never made it home." He shrugged one shoulder. "His wife showed up in my office and hired me to find him."

She scanned him with her cool gaze, her face a stoic mask. "Why do you think I'd know about him?"

Nik dropped his chin and stared at her from under lowered brows. "Come on, Felicia. Give me a little credit as an investigator. I tracked him here and you're already twitchy about him. Where is he?"

She sighed, but the mask didn't slip. "In the city morgue."

Nik blinked. "Where?"

"The morgue, Master Canin. Richard Johnson is dead." She scowled. "Exsanguination. Such a waste."

Only a vampire would think of exsanguination as a waste. Nik went over the timeline in his head. "How do you know how he died?"

"Because I found the body. In the Underground."

That must be where all the blood I smelled came from. "He was killed here?"

Felicia nodded, sitting in the chair behind the desk. "I cleaned up the mess, dressed the body, and dumped it in the alley at the Hump & Bump. We can't have cops in the

Underground, Master Canin. You know this."

"Yeah, I also know you can't let a murderer get away with this because what's to stop him from doing again?" Nik scowled. "Where was the body when you found it?"

"In a cage suspended from the ceiling."

"Chewed bones." He shook his head. "We gotta find the perp, Felicia. Talk to Lady Aislynn and get her take on it. I suggest you let Detective Wolffe back in here to investigate."

"But he's a cop."

"He's also one of the Elder Races and knows how to keep a secret. Let him take a look at the original crime scene and he'll catch the bastard."

Felicia tilted her head, her expression thoughtful. "You have a lot of faith in Detective Wolffe, Master Canin."

Nik snorted. "I should. He's my brother."

"That isn't always enough, trust me." She shook her head and the corners of her mouth dropped. "Family doesn't always play fair."

Nik nodded. "True, but I know Chayse. He might be a dick in other ways, but betraying the Elder Races isn't his thing. His beef lies with something else. Give me a day and I'll find out more. In the meantime, talk to Lady Aislynn. We'll both have questions for her."

CHAPTER FIVE

The predawn sky appeared like a dappled blanket overhead as Nik trotted up a ridge line above Red Rock Canyon in his Brother form. The air tasted cold and wintery, a rarity in the Mojave Desert, but a welcome one before the heat settled over the valley in a suffocating haze. Snow still coated the upper heights and he wondered if more would come this year. *Goddess knows we need it.*

Chayse had told him to meet him on the canyon rim, just beyond the choice climbing spot. While it was a haven for rock climbers in the summer, the winter snows often closed the wall down and few humans ventured so far back into the park this time of year.

Nike wound his way through the scrub and boulders dotting the jagged spires surrounding the park, choosing one of the hiking trails to save his paws. The snow lay thick in the shadowed areas, but some of the open spots had melted. A sound carried across the silent rocks and he froze, listening hard.

Nik lifted his muzzle and sniffed the wind. The scents of sweat, unwashed human, and garlic perfumed the breeze and he sneezed. *Campers in Red Rock at this time of year? Hardy souls.* The latest snowstorm had dropped a good two feet, but he rounded the bend and found a tent nestled in one of the few cleared flat spots. He crept closer, listening hard.

An unearthly glow showed over the next ridge as the moon edged toward the sky and the cold air made it seem brighter than usual despite the light pollution from the city. *Gotta love the lights of Vegas.*

Rhythmic grunts alerted him long before he closed in on the campsite. The scent of sex hit his nose along with the previous odors and he shivered. What he'd give to have someone willing to fuck him out on a cold, clear morning. He yipped in apology for disturbing them and padded away, grinning.

The tent stilled and someone whispered, "Did you hear that?"

Nik held back his bark of laughter as he headed up higher in the park.

****

Chayse trotted through the underbrush above Red Rock Canyon, enjoying the brisk spring air. Gentle dawn sunshine gilded the rocks and scrub pines around him, but the shadows remained cool beneath the overhanging bows.

A newly torn branch leaning against a tree caught his eye. He paused, dropping his muzzle to the ground at the base to investigate. *Once a CSI always a CSI.* Not that this was a crime scene, but he always learned something new by seemingly innocuous artifacts left behind by someone's actions.

A warning *wuff* brought Chayse's head up, his ears flagging forward. A pair of green wolfish eyes met his own. Nik.

:Hello, Brother,: he growled. *:I'm here. What did you want to talk about?:*

:Good to see you, too.: Nik cocked his head to one side,

his tail lowered in neutrality. *:I didn't think you ran in the woods any more, little brother. Glad I was wrong about that.:*

Chayse felt his lips pulled back from his teeth. *:Just because I like city life doesn't mean I've forgotten my true self,* brother.:

Nik didn't sneer, but his expression filled with disdain. *:Could've fooled me. You've managed to forget you had a brother.:*

:I haven't forgotten, I just don't need to hang out with you.:

:You mean, share.: Nik shifted his weight onto his hindquarters and Chayse tensed. *:What the hell happened to you? You graduated from the Academy and suddenly you're too good for your 'twisted' brother?:*

:I never called you twisted, Nik.: Chayse growled, sidling to keep from presenting a large target to the other wolf.

:You didn't have to. It was implicit in your decisions to run from your needs.:

Anger built in Chayse's heart. Why did he have to defend his decision to anyone, most of all his twin? He eyed his brother's stance. Nik looked relaxed and nonchalant, but their connection wasn't so diminished that Chayse couldn't feel his preparation.

:I didn't run from anything.: Chayse flattened his ears.

:You ran from everything, *and you owe me years!:*

Nik leapt, his canines flashing in the sunlight as he slammed into Chayse. Chayse snarled and rolled, stepping on the broken branch in his bid for freedom. He snapped at his older brother and Nik twisted away, but Chayse's claws raked down his flank, Nik yelped.

:I'm not going to argue this with you again!: Chayse kept pace with Nik as they circled over the fragrant ground covered in ponderosa pine needles. *:I made my decision for my own reasons.:*

:You stopped sharing because of a job!: Nik lunged, snapping just short of Chayse's shoulder. *:You did it to please 'the man', not because it was something you wanted.:* Nik rushed him again, slamming his shoulder into Chayse's side and knocking him into the underbrush.

Chayse grunted and rolled, but Nik pounced and struck at his exposed throat. Chayse met Nik's jaws with his own, snarling as he warded off the attack. He shoved his hind feet into his brother's belly and threw him off, writhing out from under him.

:That's not why I stopped sharing, Nik. It wasn't the job.:

:Bullshit!: But Nik didn't stand with his usual confidence.

They faced off, panting as they eyed each other. Chayse didn't want to argue with his twin, but his reasons for changing his sexual lifestyle stemmed from protecting his brother from a deadly addiction. He'd explained it as the need to fit in with the police force after he graduated from the Academy, but the reality had been much darker. Now, looking at the hollow expression Nik's face, regret stung almost as deeply as his need to protect.

Admit it, you feel the loss of Nik, too, his Brother wolf remarked, urging Chayse to reunite with the other half of his soul.

Groaning, Chayse shook his head hard as if to silence the heartfelt voice. He didn't want to listen to his heart. He didn't want to hear the ringing truth in it. *It's too dangerous to let him in again.*

:Listen, Chayse. We have to work together on this case, even if we come at it from different sides.: Nik dipped his head a little; not enough to be submissive, but to offer a temporary truce. *:There's something I need to tell you about the strip club. It's more than just the pretty girls and boys dancing on stage.:*

Chayse cocked his head to once side. *:Is it*

prostitution?.:

Nik shook his head. *:No. Something else.:* He flattened his ears and sat down. Chayse tilted his head in surprise. *:There's an underground club, a special place for people who have alternate needs and pleasures. People who like sharing and...other things.:*

:Other things?.:

Nik whined. *:BDSM. Bondage, Dominance, stuff like that.:*

Chayse flattened his own ears. *:How do you know about all that?.:*

Nik sighed and scanned the woods around them. *:Because I'm a Dominant in Lady Aislynn's Underground club.:*

Chayse's rump hit the ground hard. *:What? How did that happen?.:*

:How do you think it happened, jackass? You left, remember? You disappeared and cut yourself off from me. Your twin!: Nik snarled and his ruff stood up. *:Did you think I wouldn't notice? Did you think I wouldn't try to find a way to fill the hole in my life, my world?.:*

Chayse dropped his head, glancing away from his angry brother. *:So, do you like hitting people and pain, and stuff?.:*

Nik growled. *:Not everyone in the lifestyle is a masochist, Chayse. Dominance isn't always about pain no matter what the media tells you.:*

:And you just sort of fell into this after...after I left?.:

:Yes and no.: Nik's ears came back up. *:I did kinda fall into it, but then I trained under another Dom before I took on a sub of my own.:*

:Wait, wait. You trained? They have classes for this sort of thing?.: Chayse shook his head.

:Of course they do. You have to learn how to do this right or people can get hurt or sued.:

:And you have a submissive?.:

Nik shook his head. *:No, I trained submissives for a*

while, but never collared anyone.:

:Collared? As in "dog collar?".: Chayse snorted and his tongue lolled in a canine grin. *:Even for Moon Singers, that's kinda sick.:*

:No more sick than cutting yourself off from your twin for no other reason than your job couldn't handle your sexual tastes.: Nik bared his teeth. *:That makes us even.:*

Chayse glanced away again. *:It wasn't the job that made me change.:*

:You tried to sell that before, but I'm not buyin'.: Nik's shoulders dropped and his tail lowered. *:Just tell me why, Chayse.:*

:To protect you, brother.:

Nik coughed. *:Protect me? From what?:*

:From Celine.: Even her name tasted like rotting shit on Chayse's tongue. Cold fear and nausea churned in his belly from just her memory. *:Leaving you was the only way to keep her from feeding off your life essence and killing you. Just like this Lady Aislynn at Eve's Paradise.:* Anger surged and he coughed out his disgust. *Eve's paradise, my fuzzy ass. More like Eve's Parasite.*

Nik tilted his head with disbelief. *:What are you talking about?:*

:The proprietor, Lady Aislynn. You know she's not human, right?:

Nik snorted with derision. *:Yeah, I got that. I don't know what she is, but her energy is off the charts.:*

Chayse's ears flagged forward in surprise again. *:You don't know what she is?:*

:No. Do you?:

This was a first. Chayse rarely knew something his older twin didn't and he took a moment to savor the delicious novelty.

Nik growled. *:I know that look. Spill it, jackass!:*

Chayse grinned, his tongue lolling, and barked a laugh. *:Is this what it feels like to know something no one else* *does?:*

Nik added a snarl and snapped at Chayse.

:All right! Keep your fur on. She's a succubus.:

Nik yipped. *:She's a what?:*

:A succubus. You know, a female sex demon who feeds off the life energies of those she has sex with?:

His brother sat down hard, his face a mask of astonishment. *:I thought succubae were myths.:*

:No.: Chayse lost all his humor.

Nik's eyes narrowed. *:How do you know?:*

Chayse looked away, trying to stave off the memories of the one addiction to which he'd succumbed. He'd been living in Las Vegas, sharing lovers with his brother for years. But Celine had been preternaturally beautiful, and considering his werewolf heritage, that said something about her charms. He'd fallen for her and let her feed off him for a few months before he realized what he'd gotten into. It had taken everything in him and the help of a *Morukai* shaman to get him free of his addiction. From then on, Chayse had cataloged the scent of succubae until he could recognize it at a thousand paces.

:I'm not as 'squeaky clean' as you may think, big brother. The point is, watch your back around her. Don't get on her radar. It could kill you.:

Nik snorted his derision and shook his head.

Chayse bristled. *:I'm serious, Nik. Stay away from Lady Aislynn.:*

Outrage curled through Nik and he growled. *:Giving orders now, little brother? First you ran away to 'fit in', now you're telling me who I can be with?:*

:I'm trying to protect you, asshole. You don't know succubae like I do. They're deadly.:

Nik presented his ass to Chayse in disdain. *:So you said. How do you know?:*

:Because I was addicted to one. I was addicted to Celine. That's why I 'ran'.:

29

Nik snorted. *:Come on, you ran because Celine was a succubus?:*

Chayse bared his teeth, but his ribs expanded as he took a deep breath. *:Yes. She was. That's why I couldn't share her with you, Nik.:* Nik started to speak, but Chayse growled in the wolf equivalent of holding up a hand. *:I was too addicted to her to share and I would have turned on you to keep my fix to myself.:* He swung away and his tail clamped to his hindquarters in shame. *:In my lucid moments, I knew I had to keep her away from you so you wouldn't follow me down the dark spiral. But most of the time I was jealous of her attention to you, and so I had to take her away. For both our sakes.:*

:Why didn't you say anything, Chayse? I could've helped you—:

Chayse wheeled on him, his teeth bared in a snarl. *:No one could help me but a* Morukai *shaman! And it was a very near thing. You think I wanted to stay away?:*

:I don't know, Chayse.: Nik met his anger with his own. *:Since you stopped talking to me altogether, I had to guess.:*

:I did it to save you.:

:Oh yeah? What's your excuse now?:

Chayse sighed and dropped his gaze as well as his shoulders. *:I'm not completely well. I'm better, but I still have weaknesses. I don't want to infect you with any of it. I'm getting stronger, but I'm not to one hundred percent yet.:*

Nik snorted, but didn't press. *:Fine, then let's talk about the case.:*

:Fine. Just watch your back around Aislynn. She's not as harmless as she appears.:

Nik nodded, but Chayse didn't think his twin believed him. *:All I know is the murder in the club is bad for business and not something we want the human cops involved in.:*

:They're already involved because it was a human murder, Nik.:

:Are you lead investigator on it?:

Chayse nodded slowly. *:Yeah, why?:*

:Because I can convince Felicia and Lady Aislynn to let you into the Underground to do a complete investigation of the original crime scene. I don't think they'll let anyone else in.: Nik tilted his head and whined a little. *:But it means you have to go and talk to Aislynn about it. I told Felicia we'd both have questions for her, but if you want access, you have to come with me.:*

Chayse ground his teeth, but swallowed against the disgust trying to rise from his gut. *:When?:*

:I'll text you the time and meet you there.: Nik paused and wuffed the last of his disbelief. *:Is Aislynn really a succubus?:*

:Yeah, she really is. Watch your back around her.: Chayse hoped his brother would listen to his warning. *Because I don't know if I can save him again.*

:Will do. Talk to you later.: Nik took off toward the city.

Chayse nodded, but his gut still cramped at the idea of returning to the succubus's lair. *Maybe it won't be so bad with Nik there.* But something told him he was looking at a tarnished silver lining.

CHAPTER SIX

Nik met Chayse at the Fremont Street Precinct late the next morning and climbed into the passenger seat of Chayse's Chevy Volt. They might have had their differences over the years, but they still agreed on cars.

"Nice. When did you get this sleek beastie?" Nik caressed the creamy leather seats.

"A couple of years ago." Chayse pulled into traffic, heading for the 95.

"How many miles per gallon does it get?"

"When just on electric, it gets two hundred and fifty. When I use the gas engine, somewhere between forty-five and fifty."

Nik whistled. "Very nice. How long does it hold a charge?"

"About the first forty-five miles of driving."

The conversation sounded normal, but it had been so long since he and his twin just talked, the "safe" topic of cars put off the hard issues still plaguing them. Chayse wasn't sure he could ever be normal with his brother again, and his stomach threatened to rebel over the idea. *Get over yourself. It's been five years.* He didn't know if Nik wanted to fix the rift between them, but with another succubus in the mix, Chayse wasn't willing to take the chance.

They continued the inane conversation until he pulled into the Eve's Paradise parking lot and shut off the car. He stared at the front entrance, innocuous in its elegant art deco façade. The entrance had a reflective glass portico so VIPs could get out of their ride protected from sun or rain, but the rest of the building remained plain stucco. There were only a few other cars in the lot, but the club wouldn't open officially for another hour.

"Come on, let's get this over with," Chayse grumbled. He didn't want to return to the strip club again, but his brother insisted it was the only way they'd get any real answers.

They stepped out into the winter sunshine. The temperature remained warm despite the time of year and they strode across the lot under the portico before they started to sweat. They pulled open the sleek oak doors carved with sensuous women frescoes and stepped across the threshold, the cooler air of the club greeting them.

Nik pushed past him and stood for a moment to let his eyes adjust after the comparative brightness of the Las Vegas spring outside. Black and red streamers, stylized hearts in red and magenta, and brilliant red and white tinsel sprays festooned the walls of the club in a Valentine's Day display. Bouquets of tiny orange, pink, and yellow flowers perched on each table before the stage, and paper heart doilies sat beneath them.

Very festive. It should put the patrons in the right mood. Too bad he couldn't appreciate it.

"Beautifully done, Felicia. I'm pleased."

"Thank you, Mistress."

The voices weren't loud, but his werewolf hearing caught them anyway. His gaze strayed to the bar where Lady Aislynn stood in a long, narrow skirt slit nearly to her hip and surveyed the decorations in her domain like a reigning queen. Her dark hair hung straight down her back except where two mother-of-pearl clips held it to the sides of her head. A black and red corset with thick buckles bracketed her ribcage and pushed her breasts up into tempting, delicious mounds. Chayse's mouth watered before he could slam a lid on his addiction.

"Oh, marvelous." Felicia's expression hardened. "It's the cop and the PI I mentioned before."

"Are they?" The succubus tilted her head and her lips quirked into an amused smile.

"This is turning into the Nightmare Before Valentine's Day with the murder and all." The vampire set her clipboard down. "I'll take care of them, Mistress."

Aislynn held up one hand, surveying her prey, and Chayse locked his knees to keep from bolting back out the door.

"I'll speak with them. Please finish up preparations for tonight."

Felicia paused, eyeing Aislynn. "Yes, Mistress."

The succubus approached as the sounds of slender heels ripping at the carpeted floor reached Chayse's ears, and he fought to hold back a snarl.

Ten grand says she'll rip your heart out and bleed you dry.

"Welcome, gentlemen." Her voice spread a balm over every hurt in his soul, promising comfort and understanding, and he felt his brother's tension relax. *Fool.*

Chayse kept his eyes on her boobs to keep from being snared by her seductive gaze.

"What can I do for one of Metro's finest?"

"We have a few more questions about the crime committed in your establishment."

Chayse had never heard Nik speak so graciously. He glanced at his "rougher" brother and grimaced. The ignorant idiot was a goner already, wearing a dreamy expression.

"Of course. I want to help in any way I can. Why don't

you come to my office so we don't disturb the staff."

Nik followed after the sultry woman like a dog on a leash. Chayse just hoped the succubus wouldn't make a play for his brother. Because estranged or not, he'd protect Nik from her, even if it meant murder.

They followed her through a door beside the bar and up to a remarkably austere office overlooking the club. While the décor remained feminine, the room had been arranged with comfort and practicality in mind. An elegant, but simply constructed antique desk stood before a well-worn and comfortable leather armchair. The wall across from the bank of windows supported a plush couch with chenille throws on either arm where visitors could sit.

"Please, have a seat," the succubus offered as she retreated behind the desk.

Chayse sat in one of the straight-backed wooden chairs before the desk, studiously ignoring the female demon's eyes.

"Now, what would you like to know that hasn't already been asked?"

"Can you tell us where the body was actually found?" Nik asked. He leaned his elbows on his knees and Chayse scented his interest in the undoubtedly beautiful woman.

"We found the body in the lap dance room." She delivered her answer with ease, but Chayse scented something off about it. "We don't know how he died. We assume it was a heart attack."

Damn, she sounds so fucking reasonable.

Chayse snorted.

"Is there something funny, Mr...?" She trailed off, waiting for him to supply his name.

Not bloody likely, bitch.

"Detective Wolffe, ma'am. And no, I don't find anything funny when people lie to me."

"Easy," Nik muttered, but Chayse ignored him.

"What makes you assume I'm lying to you, Detective?"

35

"Three things, actually, Lady Aislynn." He tried to keep the growl out of his voice, but his animosity for her kind coupled with the lying stretched his patience thin. He raised his gaze to her chin. "First, he had fresh bruising all over his body that couldn't have come from one of the dancers with the whole "no touch" rule. Second, his thigh was severely mutilated by some sort of knife or weapon not usually kept in a strip club. And third, he'd been completely drained of blood from a puncture of his left femoral artery, but there was no blood on his clothes or the chair where he was found. That means he was moved."

Chayse crossed his arms over his chest. "So, do you want to change your statement, *Lady* Aislynn?"

Lady Aislynn regarded him silently for several heartbeats with a serene expression. *Damn, she'd make an awesome poker player.* He almost snorted. *I bet that's how she got the money to pay for her little* Paradise.

"You make the assumption that I would know anything about the body's condition. As I told the other detectives, my assistant found the body, and when I heard about it, it was dressed and left where you saw it."

"Did you know the victim?"

"Personally? No. But I'd seen him here before. He was a regular bi-annual visitor."

"You didn't know the victim, but you knew he was a regular?" Chayse scowled. "I find that hard to believe."

"What you believe or not isn't something I can control, Detective Wolffe. Even here in my demesne." Lady Aislynn wove her fingers together and rested her hands on her desk. "What I can tell you is he attended the club with another man on Thursday night and that's the last I saw of either of them."

"Another man? Who?" Nik leaned forward with interest.

"I don't know him. He's not a member of the Club, Mr. Wolffe. This was the first time I'd seen him on the premises." She gave his brother an earnest stare.

Something in her voice around the word 'club' made him glance at Nik. Chayse scented concern and unease from his brother, and suspicion grew in his gut.

"Do you have surveillance video of the public areas from that night?"

"Of course."

"We'll need to see any security footage from the last week."

"I'm afraid that's impossible, Detective."

Chayse shivered with her voice sliding over him. *Get out of my head, bitch!* "Why is that, Lady Aislynn?"

"Because this is a private establishment and several of the parties pay good money to be anonymous. I'm afraid you'll need a warrant."

Chayse's stomach curdled. "This is a murder investigation—"

"For which you have no crime scene and until you can prove it was here, I will not have my patrons exposed to slander and ridicule." Her face remained serene. "Come back when you have a warrant."

Nik grunted thoughtfully while Chayse seethed. *Secretive, evil wench.* "I can do this, but it will take time and your club will remain closed until you agree. So you could make this easier by just giving us the footage."

"That's an empty threat, Detective Wolffe, and we both know it." She gave him a disappointed look. "You have no crime scene on my premises and no legal reason to shut me down. Go get your warrant and you shall have your footage."

Chayse stared her down, trying to find a way to get around her logic, but his brother stood and extended his hand Lady Aislynn.

"Thanks for seeing us. We'll be back with that warrant." Nik held out his hand.

A lovely smile creased her lips and she gently took the

offering. "I'll be here."

"We know he was here, Lady Aislynn. You could be charged with obstructing justice." The growl rumbled in Chayse's voice.

"You know he was here, but it only means he enjoyed a show. Everything else is assumption and circumstantial. And you deal in facts, yes?"

Her unruffled demeanor set his blood on fire and he wanted to tear her throat out. Or lick the hell out of her. *Damn the succubus addiction.* Chayse nodded sharply.

"We'll be back with that warrant."

"Looking forward to it, Detective."

Yeah, I just bet you are. Chayse followed his brother out of Aislynn's office, swearing he'd get the best of her one day.

****

Aislynn exhaled in a rush as the angry cop left her club and rubbed her eyes with the heels of her hands. *Sweet Goddess, he's exhausting.* His rage had increased the closer he'd come to her and by the end of the interview, Aislynn thought he'd burst into flames. Exhaustion prowled the edges of her awareness and she leaned back in her chair, trying to recoup her losses. She'd have to feed again tonight to keep the fatigue at bay.

She reached for her phone and punched out a text to Felicia. *Bring me some Dragon Phoenix tea, please.* She set the phone down and sighed. She hadn't needed the special tea made from the phoenix flower soaked in dragon's tears for centuries. It had a helluva kick and provided much needed energy when fatigued. *I definitely need the boost after that meeting.*

Rising from her chair, Aislynn scanned Eve's Paradise from the windows overlooking the floor, but she didn't see it. Her mind filled with the images and energies of the two werewolves who'd visited her in search of the killer. Their signatures were similar, yet so different, like wine grapes grown in the same soil, but barreled in different wood casks.

Brothers. One calm, collected, and...kinky. She didn't know which kink yet, but she'd felt his energy in the Underground playrooms in the past. The other brother carried anger, belligerence, and hurt from some past incident. *Probably involving his brother if their exchange was anything to go by.*

But while Aislynn suspected Mr. Wolffe had been involved, something else familiar tainted the detective's energy. Something rancid and sinister. *Something like me.*

Felicia's entrance disturbed Aislynn's thoughts and she inhaled the medicinal scents of the tea as the vampire placed the pot and cups on the desk. Felicia deftly filled one of the cut crystal cups Aislynn had acquired from Imperial Russia and held it out.

"Thank you, Felicia."

"You're welcome, Lady Aislynn." Felicia stood back and tilted her head with a small frown. "Are you well?"

Aislynn sipped the tea and sighed as the magic of the liquid slid through her body, returning energy. "That's better."

"Did something happen between now and your last meeting?" Felicia hovered, her expression worried. Aislynn mustered a smile at her friend's concern.

"Nothing I haven't experienced before." Aislynn dropped her chin in consideration. "But if either of those werewolves return, please make sure we have this tea on hand. The crime scene investigator has a great deal of disrupting energy."

"Will do. He definitely has something eating at him."

"Yes, he did." Aislynn nodded.

Felicia's gaze went distant, and Aislynn wondered if she'd recognized a similar soul to her own.

Too bad I haven't found someone to take her mind off Taggart. Aislynn mentally waved the thoughts away. *That was a hundred and forty years ago. It'll work itself out.*

Aislynn sighed. "Speaking of which, tell me how you found Mr. Johnson again, and spare no details. I need to be prepared for when Detective Wolffe returns with his warrant."

Felicia sighed and sat down in one of the chairs across from Aislynn's desk. "I found Mr. Johnson hanging in the Iron Maiden cage in the Gothic dungeon at about eleven-forty-five Thursday night. Mistress Dee lay against the north wall, out cold from a blow to her head. A large pool of blood, roughly four feet in diameter and half an inch deep, covered the floor beneath the cage." Felicia scowled. "Such a waste."

Aislynn stifled a smile. Vampires tried not to squander their own energy source. "Go on."

"Mr. Johnson's spirit had long fled and his body was badly damaged, specifically his left thigh. Because of the damage, he'd bled out from the wounds in his leg, caused by something unsharp like a ball point pen." Felicia held up her hand with her index finger curled to her thumb to make a circle. "It had to be sharp enough to break the skin, but not sharp enough to cut cleanly. The murderer must have hit the artery. Mr. Johnson was dead in minutes." She shook her head in disgust. "I checked Mistress Dee and she came around soon after, about eleven-fifty. She said she'd been hit from behind and hadn't seen her assailant. I took her to rest in the after-care room and returned to the dungeon to clean up the mess."

"Did you touch the body?" Aislynn shuddered. Even as a succubus, dead shells gave her the creeps.

"Not at first. It was easier to hose down the walls and floor before I worked on the cage." Felicia's hands tightened into fists on the arms of the chair. "When I did move the cage, I wore my leather gloves and laid the body on the steel work table before washing the cage. I carefully cleaned and dressed Mr. Johnson before transporting him to the alley outside the Hump & Bump strip club down on Highland."

"And that's the last you saw of him?"

"Yes, Lady Aislynn. I returned here to the club around one and checked on Mistress Dee. I contacted one of her regular subs to come for her and resumed my duties supervising the Underground that night."

Aislynn sipped her tea and tapped the desk. "What of the man who'd been with Mr. Johnson in Eve's earlier?"

"He left around ten and I didn't see him again upstairs."

"Check the security footage in Eve's." Aislynn's anger surged and settled into a cold lump in her gut. Humans committing murder in her sanctuary and playground brought police and endangered her patrons. Not to mention the safety of the Elder Races who came to play in Vegas without fear of persecution from the humans. "I want to know how he came into Eve's and got anywhere near the door to the Underground between the hours of ten and midnight. Either we'll catch the bastard or we'll hand him over to the cops."

"Really? We'll let them take care of him?" Felicia raised her eyebrows in surprise.

Aislynn nodded. "The detective is a werewolf. He won't betray the other Elder Races who come here."

"Let's hope not."

"Right. Bring me the information as soon as you have it, Felicia. I don't want the cops to get into the Underground if I can help it, even with the discretion of Detective Wolffe." Aislynn grimaced. "But if anything shows up on digital capture, the police can have it and do their own hunting."

"And if they cannot find the murderer?"

"Then we'll have our own hunt." But she suspected the werewolves always got their man.

CHAPTER SEVEN

Nik stepped through the revolving door of the Desert Oasis Hotel and Casino on the Las Vegas Strip for the second time that week, bracing himself for the overwhelming scents of sweat and desperation. Despite the opulent interior and the peaceful décor, the constant chimes of the slot machines filled the air with insistent discordance. Nik usually avoided the big casinos on the Strip because the sounds and smells damn near drove him insane. *Thank the Goddess most of the people I investigate avoid them, too.*

Unfortunately, Richard Johnson of Nebraska had stayed in the Desert Oasis with his company for Nebraska Tractor Consortium conference along with his brother-in-law, Paul Hemmings. Because of the murder in the Underground, Nik needed far more information than he had the first time he came in. And according to Nik's buddy on the Desert Oasis's security staff, Dick and Paul had been seen together a lot in the last few days.

Sounds like a kids' book. See Dick die. Where was Paul, Dick?

Nik flashed his PI badge at the registration desk. "I'm here to meet Mr. Rufus McKinley for a security appointment."

"Just one moment. I'll call him up for you."

"Thanks."

Nik stood to the side as an obese couple bellied up to the desk, wheezing with exertion and excitement. Nik caught the scents of alcohol and rancid sexual release from the man, while the woman smelled of candy and avarice. *Gotta love Vegas.*

"Hey, Nik. How's it going?"

A tall man with lively green eyes and red hair cut short enough to be called stubble gave Nik a quick wave. Despite his size and his seriousness, the Leprechaun couldn't quite hide his perpetual merriment. Nik always loved the myth encouraged about Rufus's people. While Leprechauns were definitely secretive and merry, they came in all sizes and intelligence levels.

"Hi, Rufus. How's the rainbow rehabilitation going?"

"Shut up." The redhead grinned and grasped Nik's hand palm up, acknowledging Nik's alpha status among werewolves. "You're just jealous you haven't found yours yet."

McKinley's lilting accent still came through when amused. Or aroused. The Leprechaun didn't share Nik's proclivities for sharing, but he got a lot out of dominance and control. Especially by his lover, Master Mulroney. Mulroney stood only five-foot-eight, but his presence could fill a room and make Rufus appear diminutive.

"I'm working on it." Nik matched his grin and released the larger man. "You got the footage I asked for?"

"Yeah. Come on back to my lair."

Nik laughed as he followed the redheaded giant through the security doors and down a maze of beige corridors without any decorations. The "invisible" people walked these halls and made the whole illusion of the Strip possible. *Tourists never see the real world of Vegas.*

Another locked door with a security keypad opened to a

darkened room full of surveillance monitors and more security personnel. All were human and barely looked up when Rufus led Nik through to a smaller side room with banks for disk storage. A DVD player attached to another set of monitors and a keyboard sat to one side. Rufus closed the door and waved his hand over the knob. Green sparkles blinked in the air briefly, sealing the portal without the sound of locks engaging. *That kind of magic is definitely useful.*

"Okay, then. Which days would you like to see?"

Rufus sat down at the console and unlocked the computer as Nik flipped on his PDA, scrolling through the notes on the screen.

"According to his wife, Mr. Richard Johnson stayed in room 2115, and the front desk said he was last seen leaving the hotel around seven-fifteen last Thursday night." Nik crossed his arms over his chest. "Can you cue up the feed from the hallway outside his room starting around six-thirty? I want to see who he talked to and when he actually left."

"Righto."

Rufus skimmed his long-fingered hands over the keyboard and images zipped across the largest screen. Boring comings and goings of various guests cascaded in a pageant until the time counter in the corner read 18:30.

"Here we are. Six-thirty, Thursday, February sixth."

Nik focused on the screen. For the first ten minutes, no one approached the victim's door, though several other people passed on their way to the elevators. A pair of women in skimpy bikinis sauntered down the hall just before things got interesting. At 18:42 a silver-haired middle-aged man in a sharp charcoal gray suit knocked on Johnson's door. A second middle-aged man with a trimmer waistline than the first greeted his visitor with a friendly smile. They talked for five minutes before the man in gray walked to the room next door and entered.

"Do you have another angle from the other end of the corridor? I want to see his face."

"Let me see what I can find." Rufus clicked the keys like a virtuoso and soon another monitor lit up with the opposite view of the same hallway. "There you are."

"There go the women in bikinis...Ah, bingo." The man in gray paused to watch the women pass, his body language suggesting he found them repugnant. *So, he's disgusted with women, or just scantily clad women?*

The time stamp on the feed showed it around to dinnertime when most business folk got ready to relax, but the man's suit remained impeccable with the shirt buttoned and the tie knotted tight. Again, they watched him stop at Johnson's door and speak with the trimmer man. At the end, the visitor turned toward the camera and walked to the neighboring room, disappearing inside.

"What room number is that?"

"Uh, 2117, I think. Let me check." Rufus brought up a map of the hotel towers. "Yeah. 2117 is the next room on that side."

"Right. Can you go back to when we have a shot of his face and zoom in?"

"Yeah. Hold on."

The images reversed to time stamp 18:47 and the man's face came into view. Rufus manipulated the data and zoomed in until the face filled the screen.

"Can you give me a bust shot and print it?"

"To be sure."

"Great. Then let's see what happens after this."

The printer in the corner of the room hummed as it spit out a 5x7 photo of the man in the gray suit. Nik snagged it and tucked it into his jacket pocket, his gaze returning to the screens.

Both views showed the man in gray and Johnson leaving their rooms at 19:08 and heading for the elevators. Rufus cued up the lobby cams and found the pair as they sauntered to the concierge desk, talking. They paused there, engaging the staff about evening plans. After a few minutes, the two men left through the revolving doors at the time stamp of 19:16.

"Is that the last time we see them?" Nik made some notes in his PDA.

"See, that's the thing. Normally, I'd say yes, but after your request, I checked to see if they came back, and something sparked my recall." Rufus accessed the data for later in the evening. The time stamp jumped to 22:21. "Check this out."

The view showed the lobby and Johnson's neighbor walked in alone, his motions clipped as if anger rode him. He said nothing to anyone near him and made no other motions until he stepped off the elevator on his floor. Before he'd taken more than three steps, he slammed his fist into the wall beside the plastic potted palm. Everything in his body language showed fury. *What's his problem?*

The impact seemed to bring him back to himself and he jerked his clothes back into place. He rolled his shoulders and stalked down the hall to his room, letting himself inside.

"Wonder what set him off."

"Dunno." Rufus shook his head as he stopped the feed. "But something sure made him mad."

Nik frowned. "Did the camera catch Johnson returning at all that night?"

"No, not that I saw."

"Did you watch much more?"

"No, too much else kept me busy."

Nik nodded and leaned forward onto the desk beside Rufus. "Let's go forward to around ten-forty-five and see if anything more happens." Nik's Brother wolf sat up and sniffed the air, his instincts screaming. Something didn't feel right.

Rufus mumbled something about inquisitive

werewolves and cued the video. It played in monotonous regularity until 22:53 when Johnson's neighbor reappeared.

"There he is." Nik pointed at the screen.

"Hello there, boyo." Surprise filled Rufus's voice as he zoomed in on the door.

Instead of a suit, the man wore droopy jeans resembling overalls, a blue windbreaker, and a John Deere baseball cap. He walked directly to the elevators without looking anywhere but at his feet. Another guest waited with him, but he wore a distinct "leave-me-alone" vibe.

They followed the man through the hotel lobby, striding with his head down and his footsteps quick. His demeanor said man on a mission rather than on a sight-seeing trip to Vegas. He got into a taxi and disappeared from view.

"I'll bet that's the last we see of him." Rufus clicked the keys and swung the mouse to close the files.

"Wait. Let's keep going to see if he comes back."

"That guy? He's sneaking off to a brothel."

Nik sucked in his bottom lip. "Maybe. Just keep your eyes on the screen."

Rufus sighed, but let the lobby feed continue. They watched the repetitive images of the various guests in the casino floor and Nik scanned the faces and bodies for anything familiar. The crowds thinned just after the clock showed midnight and Nik almost missed Johnson's neighbor returning to the bank of elevators. He'd removed his windbreaker and ambled in with the swagger of a tourist.

"Wait. Go back. Isn't that him?"

Rufus scowled at the image as he reversed it a few seconds. "The hayseed? You sure? He doesn't have a coat and he's walking like he's just gotten laid."

Nik nodded while his Brother wolf growled. "Just look at the cams in the hallway outside Johnson's room."

The Leprechaun sighed and clicked the keys to the view of the hallway. After a few moments, the man in the overalls strode straight to the neighboring door. Everything about the man spoke of satisfaction and contentment. *Maybe I've got it wrong and he did go out to get laid.*

"Stop it right there." The man had looked toward the camera, but more than that, Nik spotted something dotting the legs of the overalls. "Can we get a closer look?"

"Yeah, let me just do something here."

Rufus enhanced the resolution on zoomed in closer. The dark spots looked almost black in the light of the corridor and the facial expression resolved into clarity. Relaxed satisfaction. Nik wished the video came with scents because he'd give much to know how the man smelled. *Think it was sex that gave him that look?*

"Oh, yeah." Rufus snorted, reading Nik's mind. "That guy got laid, all right."

"Maybe…Can I have a copy of that still?"

"Sure. I'll send it to the printer."

"Thanks."

"Just tell me one thing, Wolffe. What's this for, anyway?"

Nik shot him a dry look. "Investigation."

Rufus snorted as the printer hummed. "Yeah, but you never go this in depth for just one of your jobs. What's the big deal about this one?"

Nik tucked the photo into his pocket next to the other one as he gathered his thoughts. He could play it off as just a missing-persons case, but Rufus was a friend, and a member of the Underground. What happened there affected them all.

"It affects the Underground."

Rufus hissed a surprised breath and his eyes narrowed. "How?"

"Johnson and a companion were seen at Eve's Paradise, and I think this guy was the companion." Nik shook his head. "Either way, he's the last one who saw Johnson before he disappeared. And the Goddess knows, we don't want human cops getting downstairs."

"No, we don't." Rufus cleared the screens of Johnson's neighbor and then cleared the cache of their tracks in researching the files. "I'll keep this to myself. Let me know if there's anything else I can do to help protect the Underground."

"You wouldn't happen to know the registration info on the guy in room 2117, would you?"

"No, but I can get it with a little sweet talkin' persuasion, to be sure." Rufus winked as he turned on his Leprechaun charm.

"Good. Let me know ASAP. And thanks for these." Nik patted his pocket as Rufus waved over the doorknob.

"Not a problem, Nik. Let me know how things work out." Rufus showed him out of the security office.

"Will do." Nik headed for the exit and considered his options. Johnson lay in the morgue and the man in the overalls probably knew something about it. All they had to do was find him. *Time to talk to Chayse again.*

CHAPTER EIGHT

"Get your warrant yet?"

Chayse looked up to find his brother leaning against the lab doorway with a visitor's badge clipped to the lapel of his leather jacket.

"What are you doing here, Nik?" Chayse couldn't recall the last time his twin had darkened Metro's halls.

"Can't I visit my own family?"

"Not in the last few years."

Nik grimaced and shoved his hands into his jeans pockets. "Didn't get the feeling I was all that welcome five years ago."

"What's changed now?" Chayse tried to keep his voice even. Despite the time and history between them, he missed the camaraderie they'd shared.

"Now it seems we're working on the same case from different angles. It's just that Johnson isn't so missing anymore."

"You told your client yet?"

Nik shook his head. "No. I wanted to bring her more than, 'he's in the morgue'."

"Metro can't hold off from contacting her much longer, Nik. She's next-of-kin."

"I know." Nik nodded, pulling out a photo from his pocket and sliding between his hands as his thoughts chased each other through his eyes. "I'll tell her it's a murder as soon as I'm done here."

Chayse eyed the photo and raised an eyebrow. "And why are you here, again?"

"I'm here for your help."

Chayse's mind went into a momentary freeze. *Nik needs my help?* "For what?"

Nik extended the photo to Chayse. "This guy stayed in the room beside Johnson the night he disappeared. He went out with Johnson around seven fifteen that evening."

Chayse studied the satisfied expression on the face of a man in overalls. A series of spots marred the blue denim like mud splatters. "Johnson went out with this guy?"

"Yeah. I checked with my sources at the hotel. Johnson and this guy went out dressed in suits."

"What time was this again?"

"Time stamp has them leaving at 19:16."

"Did they come back together?"

Nik shook his head and pointed to the photo. "That guy returned around ten-twenty and had a tantrum in the hallway outside his room before going inside."

"Maybe Johnson left him in the lurch."

"Maybe, but at ten-fifty, this guy left again dressed like you see him there, in overalls, windbreaker, and the hat. Normally, I wouldn't care, but he didn't look at anyone, didn't act like a tourist or a businessman out on the town." Nik nodded to the picture. "In fact, he left like he wanted to hide from anyone who knew him, head down, on a mission. He was gone until ten after midnight, and when he got back, he wore that expression, but was missing the windbreaker."

Chayse chewed on his brother's news. For all the other issues between them, Nik's instincts about people were spot-on. Something had set off Nik's warning bells and

Chayse would be stupid to ignore them. If the hayseed in the picture had gone out with Johnson, he might at least know more about what happened to the victim prior to his death. Chayse reviewed his notes and something pricked his memory.

"Wait. What room did you say this guy came out of?"

"2117, right next door to Johnson's. Why?"

"That's Paul Hemmings's room. He's Johnson's business partner and brother-in-law. We interviewed him and he said he'd gone out with Johnson, but they split up after dinner and he returned to the hotel."

Nik's eyes narrowed. "Did he say what time he got back?"

"You know I can't tell you that."

Nik shot him a flat look. "I'm not asking for me, dumbass. Check your notes. The time stamp on the security video said he got back to his room at 22:21. That's a long time for dinner."

"They could've watched the strippers at Eve's Paradise. We know they went there."

"Yeah, but did he mention the strip club? From what I saw when he came to get Johnson before dinner, he wasn't too keen on women in general." Nik shrugged. "Could be nothing, but my nose is twitching, especially when he left the hotel later dressed in the overalls. What did the ME determine was time of death on Johnson?"

"Around eleven-thirty p.m. What time did Hemmings leave again?" Chayse's nose started twitching along with his brother's.

"Hemmings left his room at ten-fifty-three and returned at twelve-twenty. That brackets TOD pretty well." Nik dropped his chin and raised his eyebrows. "Look, just check your notes. I bet the man Lady Aislynn saw with Johnson at Eve's was Hemmings, but he said he left after dinner. Something doesn't add up. I'm gonna call my client and let her know I've found her husband. She can come ID

52

the body and I can get paid."

"That's it? You're done with the case?" Chayse gaped. Nik had never given up on anything. *Except me when I forced him to do so.*

"Hey, it's your job to find out who killed him. I just got hired to find him." Nik shrugged as he pulled his phone out of his pocket. "But my money's on the brother-in-law."

"It's pretty thin and circumstantial, Nik."

Nik snorted. "That's why you're the detective and are getting a warrant. Right?" He smirked and disappeared into the hallway to make his call.

Chayse growled and looked down at the satisfaction on Hemmings's face. *The guy looks like he just got a blowjob. Lucky bastard.* It'd been a long time since Chayse had received one of those, at least a decent one. Celine had fucked him up so much he hadn't been able to get a hard-on, much less have sex. For years after the *Morukai* shaman worked on him, the idea of touching a woman intimately triggered bad memories.

Even now, Chayse had to steel his mind against her image as he jerked himself off to get some release. Each time he tried to have sex, he could barely get through without picturing the succubus who'd nearly killed him.

Chayse shoved the past roughly away. *That's not the issue here.* He agreed with Nik. Something didn't jive with Hemmings's retelling and Nik's new evidence. He opened his notes and reread Hemmings's testimony. According to him, he and Johnson had gotten dinner and then gone to a gentleman's club, Eve's Paradise. But they'd split up and Hemmings had returned to the hotel around ten o'clock.

Accurate so far.

Hemmings had gone out the see the sights before turning in sometime between eleven-thirty and midnight. Again, not too far off from what Nik had found. And "seeing the sights" could be a euphemism for almost anything in this town. *Maybe he just doesn't want his wife to know he visits strip clubs and whores while away from home.*

Legally, prostitutes couldn't operate within Clark Country, but reality often remained aloof from the law. Metro knew some escorts worked within the county limits, but as long as no one ended up dead, the cops had bigger crimes to solve than paying for sex. As far as Chayse was concerned, the women earned every penny to put up with those willing to pay for it.

But while Hemmings wore an expression of satisfaction in the photo Nik brought, it wasn't the kind of gloating Chayse had seen on human males after a night of sex. It looked more like triumph and retribution.

He snorted in disgust. *Don't let Nik's unsubstantiated suspicions sway you. Follow the evidence.*

The evidence said nothing untoward had happened between Hemmings and Johnson the night they'd gone out together. But like Nik, Chayse's nose twitched and his Brother self growled. He studied the photo again. *What the hell are those splotches all over his legs?* Where would a businessman have gone to get that kind of stain pattern?

Chayse put in a call to the Desert Oasis for a copy of the security footage as he considered the marks on Hemmings's clothes. Mudwrestling could do it, but usually the spectators didn't get that close. Paint ball fights resulted in paint splattered everywhere, especially from the band with blue heads. *What I really need are the overalls.*

And a suspect. And motive. Hell, the original crime scene would be nice. He growled.

I gotta go visit the damn succubus again. That warrant better get here soon.

****

Luck was on their side and Chayse called Nik to come with him to Eve's Paradise to serve the warrant to Lady

Aislynn. Nik wondered why Chayse hadn't called his partner Jamison to go with him, but didn't feel like arguing. *Probably something to do with this becoming an Elder Races problem.* Goddess knew humans often mucked up what could be an easy solution within the Elder Race community. And Nik's priorities centered on keeping the Underground safe. *Lady Aislynn, too.* The last surprised him, but he chalked it up to protecting the club and her as the proprietor.

They arrived at the same time and parked on one of the side streets. The parking lot sat full of cars and limos. *Good to see Aislynn's not hurting for customers tonight.* They wound their way through the vehicles and passed both men and women entering the strip club. The sleek oak doors held back the erotic music inside, but the sound flooded over them as they stepped inside and waved to the bartender behind the bar.

Nik motioned to him to call for Felicia and settled in at the edge of the bar to wait. Patrons and waitresses jostled for position along the polished counter and Chayse growled at someone who nudged him too much. The man backed off with a startled look and Nik elbowed his brother.

"Easy."

"I hate this place."

"I know. It won't be long."

Eventually one of the strip shows started and the bar section emptied enough for them to stand comfortably. The bartender motioned for them to follow him into a side room meant for lap dances, but none of the patrons had been allowed in yet. Chayse took the lead and Nik followed, but he damn near ran into Chayse's back as his brother stopped like he'd hit a wall.

What the fuck.

Nik peered around Chayse's shoulder and swallowed a chuckle. The room in front of them sparkled with soft candle light from elaborate sconces. An oriental rug softened the wood floor and white lilies perfumed the air from a marble topped table set beside an ornate fireplace.

But that wasn't what dominated the room.

The woman stood about thirty feet away with her hands on hips, her sensual lips curling into an inviting smile. A lacy teddy covered her voluptuous curves, anchored to her thighs with matching lace stockings. She lifted one hand and beckoned to Chayse with a manicured nail as she balanced precariously on black velvet platform heels.

Damn. Whatcha gonna do, Chayse?

His younger brother stiffened and lifted his chin, a subsonic growl rumbling from him.

"Good evening, gentlemen." Her voice called up images of silken sheets and velvet kisses. "Are you here for a ménage?"

Nik's cock threatened to break his fly at the idea of sharing this lacy vixen with his brother. It had been so long. But Chayse's fists clenched at his side and his shoulders turned taut as he shook his head.

"Not today, sweetheart." He whirled, looking for the bartender with a snarl. "What the fuck, Nik?"

Nik shrugged apologetically, trying to swallow his grin. "Hey, at least it's quieter in here."

"I'd rather wait in the bar." Chayse shoved back out into the main room.

Nik shook his head and grimaced at the lovely lady. "He's on the clock. Me, too, or I'd take you up on that, darlin'. Thanks for the offer."

She inclined her head graciously as Nik trailed after his angry brother, chuckling.

Hanging out with his brother in a Vegas strip joint struck him as absurd as a summer snowstorm. Chayse represented everything straight-laced as a good cop should. *That wasn't always the case.* No, Nik had shared many women with his brother until the last one. *Who was an alleged succubus.* He wasn't sure he believed that or not.

Felicia exited the door to the upstairs offices and met them at the bar as the strip show continued. Her expression remained smooth, but her sharp gaze took in everything, including Chayse's building fury.

"Can I help you, gentlemen?"

"We have a warrant to search the premises." Chayse held up the documentation while his voice came out as a growl.

Felicia took the paper and scanned it, her expression betraying nothing.

"Very well, please follow me to Lady Aislynn. She'll need to see this before we grant you access."

"That's not how this works—"

"Ah, but that *is* how it works, Detective. This is Lady Aislynn's domain, and she must see this before permission is granted. Those are her rules." She leveled him an implacable look. "And you know she and I can enforce them regardless of the human laws."

Chayse growled something resembling an insult, but shook his head. "Lead on."

Felicia nodded and sauntered away. Nik expected her to return to the upstairs office, but jerked in surprise as she headed for the door to the Underground. *What the hell is she doing? Chayse is a cop.* He tried to catch her eye as she opened the door and preceded them into the stairwell, but she never looked back.

Chayse inhaled as he stepped across the threshold and a low growl echoed against the stone walls leading downward. "I smell blood and body fluids."

"You'll probably smell more than that, Detective, but that's not your concern." Felicia's voice had settled into her Domme range. "Your focus is on Lady Aislynn and what this warrant allows you to see. Are we clear?"

Chayse growled again, but settled when Nik thumped his shoulder. "Yes, we're clear."

"Good."

Felicia led them down a corridor Nik knew well, but rather than continuing on the straight path he'd traversed, she paused at a door reminiscent of a Gothic cathedral. The vampire woman produced a key and turned it smoothly before shoving open the door on silent hinges.

"You need a key?" Chayse snorted and shook his head.

"No, the lock is only for the overly curious...humans. We have other impediments for the Elder Races." She gestured past herself, standing out of the way. "Lady Aislynn will see you in the salon, the first door on your right."

Chayse scowled as he went through the doorway. Nik paused at the threshold and tilted his head toward Felicia.

"Are you sure?"

"No, but Lady Aislynn requested you both be brought down here against my better judgment. Harm her at your own peril."

"I have no intention of hurting Lady Aislynn, Felicia."

"It's not you I'm worried about, Master Canin. Keep a leash on your brother."

"Nik, are you coming?"

Nik grimaced and nodded to Felicia before ducking through the door. She followed him and closed it behind them, then gestured for them to proceed. Nik examined the elegant hallway laid with golden veined marble floor and oriental rugs every few feet. The walls had been painted a pale cream and recessed lighting made the place warm and welcoming.

"The salon is to your right, gentlemen."

They followed Felicia's directions and stopped in an elegantly appointed room with glass doors opening out onto a terrace. *A terrace underground?* He'd never seen such a thing though he had heard of a Las Vegas home built to be sustainable in case of some sort of holocaust on the surface. He wondered if the light cycled like the "sky" over the Forum Shops in Caesar's, changing with the time of day.

"Why the hell would a space like this be down here?" Chayse's derision poisoned the air.

"I sleep much better this way, Detective Wolffe. Safer, and cooler in the summer."

Nik shifted around until his gaze filled with Lady Aislynn standing in the doorway. She had skin the color of cream-laden coffee and eyes of silver-gray. She belted a satin robe around her waist with elegant manicured hands, and Nik's hands itched to peel it off of her.

What the hell is wrong with me? He'd seen her before. *Why am I acting like new pup with the scent of roses in my nose?* Chayse's voice reminding him of a succubus's power returned to his thoughts. *Is that what he meant?*

Felicia pushed past them, handing Aislynn the warrant. "These men brought you a warrant to search the premises."

"Ah, yes. Thank you, Felicia."

"Mistress." The vampire bowed her head to Aislynn and stepped back.

Aislynn read over the document while Chayse stood with locked knees, his hands curled into fists at his sides. Seething anger radiated from him, but he held himself still. Nik hated to make his brother face the subject of his addiction, but the only way to solve this case was through searching the succubus's domain.

"Very well. That will be all, Felicia. I'll take them around and make sure they don't disturb the players while investigating." Aislynn gestured for Felicia to leave. The vampire grimaced, but nodded and left the room. "Now then, gentlemen, if you'll give me a moment, I shall make myself more presentable before we take our tour."

"It's not a tour, Lady Aislynn." Chayse sounded as if he choked on broken glass. "We're here to search your premises for the original crime scene."

"I'm aware of that, Officer Wolffe. But this is also a specialized club where the privacy of the members is strictly enforced." Aislynn never lost her cool and a sense of pride filled Nik's chest. *That's my lady.*

Aislynn shot him a surprised look and raised her eyebrows, but returned her gaze to Chayse when he didn't answer. "I won't be a moment."

She sauntered away into one of the side rooms while they waited in the foyer and Nik wrestled with the odd sense of proprietary connection he'd experienced. Other than the meeting a few days ago and this one, he'd never seen Aislynn. *Why the hell do I think of her as mine, then?*

"Don't let her get to you, Nik." Chayse grasped his arm and squeezed. "She's a succubus and very dangerous. Don't let her refined ways and gentle voice fool you. Once you're addicted to her, you'll never be free."

"Come on, Chayse." Nik scoffed as he shook his head. "That was one succubus years ago. How do you know Aislynn is the same?"

"Five years, Nik. It's taken me five years to recover this much and I'm not even close to being a hundred percent." Chayse's lips pulled back from his teeth in a furious grimace. "Five fucking years and I run across another damned succubus. The Goddess must have it in for me."

Nik scowled. "Let it go, man. It won't get you the answers you need for this case. Focus on that and leave your anger at the door. Aislynn might be a succubus, but she hasn't done anything to you."

"Not yet, but it's early."

"We're on official police business. Suck it up."

"Left to my own devices, she wouldn't be able to get anywhere near me, but I'll do my damn job. Just watch your fucking six, Nik, 'cause I already saved your ass once. Not sure I have it in me to do it again."

Nik shrugged. Chayse had a point about a succubus's threat level, but something about Aislynn insisted on her individuality. She was different and Nik wanted to know what made her that way. But he nodded when Chayse shook his arm. "Yeah, got it, little brother."

CHAPTER NINE

Chayse struggled to get his emotions under control. If he lost it here, the succubus would eat him for lunch. *It would be a pleasurable way to die.* He mercilessly squashed the traitorous voice. He'd already tried that...and survived. Sometimes he wondered if he'd have been better off dead. *Too late now.*

Aislynn returned to them dressed in a fairly demure pinstriped suit and low pumps. She put her hair up into a ponytail that swayed over her shoulders as she walked past them to the door. Nik followed her with a besotted smile and Chayse ground his molars but stomped after them. *It won't take too long...I hope.*

"I need you both to understand what you're about to see must remain strictly confidential, gentlemen." Aislynn paused in the hallway they'd started in, meeting their gazes with none of her usual superior amusement. "There are people here from all the Elder Races as well as the humans who have paid for anonymity and unless you find evidence of their having participated in this heinous crime, they are not to be disturbed or harassed. Everyone you're about to see is a consenting adult."

"Of course." Nik's response didn't surprise Chayse. *Under her sway already.*

Aislynn's gaze rested on Chayse. "Detective Wolffe?"

He swallowed an ill-tempered growl. "Yes, ma'am."

"Good." She turned on her heel and strode down the dark hallway.

They followed her into a room, brightly lit and decorated much like a farmyard. Fence posts of weathered wood marched along one wall, strung together with barbed wire. A large coil of extra wire hung over one post, the barbs gleaming in the "afternoon" light with sinister intent. Straw had been strewn over the floor and a pitchfork stuck out of a real haystack against a barn façade.

Someone has a hoe-down kink?

"What exactly do you do here?" Chayse surveyed the room with disgust.

"Fantasy, Detective, is what we do here." Lady Aislynn gestured in a wide sweep and they spotted the other woman.

Nik grunted and Chayse bit his lips to hold in his growl.

The woman stood against the rough bark of a tree stump, with her hands restrained with thin, cotton cord. Crimson nails contrasted with her long sleeved, low-cut black t-shirt, showing enough cleavage to hide a deck of cards. Her head rested against the tree and her scarlet lips lay parted and slack.

"Is she in pain? Who did this to her?" Chayse demanded.

"Wait." Lady Aislynn held up her hand.

A man dressed as a cowboy bandit strode into the room, spurs jangling. A Stetson shaded his eyes from the harsh light over a bandana tied around his face. One gloved hand snapped a bullwhip in the air and the woman moaned.

"Oh shit."

The cowboy sauntered around the bound woman, cracking the whip, and watching her intently. Chayse wanted to pounce on him and hold him while his brother freed her, but Nik appeared to be as fascinated with the scene as the cowboy was.

Each clap of the leather against the air made the woman squirm against her restraints and moan loader. At first, she seemed to be in pain, fear twisting her features, but Chayse scented her arousal, and watched her nipples harden against her sheer t-shirt.

The cowboy snapped the whip once more, cocking his head as he studied his partner. He ran the hard handle of the whip down her arm and she jerked in surprise, squeaking a little as she opened her eyes.

"Did I give you permission to open your eyes, pet?"

She immediately snapped them shut. "No, Sir."

"What is the consequence for disobeying me?" The cowboy's voice slid silkily in the charged silence.

"Five lashes, sir."

"That's right. You will count and ask for each one, pet."

"Yes, Sir."

"And you will keep your eyes shut until I say otherwise. Is that understood?"

"Yes, Sir."

"Very good, pet." The cowboy Dom jangled his way to the barn façade, opened it, and withdrew a flogger made from red suede.

"It's time to move on, gentlemen," Lady Aislynn whispered, and Chayse flinched. "If you'll just follow me."

As they left the "playroom" behind, the flogger cracked and the woman grunted. "One. Thank you, Sir. May I have another?"

"He won't hurt her, will he?" Nik glanced at him, but said nothing.

"Not any more than she wants him to."

"What does that mean?"

Lady Aislynn remained silent for a few heartbeats, her

face serene. "Are you familiar at all with BDSM, Detective Wolffe?"

Dread and disgust slithered through Chayse, leaving a trail of humiliation. "I've read a little about it."

"A little." She slanted an amused look at him. "Then you'd know that in a Dominant/submissive relationship there is a power exchange, and the partners are essentially equal."

"How can they be equal?" Chayse snorted as they passed another room where the submissive, male this time, crouched gagged and handcuffed before his mistress. "She was tied to a tree and he had a whip." Was this what Nik was into? Chayse shot a look at his brother, but Nik's expression had settled into impassiveness.

"He will give her no more than she wants or needs. When she wants the game to end, she can stop it with a word or gesture they have agreed upon beforehand."

Chayse shook his head. "Come on, just one word, and he'll stop?"

"That's how the game is played. The Dom needs her to need him. He is essentially her slave. Nothing that happens between them is outside of their carefully constructed rules. She needs him to take control, just as he needs to serve her by taking that control."

"That just doesn't make any sense." Chayse couldn't fathom anyone having control over him. The idea frightened him, disgusted him…and excited him. He clenched his jaw. "If she's his submissive, how is he her slave?"

"Because he will do everything she wants him to do, including tying her down or flogging her. She requires that of her lover, and he will do everything in his power to make her happy." Lady Aislynn offered Chayse a wise smile. "It seems counterintuitive, I'm sure, but he literally needs her to need him, and he will assume the role of her Dom just to please her."

"Which in turn pleases him."

Lady Aislynn's smile widened with approval as she looked at Nik. "Yes, exactly, Mr. Wolffe." Nik damn near preened under her gaze and Chayse wanted to smack him.

Don't let her get to you, dammit. She's a succubus, remember?

He tried to catch his brother's eye, but Nik's attention wandered to another room. The décor resembled a gothic dungeon and a woman stood strapped to a large X-shaped cross wearing nothing but fishnet stockings and black stiletto heels. Another woman dressed in tight leather pants and corset wielded two floggers, alternating her strokes on the bound woman much like a windmill. The bound woman made no noise, but she'd jerk every now and again, her skin pinkening with the blows.

"You may come now, darling." The rich sultry voice carried over the slapping leather and the woman bound to the cross tensed then wailed her orgasm, her body shaking against her bonds.

"That's it, darling. Sweet darling." The Domme stroked her hands over the glowing shoulders of her submissive, a sweet smile of satisfaction curling her lips.

Chayse scented arousal and contentment coming from both women, and his cock hardened in sympathy. He wanted that, the satisfaction of serving a lover, of being served by a lover, but he didn't think he could submit to anyone. The idea of being tied down frightened him. Even when he'd shared a woman with Nik, he'd never been restrained.

"There is great release in allowing someone else to control your sexual pleasure, Detective Wolffe," Lady Aislynn whispered, and he jerked away from her.

"Leave me alone!"

She stepped back and nodded her head slowly. "Have I done something to offend you?"

He refused to meet her eyes. *That's how succubae draw*

you in. "My mother taught me if you can't say something nice, don't say anything at all."

Her expression remained curious. "Forgive me. I didn't intend to intrude." She retreated from him and they continued their path through her club, while Chayse seethed.

I'll never let another succubus fuck with me. It took hell to get out of that mess. I shouldn't even be here now.

She opened an unassuming door resembling a broom closet with a plaque that read *Staff Only* affixed to the surface. The room on the other side was anything but a closet.

The door led back to a foyer with marble floors and polished cherry furniture. Fresh roses graced a tall vase on a small circular table beside a framed mirror. They passed through to a living room housing comfortable furniture upholstered in earthy colors over soft, cream colored carpeting. A see-through fireplace held court in the center of the room. *This must be another apartment or the other end of the one we saw before.*

Chayse had been expecting something Victorian with heavy brocades and lion-footed furniture, not this homey, comfortable apartment. Some of his tension melted away as Lady Aislynn drew them through a door to the right behind a loveseat he estimated could seat at least three.

Aislynn's office had the same comfortable décor as the rest of the apartment. A rich cherry desk faced two comfortable leather chairs with a matching one behind it. There were no windows, but bookshelves lined the walls with magnificent landscape art placed at gentle intervals. Chayse recognized Thomas Kincade and Ansel Adams, but the others, watercolors, oils, and photography, escaped his knowledge.

"Please, gentlemen, have a seat." Lady Aislynn paused behind the desk and Chayse kept his gaze on her chin. "Can I get you anything to drink while we discuss our business?"

"No thank you, ma'am," Nik said, openly staring at her luscious curves.

"No." Chayse wanted to thump his brother, but tightened his hand into a fist at his side. "I'd just like to get this over with."

"Glad to see you got the warrant. I'm surprised it came through so soon." Lady Aislynn retreated to a little coffee maker in the corner and filled it will water, her motions graceful and sensual. She prepared a teapot and mugs as if at an intimate tea party. Chayse told his dick to ignore her. *It's just calculated to get me hot for her.*

"It gets better, you know."

"What?" Chayse looked up, startled. Lady Aislynn assessed him from across her desk. She leaned back in her chair, presenting him with a delightful view of her creamy breasts.

"The addiction. The longer you're away from her, the better it gets."

Chayse narrowed his eyes as he stared at her chin. "I don't know what you're talking about."

Aislynn offered him a sad half-smile. "Not all of us actively choose to enslave our lovers, Detective. Some of us try not to ensnare anyone." She tipped her head and swept her hand around the room. "That's why I built this BDSM club. I can take sips of every sexual encounter in my club without harming anyone. It sustains me and hurts no one."

Chayse felt this blood leave his face as his stomach curdled. "You feed from *everyone*?"

"I have to survive. I'd much rather do it without killing anyone, and this is the best solution." She gave him the sad smile again. "It also ensures I don't allow anyone to become addicted to me."

Chayse gritted his teeth and looked down at his fists. He tried to remember the breathing exercises Master Kindle had taught him for calm. "Those are pretty words, madam succubus, but we both know they don't always hold true."

Aislynn's expression turned sad as she nodded.

"How did you free yourself from her grip?" Her voice held a note of admiration.

Fury ripped through Chayse and he raised his gaze to her chin as he flashed her an angry grimace.

"I didn't. A *Morukai* healer found me, sick and jonesing, took me in, and helped me detox." Rage seethed like a living thing beneath his skin, increasing his heartbeat and making him sweat. "He helped me reclaim myself. He taught me how to identify your kind and avoid them. I don't know why I'm allowing myself to be anywhere near such a monster as you, but I'm here, and I'm strong enough to withstand your machinations."

"I'm sorry one of my kind has hurt you so badly." She didn't smile. He scented honest sadness coming from her, but he refused to be drawn in. *That's how they get you, the bitches.* "I cannot change what I am, but I can change how I choose to get my sustenance. I take a little from everyone, rather than killing my lovers."

Aislynn leaned forward. "I'll let you in on a little secret, Detective. The deaths still haunt me, and I wish I'd been smart enough to prevent them. This club is my solution. If you have a better one, I'm all ears."

"You could die," Chayse snarled.

"Sometimes, I wish I could."

"I can help with that."

"Chayse!" Nik snapped, his own anger finally kindled.

"You have no idea what she's capable of!" Chayse shot out of his chair, rounding on his brother. He pointed at Aislynn. "You think she's sweet, demure, gorgeous, ordinary. But she's not. She's a monster, something so horrible and dangerous, even a Moon Singer has to be wary. You give her the okay and she'll be on you so fast, you'll be dead within a month." His lips curled with furious derision. "Stay away from my brother, bitch, or I swear I'll tear your throat out, and bury your body where even the other detectives can't find it."

He whirled away from them and stormed out the door, his body shaking with his fury and need. Chewed bones, he wanted Aislynn, and he knew it was his old addiction coming to call. He wished he could shield his brother, but he could barely control himself around her.

Fuck, will this damn addiction ever go away?

CHAPTER TEN

Aislynn watched the young, handsome cop fly out her office door and part of her yearned to go after him and soothe the raging pain she felt from him. *Dear Goddess, he's been hurt so badly.* She wished she could help him, comfort him, but she was the monster he feared.

He'd meant his threat with every fiber of his being, but it had only excited her. He had power and passion, two qualities her last few lovers had lacked. She couldn't help but desire him.

Of course I do. I'm a succubus, cursed by the Goddess since the Garden of Eden.

Aislynn mentally slapped herself. She had no time for self-pity.

"I'm so sorry, Lady Aislynn. I've never seen him this worked up."

"It's all right. He's right about my kind, Mr. Wolffe." The PI raised his eyebrows dubiously. "Most succubae are either too young to have much experience holding back the urges, or have little to no conscience. He cannot know I'm different. His experience says otherwise."

"What makes you different?" Mr. Wolffe fixed her with his pale green gaze.

"I'm old enough to regret my past actions."

He bit his lips and she suspected he wanted to ask her age, but had been taught differently. She wished she could lay all her remorse and frustrations at his feet, but she knew very little about this male, or his angry brother, and she was too old to act rashly.

"Perhaps you could tell me a little about you."

"About me?" His eyes narrowed and a little zing of pleasure zipped up her spine. "Like what?"

"I've seen you here at my club before, only I don't recall a 'Mr. Wolffe' on the register. I believe you are called Master Canin, a Dom of some repute."

Wolffe crossed his arms over his chest, an unconsciously defensive motion. He offered her a dead stare for several heartbeats in a battle of wills, but Aislynn wasn't intimidated. In fact, he intrigued her. She'd seen him many times, always with a different sub in tow as if he hadn't found his perfect partner. She'd never shown herself to him, but he'd often turned his head toward her as if he sensed her attention. She'd watched him, curious to see what kind of Dom he was, but though he brought them to their pleasure, he never seemed to reach contentment.

"I've carried that moniker a time or two." Amusement curled through his voice, but his expression remained serene. "I thought I sensed someone watching me, but I never saw you. I was very sorry to hear about the murder in the club."

"Thank you, Mr. Wolffe. It has disturbed the players, but we are all coming to grips with the situation and I'm sure it will be resolved soon."

"Do you play at all, Lady Aislynn?"

The question appeared merely curiosity, but the gleam in Wolffe's eyes suggested he hoped she'd reveal more with her answer.

"No, though I'm familiar with the games." She gave him a half-smile.

SIOBHAN MUIR

"Maybe you haven't found the right Dom."

"What makes you think I'd be a sub?"

He cocked his head and his green gaze swept over her body, eliciting pleasure from the base of her neck all the way down to her pussy. Her nipples tightened for the first time in centuries with his luxurious perusal and she wondered if he'd be worth the effort to play with.

Don't be daft, Eva! You'd kill him at your first orgasm—or his.

Her private name for herself reminded her of simpler times as sorrow doused her arousal and she swallowed against the sudden lump in her throat.

"I think you'd make an excellent switch for the right partners," he mused, but the lust dampened as if he could sense her sorrow. "I can see you need someone to make the decisions after the years you've kept this place running. Someone to help you reach that pleasure you want and so richly deserve."

How arrogant of him. I've never wanted to be told how to take my pleasure, not even that first time. But the certainty in his voice and the confidence in his eyes shook her to her core. Her pussy clenched with the idea of being his sub, of attending his demands so he could serve hers.

"But I can also see you as a compassionate Domme, well-attuned to your lover's needs and desires."

Aislynn smiled, but the pain of her past made it bittersweet. "I don't take lovers, Mr. Wolffe. I'm a succubus. If we take a lover, we usually kill them whether we wish to or not. As your brother pointed out so clearly."

Wolffe grunted and his expression lost some of the wise amusement. "My brother has been holding out on me."

"Perhaps we should conclude our business at a different time. I'm sure your brother could use some understanding company." She rose and gestured toward the door, hoping to distract him from pursuing the idea of her as a switch. "I'd prefer if he didn't destroy my club in his

72

anger. Please make sure he gets home safely. I fear the addiction to succubus energy is riding him fairly hard."

Wolffe eyed her narrowly as he stood. "So you can see his addiction?"

"Oh yes. His energy signature is patchy, like a staticky signal from a radio. The succubus who got to him did a great deal of damage, and while he's mastered his urges, he hasn't fully healed from the experience."

Wolffe's brows lowered and his face hardened. "Will he always be this way?"

Aislynn tilted her head in consideration. "Honestly, I don't know. Werewolves have true mates, correct?"

The PI's expression turned wary. "Why?"

Aislynn snorted with derision. "Come now, Mr. Wolffe. I'm not trying to ensnare you, merely offering a solution to your brother's problem. And even without you saying anything, I can tell what you are. Do werewolves true mate?"

His jaw clenched. "Yes."

"Then there is a chance when he finds this true mate, she'll fill the spaces left by the succubus, and the addiction to such energy will be broken. However, it will only be replaced by an addiction to his mate's energy. He'll always be an addict, Mr. Wolffe."

He looked liked she'd driven a dagger into his chest, and Aislynn's heart contracted, both for him and for his brother. Such fine males shouldn't have to experience that kind of pain. She wished she could hold them both, comforting them in all the ways they needed, physical and emotional.

What is wrong with me? She embodied the evil they feared. They wouldn't want to be anywhere near her. *And I never form attachments to my clients.* She almost grimaced. *They're not my clients, not even 'Master Canin'. Why in hellfires do I care how they feel?*

"You should go talk to him. He needs you right now."

Wolffe gave her a look that said *Are you serious?*

"Just listen to him. Don't judge. This kind of addiction is like any other. They can't help it. But your brother is strong if he managed to get out of it and find some help. He could use your support. Family is very important in these situations, and I suspect it's even more so for him."

"Oh yeah? How would you know that?" Mr. Wolffe crossed his arms over his chest.

"Because I can sense your connection to him." She gave him a half-smile. "You're twins, are you not?"

"Fuck." He shook his head, but said nothing else.

"He needs you, Mr. Wolffe. Just listen to what he has to say. Let him know you have his back."

"He already knows that."

Aislynn merely lifted an eyebrow.

"Shit." He swung toward the door, but paused, pointing at her. "We're not done. I still have more questions." She suspected he didn't mean about the case.

"I look forward to seeing you both again, Mr. Wolffe."

He rumbled a derisive growl and strode out the door after his brother.

Aislynn sighed and slumped against her desk. Sorrow and regret chased each other through her mind as she recalled the white hot fury in Detective Wolffe's eyes. His aura had been full of puce strings of light, faded but present. He'd fought much of the battle to rid himself of the other succubus's hold, but wounds remained, and Aislynn grieved for him.

He'd obviously spared his brother the same fate.

"Strong male," she whispered.

The sound of her own voice in the silence of her apartment brought her back to the present. She'd need to feed soon, but the club wouldn't open for another twenty minutes according to the clock.

Sighing again, she pushed herself to her feet and strode to the kitchen. She tried to take an interest in the food within the ice box, but nothing sparked her interest.

At least, nothing edible. I'd happily enjoy some rough werewolf sex.

Aislynn drew herself up short. *No. They've been hurt enough. And they're both essentially cops. No werewolf sex for you.*

She wrapped her hand around a glass bottle of iced tea and enjoyed the cold seeping into her palm as she retreated to her "outdoor" garden. Palm fronds rattled gently in the forced breeze from the internal fans while misters simulated rain on her plants. Her garden lights shined around the perimeter in the false gloom.

Aislynn stepped from beneath the patio cover into the man-made downpour and closed her eyes, allowing the water to soak her clothes to her skin. The rain washed away her worries and stresses for a moment, reminding her of the few times she'd walked along deserted roads in a rainstorm. Shoes in hand, soaked to the bone, looking for love.

Many people came to Vegas looking for love or something like it. She'd concocted a plan to give them what they wanted. Eve's Paradise, her strip club, delivered the illusion of love. The Underground catered to all forms of it.

And kept her inner succubus fed.

Aislynn's guts cramped and she gasped, folding in on herself. She'd known she needed to feed, but it was too early to go through this kind of withdrawal. The rain pelted down over her back and dripped into her face as she staggered back under the awning. She lost her grip on the iced tea and the glass shattered on the wet concrete, but she was too weak to care.

She dropped to her knees and crawled across the threshold, trying to see beyond her darkening vision. Each motion took extra energy and sapped even more of her strength. *Heaven's glories, what is wrong with me?*

Every muscle protested and her stomach threatened to vomit up the tea she'd managed to drink. She clamped her lips together and forced herself toward a phone. Contacting Felicia was her only hope of making in through whatever she suffered.

Just a few more steps...Steps? Ha! I can't even find my feet.

Hunger gnawed at her awareness as if she'd starved herself for weeks. But she'd been feeding regularly. Confusion swamped her as she kept one goal in mind: must reach a phone.

Aislynn crawled to her kitchen, but the phone on the counter seemed a million miles away. Whimpering like a newborn puppy, she stretched her hand toward the flickering view as she braced against the island wall.

Dizziness threatened to suck away her balance as her fingers scrabbled for the plastic device she'd left on the counter. *It's got to be there. I left it right on the counter.* Desperation surged and she lunged for purchase, her hand closing on the smooth lump of electronics.

Aislynn whimpered with relief, dialing the number blindly.

"Hello, Mistress."

"Felicia." Aislynn's voice wouldn't rise above a whisper. "Help me."

"Where are you?"

"Apartments."

The line went dead and Aislynn dropped the phone, pressing her forehead against the cold tile of her kitchen floor. *Felicia will come and it'll be all right. Yes, just keep telling yourself that.*

A soft pop of displaced air announced Felicia's arrival and the vampire ran into the kitchen.

"Dear Goddess, what happened, Mistress?"

"Don't know." Each word took most of Aislynn's breath. "Drained. So hungry. Need to feed."

Cool hands wrapped around her waist and lifted, pulling her close to the vampire's body. Felicia hadn't fed yet that day, her skin pale and cold, but she cradled Aislynn like a precious offering.

"Hold your breath, Mistress."

Aislynn had just enough time to heed the warning as the room disappeared entirely and fiery bands of panic gripped her chest. A silent scream welled up in her throat, but exhaustion engulfed it and she wallowed in frightened misery. Her need to breathe surged just as they popped out of the nothingness into a solid room, and she gasped in relief.

"Be easy, Mistress. Master Cory has just started his session with Quentin." Felicia set Aislynn down on a cushioned bench outside one of the dungeon playrooms. The door flashed closed in the red "do not disturb" light, but proximity was all she needed. "It won't be long now."

No sound emanated from the room beyond, but the sweet flow of sexual energy seeped into the flesh of her back. Aislynn slumped against the wall as she sank into the erotic current. The cramps in her belly loosened and the stars along the edges of her vision faded. She kept her eyes closed, but the world stopped spinning as her dizziness retreated.

"Oh, thank the Goddess," she whispered.

"Mistress, what happened? Why were you so drained?" Felicia's expression tightened with concern.

Aislynn managed a week smile. "I'm all right. Thank you for your help."

"You're welcome, Mistress." But the worry didn't leave her gray eyes. "Please, tell me what happened so I can prevent it in the future."

Felicia's protectiveness warmed Aislynn's heart, and she sent a prayer of gratitude to the Goddess for dropping the vampire in her path. Felicia's Roman Senator husband had accused her of deliberately turning everyone on but him. The poor bastard had been gay and homophobic, never a good combination, and he'd killed her with a leather awl to the temple in a drunken rage.

Aislynn found her as a newly risen vampire, struggling to come to terms with her desperate hunger from her body's attempt to heal the damage. Aislynn had fed her a little of her own blood, then taught Felicia how to hunt discreetly. The vampire swore Aislynn had saved her life and remained devoted to her forever. Her protective streak ran a thousand miles wide and she'd move heaven and earth to help Aislynn.

"I don't know, Felicia." Aislynn rocked her head against the wall. "I was fine. I'd taken the gentlemen to my office to discuss the murder."

"And?"

Aislynn stared at the rough cut stone wall and sifted through her memories of the beautiful males who'd shaken her world. Why had they impacted her relatively steady life? Men had come and gone during the centuries she'd lived, but none had made much of an impression. Nik and Chayse Wolffe waltzed into her strip club, and her whole world turned upside down.

What is wrong with me? Why am I so drained?

"And Detective Wolffe hates succubae." She dragged a hand over her breast, rubbing a nipple as the energy from the dungeon ramped up.

"Hates them?"

"Yes. Apparently, he's a recovering succubus addict."

"Dear Goddess. And he knows what you are?"

Aislynn nodded. "He's a werewolf. He's aware of my...affliction."

Felicia waved her hand with disgust. "Why should that be a problem? Plenty of males have feared you over the centuries. Why is this one any different, Mistress?"

"I don't know." Aislynn shifted her hips as the sexual energy increased again. Goddess, she could only take a little more, but she desperately wanted to sink into all of it and rest. "But until I do, you must not let me be alone with them for any length of time."

Felicia raised an eyebrow. "You want me to impose restrictions on you, Mistress?"

"Just when around the Wolffe brothers. There's something…dangerous about them."

"Dangerous, how?" Felicia eyed Aislynn narrowly. "Because they're cops?"

"No." Aislynn snorted with derision. "No, it has to do with their energy." She hesitated as she struggled to put her feelings into words. "Because Detective Wolffe was addicted to a succubus before, his energy is patchy."

Felicia sucked in a breath. "Dear Goddess."

Aislynn nodded. "He hasn't completely recovered from it and his aura is raw. Plus, he's very, very angry."

"Why is that a problem, Mistress? You've dealt with angry men before."

"Not like this. He knows what I am, so he's more guarded than most, and his anger is fueled by that knowledge." She paused and shut down her receptors from the energy pulsing behind the door. *Enough for now.* "It's potent, his fury, and it somehow taps into my energy."

"How? That's never happened before."

"I don't know. Perhaps it has to do with the last succubus and our similarity. Whatever the reason, it drains me as if my aura can fill the gaps in his."

Felicia lifted her chin in surprise. "You're tied to him already?"

"No, I couldn't be. I didn't feed off him." Aislynn sighed in relief as her hunger subsided. But fear followed. Felicia's question dug deep in her gut. "I don't know why my energy goes to him. I haven't noticed it going to his twin."

"They're twins?"

"Yes."

"Oh my."

"It's not from them both. The officer seems to have cut

off the flow of energy to his brother." Aislynn grimaced. "Probably to protect him from the manipulations of the other succubus."

"Saints preserve us," Felicia muttered, shaking her head. She offered her arm as Aislynn rose, and they strolled slowly toward the stairs leading up to the club. "Do you think he steals energy from everyone?"

Aislynn frowned. "I don't know. I haven't sensed that, but I've had limited exposure to him. It could be only when he's feeling powerful emotions. Or it could be only that I'm so sensitive to the energy."

Felicia hissed a scoff. "You've never been like this, Mistress, and there are plenty of damaged beings that feel powerful emotions who have come through our doors. It can't be only that."

"What would you suggest, Felicia? That it's because he's a member of the Elder Races?" Aislynn's voice cracked like a whip.

"No, Mistress. Forgive me my tone. I didn't mean to offend."

"Very well." Aislynn inclined her head, but irritation still stung her throat. "You may continue."

"I don't believe it is only his species that is affecting you." She pursed her lips as her thoughts ran behind her eyes. "Perhaps you'd permit me to do some research."

"Research on what?" Aislynn's gut clenched in some unnamed dread and she smoothed a hand down her dress.

"On energy transfers, especially pertaining to emotional vampires." Felicia grimaced at the pejorative term. "Perhaps there's a way for you to better defend against this young werewolf without unnecessary restrictions, Mistress."

Aislynn suspected her vampire assistant wanted nothing to do with Topping her Mistress, and nodded as she hid her smile. Felicia's expression cleared. "You may do so. In the meantime, we will be careful of the Wolffe brothers. Now then, my energy has been restored and the club just opened. Let us get to business."

"Excellent, Mistress."

Aislynn nodded in greeting to a Dom leading his rather demurely dressed sub down the stairs by a leash and collar. The tall woman kept her head bowed and shuffled after her master in a hobble skirt, the fabric restricting her steps to no more than six inches apart. Aislynn inhaled their arousal and excitement as it surged when they reached the floor below.

Something always excited her about a committed D/s relationship. The trust, love, and ultimately, compassion of the partners resonated deeply within her heart. She yearned for that kind of connection in her own long life, but her species forbade such a link. *Stop being such a sap, Eva. You don't need that.* But the desire burned in her gut and her mind filled with a vision of the Wolffe brothers.

Whoa back, girl. Don't even go there.

Aislynn barely stopped her grimace as she stepped out onto the club floor. Her stomach churned with the mixture of desire and need, but fear prowled the edges of her emotions, screaming a warning. The PI might be willing to be hers, but the detective hated her kind with a passion usually reserved for pedophiles and cesspools. In addition, she sensed both brothers were alpha, and such males rarely shared their women.

But I want both *of them.*

Keep dreaming, Eva.

A derisive laugh rattled out of her chest and Felicia looked over at her.

"Are you well, Mistress?"

"Of course, Felicia."

Goddess of all, she wished. Taking a deep breath, Aislynn smoothed her hands down her suit and hoped serenity filled her expression as she faced the evening crowd visiting Eve's Paradise that night.

CHAPTER ELEVEN

"Hey, Chayse, hold up, will you?" Nik grabbed his younger brother and spun him around. The brilliant lights of the Welcome to Fabulous Las Vegas sign illuminated every drop of sweat soaking his hair, and his chest rose and fell like a bellows. Chayse bared his teeth and Nik let go. "Talk to me, man. What the hell is wrong with you?"

Nik had gotten lucky to remember the one place they'd gone together when they wanted to think. Chayse had always loved the little pool of serenity of the sign in the midst of the crazy Las Vegas Boulevard. Most nights found happy tourists there, and gave them some of the joy they often missed when dealing with the black heart of the city.

"She's evil, Nik. You don't understand." Chayse stared at the newly married couple having their portrait shot at the Sign.

"You're right. I don't understand. Why don't you help me get to where you are?"

"What?"

"Explain it to me, Chayse. I just drove all the way here from Eve's to track you down. What the hell is going on with Lady Aislynn?"

"It's not Aislynn!"

"Then why are you such an asshole to her? She didn't do anything to you."

"It's not *her*, it's what she *is*." Chayse growled at Nik's blank look. "It all started with Celine—"

"Yeah, I know. She was a succubus and addicted you."

"She damn near killed me! Aislynn's a succubus, too. You know what they do, right? They drain their victims of their life energy, while addicting the same victims to wanting more of their 'love'." The wedding party turned their heads toward them as his voice rose over the dull roar of traffic on the Strip. "Fuck."

"I don't think she wants to kill you, Chayse."

"That's just your dick talking. You don't understand how dangerous she is."

Nik huffed a frustrated sigh and glanced up at the sign as if gathering his patience. "Can *you* tell when a succubus is trolling?"

Chayse paused, replaying the memories of Celine in his mind. Had he felt different those times when around her? Aislynn had a similar energy, but the signature of it was smooth, practiced. Celine's had been jagged, grabby, and so damn seductive.

"Yes."

"Did you sense that from Lady Aislynn?"

"No." It made his gut churn to admit it.

"Then maybe it's not just my dick talking." Nik crossed his arms over his chest. "Look, Aislynn said she regrets her past actions and doesn't want to hurt anyone. Something tells me she's not kidding. She never once tried to reel you in. She didn't even try with me after you left." He turned his viridian gaze to meet Chayse's. "I can't understand your addiction, Chayse. I won't even pretend to try. But I do want to help." He dropped his gaze. "I've missed you, brother."

Chayse felt like he'd been slapped. He'd cut off his brother to save him, but it had damn near ripped the heart right out of him. Here Nik offered him an olive branch and Chayse wanted to take it more than he wanted the succubus's sweet energy. But he was too afraid he'd drag Nik down into the morass of desperate need he still felt.

"Yeah, me too."

"Then let me back in, man. You don't have to do this alone."

"Yes, I do. It's better if you steer clear."

"Dammit!" Nik swung away from him and left the twittering wedding party. Chayse followed, his brother's pain and frustration pulling him like a tether.

"I'm sorry, Nik."

His darker, bad-boy brother shook his head, cutting off what more he would have said. "Shit, man, we have to solve this crime. If you let me in, maybe together we can resist Aislynn's pull."

"'I can resist everything except temptation'. Oscar Wilde."

"Yeah, well, Oscar didn't have a twin. I got your back, brother."

"Yeah, but who will have yours?" Chayse resisted the urge to punch Nik's shoulder.

"Together we're stronger than we are alone."

"What are you, a fortune cookie?"

"No, and I'm not wrong. For once, listen to your older brother."

"You're only older by fifteen minutes."

Nik grinned. "I swear you were in there bleaching your hair just so you could look cuter to Mom."

Chayse laughed at the old argument and some of his fury lifted. "I had to look different. Not all of us could be the dark-haired, green-eyed bad boy."

"That's 'bad-ass', Pale-Face."

"Kiss my ass, Smudge." They both laughed and Chayse could breathe again. He turned his attention to the wedding party still prancing around beneath the sign and he wished he could be so worry-free at the moment. Nik's deep inhalation brought him back to the present.

"We can do this if we do it together, Chayse." Nik shot him an earnest stare. "But you have to open up to me again. You can't keep me in the dark. We're stronger together. You know that. Remember how we tag-teamed mom and dad?"

Chayse chuckled.

"Exactly." Nik nodded sharply. "You know what to look for and I can anchor you. We can protect each other. Besides, I really don't think Aislynn is trying to snag you. I think she's trying to live as quietly as possible, and reeling you in wouldn't be very quiet."

Maybe not, but I can feel the addiction calling out to her. But he missed his brother and the easy times they'd had together. And he missed the sex when they'd shared women. All the sex he'd had since Celine paled in comparison, but he didn't think it was only about her. Something had been missing without Nik.

Chayse rubbed the back of his neck with one hand. "No, probably not."

"Hey, if it makes you feel any better, I'll go with you when you talk to her. No reason why you have to go alone."

Chayse's initial reaction was the anger he'd lived with for so long, but he shoved it away. *Nik is only trying to back me up. I'm the only one who thinks I'm weak.*

"Thanks, I might take you up on that."

Relief blazed from Nik's smile and he jerked Chayse into a hug. "I'm here, Chayse. Don't force me out again, okay? You only have to be alone if you want to be."

Chayse closed his eyes and rested against his twin's chest for a few moments, feeling relief for the first time in half a decade. He'd missed being close with Nik and so wished he could open himself back up to their shared connection. He almost let it open on its own, but his gut cramped. *I'm not ready yet.*

"Thanks, Nik." He pulled back from his brother. "I'm not quite done with what I need to do, but when I'm ready, I'll let you know."

"That's all I can ask." Nik slapped his shoulder and turned his gaze on the happy wedding party making way for another group. "You should go back to Eve's and finish the tour. I suspect Lady Aislynn will show you the real crime scene if you can behave yourself. I can go with you."

Chayse shook his head. "Nah, I'll be fine. Just give me a few hours to get my head on straight and check with the lab. The original crime scene is important, but maybe there'll be some trace on Johnson's clothes. What would be ideal is if we could find that jacket Hemmings was wearing in the video, or even his overalls, but my bet is they're both rotting in some landfill somewhere."

Nik tipped his head. "I have friends in low places around here. Let me see what my contacts say about any clothes left in the vicinity of Eve's. I might be able to shed some light on that."

"Yeah?" It had been five years. Goddess only knew what kind of friends Nik had made in his line of work. "If you find anything call or text me at the station. I'm headed there now."

"Will do. Seriously, though, if you need me to go with you when you go back to Eve's, I got the time. Anytime. I got your back."

"Thanks, Nik. I'll remember."

Chayse waved and headed for his car. It felt good to be working with his brother again, even if their connection was still tentative. He just needed some time to be sure Aislynn had no designs on him or Nik. He didn't trust the succubus any farther than he could spit a dead sewer rat, but maybe Nik was right and together they'd be able to protect each other. *Let's hope so because we still have to return to the belly of the beast.*

****

Nik watched his brother leave and some of his tension released. *At least Chayse is talking to me again.* He could give his brother the time he needed to find his center after all that had happened. He marveled at Chayse's strength to survive and recover from addiction and kicked himself for not realizing earlier. He remembered Celine had been clingy and focused on Chayse, but when his younger brother had tired easily, she'd turned her attention on Nik. Chayse had grown jealous and told Nik to get the fuck out, cutting him off cold.

Five years and I never saw what the hell was going on.

He'd let his brother down and let him face the horror alone.

Chewed bones, I was stupid. Some twin I turned out to be.

Nik strode toward his truck. At least he could help Chayse now, not only with Aislynn, but with the case as well. He'd made contacts with the homeless folks who lived in the flood tunnels below the city. They were always on the lookout for decent clothes thrown away in the dumpsters, especially around the strip clubs. It wouldn't be hard to get in touch with a few of them to see if they'd snagged a nice windbreaker, especially at this time of year when the winds through the city made Chicago look like a joke.

As if to prove his point, the wind grabbed the veil of the current bride in front of the sign and whipped it like a flag across the faces of her bridesmaids. *Yeah, they'll definitely be looking for a windbreaker.*

He threw the truck into reverse and headed north toward an enclave of permanent homeless closest to Eve's Paradise. Hemmings would've taken a taxi, but he wouldn't have worn a spattered windbreaker in the back without inciting questionable looks. Their best bet of finding the windbreaker would be around the club.

If the sanitation department didn't get it first. He didn't know the trash schedules of the area around the strip clubs. *Let's just hope didn't get the jacket.* The homeless searched for goods every night. They would've found it before the Dumpsters were emptied.

Something about Johnson's brother-in-law and erstwhile strip club companion made his nose twitch. He had no proof, but he'd bet a year's worth of truck payments it had been blood on his overalls. In any case, they needed to talk to Hemmings in person. Nik needed to smell if the man lied about his involvement in Johnson's death, if only to protect the Underground.

And Aislynn.

Nik clenched his jaw. He'd been having thoughts like that for the last few days and the damn ringing in his ears only disappeared when he got close to Eve's and Aislynn. What the hell was that about? If Chayse told him the truth, she represented an evil so old, it showed up in all the religious texts around the world. An evil capable of snaring the unwary and addicting them.

Am I just addicted to Aislynn like Chayse was to Celine?

He bit his lip as he waited to take a left off Las Vegas Boulevard. Even in February, turning left from the LVB was a bitch. The neon lights from Caesar's and Harrah's painted brilliant splashes across his shiny hood as he considered the question.

Instead of being drained or tense after encountering Aislynn, his energy increased and his mind cleared, allowing him to focus longer. The ringing faded into an easily ignored hum and all the tension in his body dissolved.

Chayse maintained that was the magic of the succubus doing its work, but wouldn't he feel drained and drugged, groggy and slow after being near her? Nik shook his head as he took a right on the side road leading down toward the off-Strip strip clubs crouched like fancy warehouses just outside of the glittering blaze from the big casinos. He liked the flash and magic of the main Strip, but these quieter spaces suited him and his work better. *Or maybe just Eve's suits me better because of Aislynn.*

He couldn't argue with the thought.

Nik pulled into the parking lot in front of Eve's Paradise and parked at the far end. Cars and limos again filled the most of the spaces, but the end of the lot had few cars. He locked his truck and pocketed the keys as he headed for the neighboring alleys. Most of the homeless visited the back alleys of the Strip, but ended up sleeping farther away from the lights and noise.

From the scents wafting out of the darkness of the nearest alley, Nik recognized Lucy and Mickey, two of the resident scroungers who periodically supplied him with information. They never thought of themselves as homeless, just forgotten by the world at large.

Nik paused beside a particularly pungent dumpster and waited for the occupants of the alley to become aware of him. Scaring them would put a crimp in the flow of information. Mickey had PTSD and quick movements made him strike out.

"Evening, Mickey, how's it going?" Nik made sure what little light poured into the alley hit his body.

Mickey paused without looking at him, but came no closer to where Nik stood. "Whozzat?"

"Nik Wolffe. Private eye."

"Oh yeah. Nose like a bloodhound, ears like a bat." Mickey bobbed his head. "Whaddaya need, Nik?"

"I'm lookin' for something. Either you or Lucy find any clothes in the dumpsters around here on Thursday night or Friday morning, early?"

Mickey squinted, suspicion still present despite the

years he'd known Nik. "Why?"

Nik shrugged. "We think it belonged to a murderer, a guy who killed someone in Eve's."

Mickey's eyes widened and Lucy appeared at his elbow, clutching his arm. "Someone died at Eve's?"

Nik nodded. "It was bad, but the murderer wore a windbreaker jacket, men's large or extra large, with reflector stripes down the arms. Either of you come across that on your forays on Thursday and Friday?"

The two forgotten looked at each other before Lucy nodded. Mickey sighed and his shoulders slumped.

"Yeah, we seen it. Was in great condition and cut the wind good. Had some smudges on it that were kinda sticky, but it didn't smell bad at all. In fact, it smelled new."

"You still have it?" Nik's heartbeat increased.

Mickey hesitated, but Lucy nudged him. "For Eve's. This is important."

One of the reasons Nik liked the Underground was for their efforts with the forgotten. Periodically, the strip club had breakfast and dinner buffets "left" out beside the freight doors for the people who slept in the alleys and beneath the overpasses. Felicia said they'd built the events into their operating budget.

Mickey sighed and swung his dilapidated pack around his body, his gaze sliding around the alley to make sure no one saw him but Nik. Lucy stood sentry while Mickey pulled out the windbreaker, the nylon squeaking as it slid past the teeth of the zipper. He held it against his chest for a moment, still wrestling with the decision to give it up.

"Tell you what, Mickey. You give me that jacket, and I'll make sure I get you a replacement. One that isn't evidence in a murder."

The forgotten man eyed Nik. "Yeah?"

"Yeah. Did that one fit you real good?"

"Nah. Arms were too short, zipper won't close."

"I'll get you one size bigger with a removable lining so

you can wear it in the winter." Nik waited. "But you have to give me that one and I'll bring you the replacement the next time I see you."

Mickey tilted his head. "Soon?"

"Yeah. Later tonight or tomorrow."

"One for Lucy, too?"

Nik narrowed his eyes. "Maybe. Do you have a plastic bag I could have, Lucy?"

"Maybe. Why you need it?"

"I need to put the windbreaker in it so it doesn't get messed up. But I'll trade you a new coat for the bag."

"Don't want a new coat. I want a down vest with a hood."

Nik swallowed his grin, happy to make the exchange, but wanting to give them the sense of control by negotiating. "How about a down vest and a warm fleece hat that won't take up as much room when you pack up your winter clothes in the summer?"

"Done. Shake." She held out a hand covered in a threadbare fingerless glove.

He took her hand and shook solemnly, making a note to head over to the nearest big box store as soon as he got the windbreaker to Chayse at the precinct.

"Thank you both." Nik unfolded the bag and held it out to Mickey.

The man hesitated for just a moment longer before he dumped the windbreaker into the bag. Nik nodded to him. "Where can I find you to bring you your new gear?"

"When you comin'?" Mickey pushed his pack behind him again.

"I can be back here tonight in about two hours or so."

"All right. Eve's has their breakfast buffet tomorrow morning so we'll be hangin' around." Lucy tipped her head. "You be sure to bring me a good vest. Nothin' bright, though. I like the dark colors."

"What size should I get so it fits you better?"

Lucy bit her lip. "Large. I like to wear layers."

Nik nodded and lifted the bag. "Thank you again for this. It's gonna help a lot."

"We won't get into no trouble, will we? 'Cause we ain't gonna give you our fingerprints."

"Nope. You're confidential sources." Nik paused and scanned the alley. "But can you show me which dumpster you found it in? There might be other evidence there, too."

"Sure." Lucy ambled off deeper into the shadows of the alley, leading him toward a set of trash bins. Only one stood undamaged, doomed to be the last one standing in the front line of garbage collection. Lucy pointed to the undented can. "That one there is where it came from."

Nik wanted to inhale the scents, but he didn't need to be vomiting over the humans next to him. "Thank you, Lucy. Would you accept a hug or is that too much?"

Some of the forgotten didn't like to be touched. Lucy eyed him for a moment then nodded. He enfolded her in a quick squeeze and released her. Satisfaction welled up inside as he snapped a picture of the trash can with his phone and texted it to Chayse. The cops would need to collect and examine the can for evidence.

"You've both done a great thing for Eve's." Nik nodded to the two forgotten. "And I'll get you your new gear by tomorrow at breakfast."

Lucy and Mickey offered him cautious nods as he headed for his truck with the bag gripped tight in his hand. His phone pinged with Chayse's response. His brother would send some techs down to collect the garbage can and test it for evidence. *We're gonna catch you, you sick bastard.* Paul Hemmings would be in for a surprise.

CHAPTER TWELVE

"The smoking gun." Nik dropped the bag containing the windbreaker on Chayse's desk. "Or as close to it as you're probably gonna get."

His brother grinned and snapped on latex gloves before peeling the edges of the bag open. He drew out a slate gray windbreaker with reflective strips on the sleeves and large, dark blotches of another substance on the front panels. Nik's nose immediately picked up the scent of dried blood along with Mickey's body odor, but they'd have to test it to see if it matched Johnson's.

"Hot damn." Chayse shoved the jacket back in the bag. "We'll get right on this. See if we can match the blood to Johnson. You're sure this is the one Hemmings was wearing in the video?"

Nik shrugged. "Looks about the same. You'll have to test it for DNA beyond Johnson's. Just be aware, I got it from one of the forgotten who lives near Eve's. His DNA could be on it, too."

"Shit. Really?" Chayse lost his smile.

"Hey, recycle, reuse. As far as he was concerned, it was a good jacket."

"Did you get a sample of his DNA to rule him out?"

Nik shook his head. "That's your job. Besides, I don't think he wants to be in the system."

"Dammit, Nik. If we find DNA, we won't be able to pin it on Hemmings if we don't have a control sample."

Nik grimaced and tapped his lips with one finger. "Has Mrs. Johnson come in to ID the body yet?"

"She said she'd be here first thing in the morning. Why?"

"Paul Hemmings is her brother. Maybe you can get her to give you a sample of her DNA and match it for fraternal epithelia. That'll at least give you enough for an arrest warrant."

Chayse tipped his head and narrowed his eyes. "Why don't you want to get a DNA sample from the forgotten?"

"Because he doesn't want anything to do with cops and he's done nothing wrong. All he did was take a trashed jacket and use it for himself." Nik shrugged. "You got your evidence and he's not identified. Win-win."

"You know that just makes my job harder."

"Hey, you're the badass detective. I have faith in you."

Chayse rolled his eyes. "Yeah, yeah. Thanks for this."

"You're welcome." Nik paused, not liking the dark circles under his brother's eyes. "Are you ready to go back to Eve's yet? I'm headed that direction after I run an errand. I could go with you."

All the humor left his brother's face. "No."

"You don't have to be alone with her, Chayse—"

"No. I'm fine. I got this." He lifted the bag. "This is a huge step forward. You go ahead to Eve's. If I need you, I'll call."

"You sure?" Nik used to take Chayse at his word, but it had been too long since they'd been true brothers. He didn't want to let his twin down.

"Yeah. I'm good. I'll get the techs on this ASAP."

Nik wanted to push the issue, but he nodded instead, rapping his knuckles against the desk. "Okay. I'll catch you later, then."

As he walked out of the precinct, he admitted he was relieved Chayse didn't want to go back to Eve's to see Aislynn. Most women didn't turn Nik's head or make him think about them all day. But Aislynn had him by the short hairs, her sweet smile and long dark hair always in the back of his mind. *Maybe Chayse is right and I'm hooked on her because she's a succubus.* But it didn't feel true. Celine had been intoxicating. Aislynn felt like a soothing balm.

Nik climbed into his truck and headed for the nearest big box store, with a shake of his head. *Maybe that's a product of her age.* She had to be experienced and carried herself with confidence.

He rubbed his chin as he pulled into the mostly empty parking lot to the big box store. His gut told him there was so much more to Aislynn than Chayse saw and while his brother had experience, he hadn't experienced Aislynn.

Aislynn is safe and strong. Nik's Brother wolf didn't speak to him much, especially since Chayse had cut him off, but when he did, he usually said something important. Nik had learned to listen.

Nik perused the winter jacket section and found a lined windbreaker in slate gray for Mickey, and a purple down vest with matching fleece hat for Lucy. It felt good to find them something useful. He couldn't save all the forgotten, but he could help a few, and he liked Mickey and Lucy. They were good contacts and watched over Aislynn in a limited capacity. *Not that Aislynn needs watching over.*

He paid for the coats and headed back to his truck. The night had turned cold as it approached dawn and he held back a yawn. He'd need to get some rest before long, but he wanted to get the clothing back to Mickey and Lucy.

By the time Nik arrived at Eve's, the parking lot sat almost empty, but lights blazed from the alley behind the strip club. He grabbed the clothes, locked his truck, and headed for the lights.

The scents of bacon, eggs, fruit, and coffee hit his nose long before he got close. Around the corner stood buffet tables holding steel warming canisters filled with breakfast foods of all kinds. A line of people in scraggly, mismatched clothing, shuffled along the length of the tables while strippers from Eve's filled their molded trays. Everyone laughed and smiled, dishing out the food with compassion and joy.

Felicia's normally cold stare softened as she held out a bowl of cut apple to an elderly man in a ragged beanie. Another woman dressed in jeans and a fleece hoodie served cups of steaming coffee at the end of the line. Her smile flashed and grabbed him by the balls.

Holy First Canid, that's Aislynn.

The proprietor of Eve's Paradise served her guests with grace and kindness, and Nik's heart swelled with recognition.

Aislynn, True Mate. His Brother wolf spoke with confidence and Nik couldn't argue.

He wanted to speak to her, but he needed to find Mickey and Lucy first. His nose led him to the end of the line.

"Hey, Mickey. I brought you your new coat."

"Is it warm?" His contact eyed the bag Nik held out.

"It better be. You won't know until you put it on."

Mickey pulled out the lined windbreaker while Lucy looked over his shoulder. Both gasped in pleasure as the slick material slid out of the bag.

"Oh, it's very nice." Lucy fingered the nylon. "Thick, too."

"And hopefully the right size. This is for you, Lucy." Nik offered her the second bag. "The bag's yours as well."

She bit her bottom lip like a kid at Christmas time as she took the shopping bag. A lovely smile creased her lips when she pulled out the purple vest and matching fleece hat.

"Did I do good?"

She bobbed her head. "Yeah. It's perfect."

"Good to hear." Nik took her smile as a gift. "Take care of yourselves and enjoy your breakfasts. And thanks for your help."

He couldn't hold back his smile as he walked the line of folks getting food from Eve's employees. Felicia interacted with more relaxation and happiness than he'd ever seen from the vampire. Musical laughter full of joy snagged his ears and he followed the sound to where Aislynn stood joking with a couple of staff members.

Nik took a moment to enjoy her without her knowledge, and the ringing always in the background of his head faded into silence. She looked younger than her age, relaxed, and happy. Nothing like the serene mistress of the Underground or the business-savvy entrepreneur of Eve's Paradise.

True Mate. His Brother wolf brooked no argument.

It was all he could do to stifle the urge to walk straight up to her and take her in a hard kiss. While his Moon Singer heritage would help him, he'd never be able to beat off everyone trying to stop him. Instead, he contented himself with approaching slowly and waving to her as he closed in.

"Mr. Wolffe, I'm surprised to see you here." Aislynn lost some of her joviality. "What can I do for you?"

"Nothing. I actually stopped by to talk to a couple of the forgotten who helped me today." He gave her a non-threatening smile. "Or last night. I didn't know today was one of your buffet days until they told me."

She nodded as she collected some of the empty food vats to return to the kitchen. "We try to do it three times in a month, but the recent events threw off our schedule."

"I bet." He paused, watching her as she worked, and couldn't believe how he'd missed the Goddess's message of their connection. "Can I help with anything?"

Aislynn opened her mouth to refuse, but paused and

tilted her head in surprise. "Are you sure?"

"Yeah." Anything to spend more time with her now that he understood who she was to him. "I'm really impressed you do this for these people. I'm happy to help, too."

She blinked then smiled. "All right. That'd be great. Are you sure I'm not trying to buy your soul with this? Your brother would see it as something more sinister."

"Hey, my soul's not for sale, but I'm happy to donate some time and effort." He winked. *And I might sell you my heart if you're buyin'.* "Besides, some of these folks are informants of mine, and while that might not make them friends, I'd still like to help them." *And you.*

Warmth filled her smile. "That would be wonderful. You can help me by taking these dirty trays back to the kitchen and bringing out clean ones."

Disappointment hit his gut, but he swallowed it and nodded affably. He suspected she tested his sincerity by giving him the most boring job. He took the trays in a large pile in through the back door of the strip club and reminded himself the sign of a true master was knowing when to submit.

Want to be with Aislynn. His Brother wolf whined and dropped his head.

I know, buddy. Give it some time. He consoled himself with being efficient and quick without missing anything necessary. He returned to the line with the clean trays and fell into place beside Aislynn while she dished out shredded hash-browned potatoes. He grinned when she raised an elegant eyebrow and happily handed out English muffins and pats of butter to the folks in line.

"You really don't mind doing this?" She shot him a look of surprise.

"I really don't." Nik nodded then lowered his voice. "And I want to spend more time with you."

The surprise changed into wariness. "Why?"

He wanted to tell her what he'd discovered, what his

heart and his Brother wolf knew, but it was too intimate for all the people around. *And more than likely she won't believe me.* Instead, he leaned close and inhaled theatrically.

"Because you smell really good." He added a grin and she laughed.

"It's the potatoes." Aislynn winked.

He laughed with her and her shoulders relaxed. "Should I start calling you Mrs. Potatohead?"

"It's Ms., actually. I'm not married."

"Well that's fortunate." He winked and leaned in close to whisper. "I'm not married, either."

She grinned and dished out potatoes to the next person in line. "Somehow, I'm not surprised."

"What's that supposed to mean?"

"You strike me as a swinging bachelor, Mr. Wolffe. Not one to settle." She said it without rancor or malice.

"That's probably true." He shrugged thoughtfully. "And the name's Nik. After dishing out food for people, I figure we can be on a first name basis. Or at least, you're welcome to use my first name."

"You're comfortable with giving me your first name?" Again she sounded wary.

"Yes, I am." *I'd like to give you much more than that.* "I'm not afraid of you, Lady Aislynn."

"Perhaps you should be." She said it so low, even his sensitive ears strained to hear it.

Nik shook his head. "My brother's afraid enough for both of us. I've seen you with people. You could be evil, but you're not." A yawn threatened to crack his jaw as the sky lightened to a rosy pink.

"I think you should go home and rest, Nik." She bumped him with her shoulder so she didn't have to put on new plastic gloves. "You're dead on your feet and we really have things well in hand here. Get some rest."

But I wanna stay with Aislynn. His Brother wolf whined

again, but he nodded as he stripped off his own gloves.

"Yeah, I'm beat. Been a long time since I've seen my bed." He cracked his neck and rolled his head on his shoulders. "Thanks again for letting me help."

"It was much appreciated."

The sound of his name in her voice warmed him from the inside out, and his cock threatened to push against his fly.

"Yeah, well, I better go before I drive myself into a light pole. Maybe I'll see you later tonight when I've gotten some rest."

Aislynn tilted her head. "I'd like that."

"Yeah, me, too. Talk to you then."

He sauntered away, tired but happy, and determined to find a way to break the news to her about being his True Mate. It wouldn't be easy. He didn't know much about succubae and their long-term mating habits, but he did know werewolves, and his Wolf had picked her. He unlocked his truck and slid behind the wheel as he sucked in another yawn. He'd be glad to hit the pillows, but he'd bet dollars to donuts he'd be dreaming about Aislynn.

Has to earn her keep as a succubus, right? He laughed and threw his truck into gear.

****

Felicia nudged Aislynn while they cleaned up the buffet tables as the sun gilded the buildings with morning light. They'd sent most of the staff home while they took the last of the food bins and dishes into the kitchens.

"What's up with the werewolf?"

Aislynn met Felicia's gaze as she came back out of the walk-in refrigerator. "What do you mean?"

Felicia hitched a shoulder as she spread cling wrap over a bowl of leftover sausages and handed it to Aislynn. "I might not be the oldest vampire out there, but I can still sense when your energy changes, and it changed around Master Canin. It became…smoother."

"Smoother?" Aislynn blinked.

"Yes, Mistress. If we were talking water, it would be the difference between laminar and turbulent flow." The vampire tilted her head and wiped down the counter with a wet towel. "Before you met Master Canin in person, your energy rippled and bounced like a river full of rapids. But this morning, with him helping you, your energy stilled and flowed evenly. Is there something I should know about him, Mistress?"

Aislynn almost scoffed, but she sealed her lips on the sound and forced herself to consider Felicia's words. She'd learned Felicia saw things about people most others dismissed or ignored. Aislynn knew better than to brush off her assistant's observation.

She pushed a broom around the kitchen floor, considering her words carefully. "I've never met anyone like Nik Wolffe, or his brother for that matter. But I can't be with anyone. My very nature and survival depends on killing my lovers."

"Not anymore." Felicia squeezed the water out of her rag. "You now have the Underground to fulfill your feeding needs. Couldn't you take a lover without killing now?"

Aislynn shook her head. "It doesn't work like that. I can still kill even if I'm fed. If I have sex with someone and we connect, I will still drain them if I lose myself in the pleasure." Sorrow pulled the corners of her mouth down and squeezed her heart. "I've looked for ways to mitigate the Goddess's decree, but the only way to keep everyone safe is to just be celibate except with my own personal toys."

Felicia bit her lip. "You've had far more experience with this than I, and I wouldn't question your knowledge. But in all the centuries we've been together, I've never seen your energy like this with anyone else. Your Nik

Wolffe calms your energy and strengthens it. You're different around him."

Aislynn snorted. "I'm sure it's just a product of recognizing him as a member of the Underground. My energy certainly isn't calm when around his brother."

"No, calm isn't a word I'd use." Felicia swiped the last counter and rinsed the rag. "The first time he was here, he drained you dry as I recall."

Aislynn nodded with a grimace as she put the broom away. "Yes. It wasn't a pleasant experience."

"He's dangerous, Mistress. You should be wary of him."

Aislynn shrugged. "I am, but not as wary as he is of me. Perhaps that's a good thing."

She flipped off the lights in the kitchen as Felicia locked the outside doors, and they retreated into the dark strip club. Without the mood lighting and music, the room sank into a tired gloom and Aislynn looked forward to curling up in her bed. But her mind ran around in happy circles when she thought about Nik Wolffe.

Don't be silly. If she was completely honest, she'd admit it ran around in happy circles for both werewolf brothers. *Not going there.*

"Good night, Felicia."

"Good morning, Mistress."

Aislynn chuckled as she headed down the stairs to her apartments in the Underground. While Felicia slept in a secret bedroom without windows connected to the business office, Aislynn preferred the comfort of the earth around her and the relative safety it provided. Plus it drowned out any traffic noise coming from the residents of Las Vegas on the surface streets.

Once she'd reached her apartments, she stripped out of her clothes and headed for a shower, needing to wash away the dirt of the night and the stress of being in charge. *What would it be like to truly submit to someone?* Oh, she'd played the game with those who needed the illusion of control, but she'd always topped from the bottom, subtly directing the play in the direction to give them pleasure and her sustenance without killing. But with Master Canin, perhaps she could let him be in command.

She closed her eyes and let the water sluice over her, soaking her hair and trailing off her breasts. She could almost picture Nik in his Master Canin guise striding around the room with his intense moss-green gaze on her. Her nipples grew taut despite the warm water and she rubbed them to relieve the excitement.

"Today you're mine, Aislynn." The rough quality to his voice filtered through her thoughts. "I'll make you tremble and lose control at my leisure. And you will lose control."

Only here, in the safety of her fantasy could she do so. *Oh, Goddess, it's been so long.* Part of her missed going all out and taking her pleasure from a lover. But the responsible side of her, the one that regretted, reminded her of the losses and the pain left from those few fleeting moments of pleasure. But here, in her mind, she could let go.

He reached out and trailed a finger across her chest just above her breasts. She swore she could feel it and threw her head back, allowing the hot water to soak her hair.

"Touch yourself, Aislynn. Show me where you'd pleasure yourself when your lover isn't here."

She slid her hand down her body, tangling her fingers in the pubic hair on her mound. She tugged on the hairs and shivered as her nether lips separated, allowing some of the water to slide between them.

"Ah, so you like your hair pulled." In her imagination, Nik nodded thoughtfully. "What else?"

She pushed her hand lower to finger her clit while she used her other hand to massage her breast, squeezing the nipple. The scents of warm water and hot arousal hit her nose as she tweaked her taut peak. She rubbed her nether lips with gentle motions, slowly increasing the pressure until her clit hardened. By the time she'd brushed it with her fingers again, it stood hard and a small gasp escaped as pleasure exploded through her body.

"Very nice, Aislynn. You're beautiful when taking pleasure in yourself." Nik's voice wove its way through her thoughts. "Chayse, take note. Let's give her the experience of two werewolves at once."

Wait, did he say Chayse? Her imagination helpfully added Nik's blond brother to the scene. He stalked up to her and grasped one hand as he led her to a bench set in the middle of the room. With nothing more than a cocky smile, he pushed her belly-down on the bench and spread her legs.

"Now, Aislynn, Chayse is going to finger and tongue fuck you while you show me what you can do with that silver tongue of yours."

Aislynn moaned as she imagined Chayse's hands sliding over her hips and ass, stroking her aching flesh. Her mind sank into the scene playing behind her eyelids and the slick, hot touch of his tongue seared into her awareness.

"Oh, Goddess, Chayse. Lick me so good." Her own voice held notes of desperation and pleasure, and he acquiesced to her demands.

Fingers peeled her nether lips apart, stroking the sensitive flesh with wet calluses. She rocked her hips and moaned just before his tongue returned. The playful tickling of his dexterous tongue pushed her arousal higher and her pussy creamed around his fingers.

"Holy First Canid, you're so fucking beautiful when you writhe like that, Aislynn." Nik stood in front of her and lifted her head until she looked up at him. "But the only moaning I want to hear is you around a mouthful of cock." He waved his erect dick in front of her nose, his leather pants open just enough to allow the thick shaft to stab through.

Oh, Goddess, he's so erotically sexy. In her waking life,

she couldn't show much emotion, but here, in the safety of her apartments, she could show everything. And she wanted to show Nik and Chayse her innermost heart. They were hers to play with, at least in her dreams.

Chayse took his time licking and tickling her pussy, each motion of his tongue against her skin a playful brush. She tried to focus on his ministrations, but Nik wasn't waiting. He pushed his cock down with one hand and stroked her mouth with the tip. Spicy, tangy pre-cum coated her lips and she licked it off in time for more to be applied.

She raised her gaze to meet Nik's and his eyes flared with lust as she took the initiative to lick the tip of his cock as it passed by.

"Ah, fuck yeah, my sweet succubus. Lick my cock before I shove it in your mouth."

She took a breath to answer, but Chayse shoved two fingers into her weeping pussy at that moment and she whimpered with pleasure at his intrusion.

"Damn, you're so wet for us, Aislynn." Chayse's voice held admiration. "I'm gonna lick and suck it all up until you come. Then I'm gonna fuck you slow and deep until you can't take it anymore.

Aislynn shivered and moaned as Nik shoved the head of his cock between her lips. The smooth, taut skin delighted her tongue and she sucked on it with pleasure.

"Oh yeah, that's it. Suck me all the way in, lady." Nik rocked forward, sliding in deeper as Chayse suckled her clit into his mouth and pulled hard.

Oh, Goddess! Pleasure spiked through her as she jerked her hips against his mouth, but she couldn't look with Nik's cock buried between her lips. She swallowed around his thick girth, bobbing her head to slide along his shaft. Chayse tugged on her clit as he finger-fucked her pussy, rubbing her g-spot with each thrust. Wet, lapping sounds combined with the hard slap of flesh against flesh, and the scents of her two men filled her nose.

Sweet Goddess, I want them both. I need them both.

She hummed against Nik's flesh, wishing she could use her hands on his balls, but at some point Nik had bound them to the legs of the bench. She lay completely at their mercy and it thrilled her.

"Oh, fuck yeah, Aislynn. Keep sucking me. I love watching Chayse eat your cunt while you suck on my cock." Nik gathered her hair off her neck and pulled her head back until she met his gaze. "Is he giving you pleasure? Blink twice for yes and once for no."

She blinked twice as Chayse shoved a third finger into her dripping pussy and she gasped around Nik's cock. She tried to keep her focus on the delicious flesh in her mouth to hold off her release, but Chayse's wicked touches kept throwing her off her game. She moaned around the tight shaft and Nik's hand clenched in her hair.

"Sonovaprick, she's gonna make me come, Chayse." Nik sounded breathless. "Eat that pussy so good. It makes her suck so hard."

Chayse growled against her soft flesh, stroking her cunt and licking her folds like a man enjoying a tasty treat. Hot, slick caresses heated her nether lips as he set up a delicious rhythm of thrusts into her pussy. *Oh heavens, I'm going to come.* The third finger and the unrelenting rhythm pushed her arousal up so fast and hard, she clamped down on Nik's shaft.

"Fuuuucccckkk." Nik threw his head back as hot spurts of cum filled her mouth. She sucked hard, swallowing his precious gift as fast as she could before her own orgasm broke over her.

Aislynn squealed around Nik's dick and she tightened her lips around him as Chayse kept thrusting. Her hips rocked on his hand of their own accord while she shot into the stars, pleasure and yearning washing through her. Her orgasm shook her to her core, but it didn't fill the aching chasm in her heart. She needed more.

Nik gently disengaged from her mouth as Chayse pulled his hand free and lapped up her release from between her legs. She shivered with the gentle erotic slide of his tongue against her sensitized flesh.

"Oh, Goddess."

"Not tonight, Aislynn." Nik crouched in front of her, his cock still proudly erect between his thighs. "Tonight it's just me and my brother, and we're not done with you yet." He slid his thumb over her bottom lip in a sensual caress. "You're gonna suck my brother's cock while I fuck you, but you're not gonna come until I tell you. Is that clear?"

Orgasm control? She whimpered.

"Is that clear, Aislynn?" His voice hardened and her pussy spasmed with desire.

"Yes, Master Canin."

"Very good." His smile warmed her from the inside out and he rose, stripping his leather pants off as he strode out of view. She turned her head to catch a glimpse of his naked ass, but he moved too quickly for her to see.

"Chayse, you ready to get your dick sucked?"

"Hell yeah."

Chayse had stripped off his pants and underwear, but left his shirt on as he sauntered to stand in front of her. His cock stretched longer than Nik's, but didn't share the girth of his brother. She licked her lips as the plum-sized head bobbed in front of her nose.

"You want this right here, Aislynn?" Chayse gripped the base of his shaft and waved it in front of her lips without touching them. "Because I'm aching to be between those sweet, sexy lips of yours. I've wanted it since I first saw you."

Oh, how I wish that was true. She looked up and met his blue gaze, astounded by the lust and desire she read in his eyes. *I have a kick-ass imagination.* But something warned her she hadn't made everything up. *Don't be silly.*

Chayse Wolffe hates succubae.

"I'm going to enjoy this, Aislynn, more than you'll ever know. Now open up for me." Chayse pressed the tip of his cock against her lips and she kissed it, wishing this was more than a fantasy. "Aw yeah, kiss my dick before you suck it."

She couldn't simply kiss the head, but had to lick it, to taste his precum leaking from the slit. Chayse moaned and she echoed it as his flavor hit her tongue. Not as spicy as Nik, almost sweeter, like a well-aged cheese, smooth and tangy. She smacked her lips, licking all the slick wetness of him and savoring it.

Oh, Goddess, I can't wait to taste him.

As if Chayse heard her thought, he shoved his cock between her lips, but stopped at just the head, teasing her with his hard flesh. She whined for more, but he only grinned and taunted her, shifting his hips from side to side. His action painted her lips with his precum and she frantically licked as much as she could reach.

She opened her mouth to complain when Nik grabbed her hips and shoved his hard cock into her dripping pussy without warning. She keened her delighted surprise as her eyes rolled back in her head. *Damn, he's thick.*

"Oh, fuck, I thought her mouth was hot." Nik groaned, but held still as her pussy spasmed around his length. "Her sexy cunt is even hotter and tighter. Did she taste sweet, Chayse?"

"Hell yeah, she did. Best pussy I've tasted ever." Chayse reached down and stroked her chin. "Open up for me, Aislynn, and I'll feed you my whole cock."

She opened her lips and he slid in with a groan of pleasure. Nik chose that moment to pull almost all the way out of her pussy and she couldn't help the whimper of protest despite the tasty flesh in her mouth. She swallowed around Chayse's shaft, slipping her tongue along the taut skin and making him moan.

Nik gripped her hips and slammed his cock into her up to his balls, driving Chayse's dick all the way to the back of her mouth. She opened her throat to take him deeper and swallowed again. Chayse growled and pulled back, holding her cheeks in his hands. Nik yanked his cock out and thrust home again, hard and deep. Aislynn gasped as her fires of lust flared back to life.

"We're gonna fuck you so hard and so deep, Aislynn, we'll become part of you and you'll never forget us." Nik's voice had turned into a primal growl. "You're ours, and always will be, and we'll never let you go." He pulled out and slammed back in, fast and solid. "Do you hear me?"

Chayse shoved his cock in her mouth before she answer, but she moaned her approval around his hard flesh. He groaned as she tongued the edges of his cock head while Nik set up a steady rhythm in her pussy.

"Aw, fuck, Aislynn, you're so damn tight and sexy." Nik's hands tightened on her hips as he rocked his pelvis. His balls slapped her nether lips with erotic tantalization.

She swallowed hard and Chayse growled. "Oh yeah, just like that. Suck on my cock while Nik fucks you. Your mouth feels awesome."

She tightened her lips at the same time she clamped her inner muscles down on Nik, and both men issued matching moans. Pride, eroticism, and delight rose in her chest as she focused on giving her bedmates as much pleasure as she could.

Fear tried to push into her mind, but she barred its entrance with the reminder that this was a fantasy. The werewolf twins remained safe from her soul-sucking grasp. Sorrow followed and she almost gave into it until Nik slammed his cock in extra hard and her thoughts splintered with a whimper.

"You will take our pleasure, Aislynn, and you're not allowed to be sad. Do you understand?" Nik withdrew and teased her entrance with the head of his cock. She missed his fullness so much, she nodded as much as Chayse's cock allowed. "Very good. Suck my brother's cock while you take mine."

He shoved back into her hot, empty pussy and they both groaned in unison. Chayse rocked his hips in time to Nik's and Aislynn savored his flavor as much as he allowed her. Nik increased the frequency of his thrusts, stoking her inner fires as his shaft dragged along her clit. But it wasn't quite enough.

"Oh, shit, I'm gonna come, Nik." Chayse threw his head back, his jaw tight.

"You wanna come, Aislynn?" Nik thrust harder. When she whimpered her affirmative, he growled. "Then you suck Chayse off and I'll make you see stars."

She focused her attention down to the hot flesh shuttling in and out of her lips despite Nik's slick shaft building her arousal into dizzying heights. *Must make Chayse come.* She wished she could slide her hand around his cock and fondle his balls, but she only had her tongue and teeth to work with. She raked her teeth over the edge of the crown and Chayse grunted with pleasure.

"Oh, fuck, I'm coming. Aislynn!" His shout turned into a drawn-out howl as he toppled over the precipice of pleasure, shooting hot cum into her throat.

She swallowed as fast as she could, clenching her inner pussy muscles on Nik.

"Aw yeah." Nik hissed as he reached around her and fondled her clit. "Come, Aislynn."

She squealed as the hot rush of ecstasy exploded in her pussy and shot to her head. Pleasure unlike any she'd experienced before filled her awareness until she floated in cloud of perfection and bliss.

"That's it, my lady, squeeze my cock with your pussy and just come. Aw yeah."

Nik's crooning words matched Chayse's growls of release, and their voices followed her back to reality and awareness. The water of the shower had turned tepid and her breasts complained about the pressure against the tiled wall. Aislynn gulped deep breaths with her eyes closed for a few more moments before she pushed herself upright.

She braced her hands on the wall and bowed her head, trying to catch her breath. She was alone in the shower and Chayse Wolffe wanted nothing to do with her. Hell, she didn't really think Nik Wolffe wanted to be near her, yet the fantasy had been realistic enough for her to orgasm harder than she had in centuries. *Not since the last time I killed someone.* It was both a sobering and amazing revelation.

Aislynn turned off the tap and stepped out of the shower. The room smelled like sex and hot water, and she shook her head as she toweled herself dry. She wanted the Wolffe brothers more than she'd ever wanted anyone, including Adam in Eden, but she couldn't have them. Not without assuring their deaths.

The sorrow Nik had thrust aside in her fantasy roared back into her mind, slamming into her like a club. She buried her face in her fluffy towel and wept for what could never be.

CHAPTER THIRTEEN

Chayse parked his car in the parking lot to Eve's Paradise and grabbed his kit, steeling himself for the inevitable. The sun hovered at the horizon, bathing the city in its sunset glow, the light flashing off the tall glass buildings on the Strip. He liked the Vegas colors, especially in the early evening, when everything looked rosy before the lights took over. *Hero hour.* Their older brother Thio often called it that as he stood with his fists on his hips and his chest puffed out. A cowboy hat shaded his eyes to make him look like the Lone Ranger.

Chayse chuckled as he strode for the front doors. His older brother had studied law enforcement and headed for the tiny town of Hershel, Nevada to become its sheriff. Dealing with Vegas had always been strange, but not as strange as being sheriff in the gateway to Area 51. Between the Men in Black and the UFO enthusiasts, Thio always had something entertaining going on. *Must be why we don't see him that often.* Hershel lay no more than fifty miles from Vegas, but his brother didn't get out much. *Neither do we, come to think of it.*

He pulled open the doors to the strip club and gritted his teeth as he stepped inside. Felicia and Aislynn stood together by the bar, and Chayse shoved his instant irritation away. *Must play nice.*

"Good evening, Detective Wolffe. What brings you here tonight?" Felicia deftly stepped in front of Aislynn, shielding her from Chayse.

"I came to finish the tour Lady Aislynn had offered. I'd hoped to see the original crime scene." *Good job in keeping it civil.*

"I didn't think I'd see you again so soon, Detective." Aislynn stepped around Felicia.

"Yes, well, my brother convinced me it would help the case if I returned."

She nodded slowly. "You know he's coming back here for his own reasons beyond the case, right?"

Chayse took a deep breath to hold the familiar anger at bay. "Yes, I know."

"I'm glad he was the one to tell you." She eyed him speculatively, but said nothing for a few more moments.

She looked haggard and worn despite the elegantly cut evening gown and the sparkling diamond jewelry adorning her throat, ears, and hair. A twinge of guilt ran through Chayse, but he brutally squashed it. *She's the monster, not me.*

"I'd appreciate it if you stayed away from my brother." That sounded cordial enough. "He doesn't know what succubae are capable of, but I do. Just leave him alone."

"Is that why you came here? To warn me away from him?" Aislynn sighed and shook her head. "You made that clear on your last visit."

"I'm here because I still have questions regarding the murder victim." His voice came out hard, just the way he liked it, and the other woman moved up protectively behind Aislynn. He flicked his gaze over her and inhaled the scents of sandy soil and blood.

Why had he never noticed the scents on Felicia before? *She must have gone hunting already tonight.*

"I didn't kill him, if that's what you're asking, Detective Wolffe."

"I know. He was drained of blood." Chayse pinned the vampire with his eyes.

"There were no puncture wounds on the body, Officer." Her voice was sultry, but it didn't grab him by the balls like Aislynn's did.

"How do you know that, Ms. Amberhall?"

"Because I was the one who found the body."

"Where did you find the body?"

"In the Lap Dance lounge."

"Fully dressed?"

"Yes."

"Then how do you know there were no puncture wounds?"

The vampire hesitated and glanced at Aislynn. The succubus said nothing, her face filled with exhaustion. Chayse raised his eyebrows.

"There were no vampire punctures on his neck or wrists, I meant. I didn't drain him."

The vampire smelled nervous even though truth rang in her words. She hid something and curiosity hummed through his veins. How far could he push her for the specifics?

Before he could open his mouth to ask his next question, Aislynn raised her hand and stilled them both. "Felicia didn't kill the victim and she did find him, but she didn't find him in the Lap Dance lounge." When Felicia moved to protest, Aislynn laid her hand on the vampire's arm. "It's all right, Felicia. He knows about the Underground, that's why I took them on the initial tour."

The vampire subsided, but her expression settled into wary distrust as Aislynn focused on him. "Felicia found the victim in one of the dungeons. He bled out there."

"Why didn't you tell us this before?"

Aislynn leveled him a dry look. "Detective, the

Underground is not a public place as I'm sure you're aware after the tour. I let you see it as a member of the Elder Races and so you could understand it better rather than rushing to judgement about it."

"But the warrant—"

"Covers video surveillance of the public areas and the specific crime scene, not our members. Each member is vetted and their backgrounds extensively checked. No one goes below stairs unless they are within the membership or brought in as a guest."

Chayse nodded slowly. "I'll still need to see your list of members."

"No."

Fury flared from where he'd banked it back. "You're aiding and abetting a murderer."

"No, I'm protecting my members from unnecessary intrusion."

"And I'm protecting the whole city from your sickness."

Aislynn reared back as if he'd physically slapped her and her eyes glittered with her own anger. "I understand your previous experiences have made you bitter, but I'd appreciate if you stopped labeling me with the horror of your past."

"All succubae are alike."

"No, Detective, they're not. Now, you can either visit the crime scene or take yourself elsewhere. I have a strip club to run and we must prepare." She took a step back.

Chayse gritted his teeth and took a deep breath before he lost the opportunity to do his job. *Find the civility.*

"Please, Lady Aislynn. I'd like to see the original crime scene."

"It has been cleaned. Thoroughly." Felicia's voice had grown as hard as his.

"I still need to see it." He kept his gaze steady on Aislynn's.

She considered him a long time before she nodded. "I'll take him down there, Felicia."

Felicia's expression grew mutinous, but she gave a sharp nod, eyes blazing. "Of course, Mistress."

"Please wait up here for Mr. Wolffe, and bring him down as soon as he arrives."

"Yes, Mistress." Chayse's sense of triumph surged, but he kept his face impassive. No sense in pissing off a vampire. Especially when she glared at him. "Harm her, wolf, and I'll hunt you down and drain you dry."

"Are you threatening an officer of the law?"

"No. I'm warning you to be kind to my Mistress or the law won't have anything left of you to find."

Chayse would like nothing better than to get into a brawl with the vampire, but he reined in his masculine tendencies and forced a nonchalant smile. "I'll take that under consideration."

"That's enough." Aislynn's voice hadn't risen, but steel filled its tones. "Felicia, please wait for Mr. Wolffe. Detective, you may follow me." She turned on her elegant heel and sauntered toward the door beside the bar. Chayse followed after her. *Like the good dog you are.* He swallowed a growl and reminded himself to be civil.

"Did you see the body before she moved it?"

"No, I was incapacitated at the time."

"How so?"

Aislynn looked over her shoulder at him. "Do you really want to know?"

Chayse swallowed hard. "Yes."

She sighed and shook her head. "There was a large orgy going on that night. It had been scheduled several weeks in advance and the playrooms were reserved. There was so much sexual energy here, I was overwhelmed and spent most of the night intoxicated by it in my apartments. I didn't know about the body until I'd come down from the high several hours later. Felicia had already moved it and cleaned up by then."

She stopped beside a playroom door, a crimson satin rope with a sign reading "Closed for Maintenance" hung across the thick wood. Aislynn unhooked the satin rope and Chayse tried not to think of what it would feel like sliding over his skin with ticklish smoothness. His mind filled with the vision of Aislynn trailing the tasseled ends over his cock and balls, teasing them to firmness.

Fuck!

Aislynn glanced at him with a raised eyebrow, but he concentrated on snapping on latex gloves from the equipment bag in his hands, trying to rein in the illicit thoughts. She unlocked the door and pushed it open on silent hinges.

The first thing that hit his nose was the scent of a strong cleaner, but not bleach—*Thank the First Canid.* She flipped the overhead track lighting on and the concrete playroom glistened with light. The floor showed no stains or liquids, and all the cupboards and racks of toys stood in perfect order. The disarray of the murder had been controlled like a Dom controls his submissive.

Chayse stood just within the room and inhaled, trying to pick up the subtle scents beneath the cleanser. Blood filtered into his nostrils along with sweat, lust, semen, and feminine musk. Some of that had to be residual from the years of playing going on in this room, but the blood scent seemed stronger, fresher than the rest. He also caught the hint of his brother's scent. *Nik came down here.*

"Has anyone been in this room since the murder?"

"No. We've kept it closed until the energy in here can be cleansed."

He raised an eyebrow as he looked her his shoulder at her. "How do you do that, exactly?"

"The ideal way is to have a *Morukai* come in, but I don't know any." Aislynn shrugged. "Can you recommend one?"

He stiffened as he heard the humor in her tone. "No."

She sighed. "I'm sorry, Detective Wolffe. I'm not making light of your affliction. A *Morukai* healer *is* the best way to cleanse a room, but in the absence of one, we use candles, incense, and prayers."

"You pray?" He couldn't help the derisive sneer.

"Every day to the Goddess."

He grunted, not sure he felt good or bad about that. Why would a succubus pray to the Goddess? He thought over Nik's words about Aislynn and wondered if his brother had been right about her. He wanted to believe she wasn't evil…

Stop those bullshit thoughts right there. That's just the addiction talking.

"Where did the vampire find the body?"

"Her name is Felicia and she found it hanging in a cage from that pulley right there." She pointed to a hook and pulley system hanging from the center of the room. The cage was missing, but the scent of blood strengthened as he approached the floor beneath the hook.

"Where is the cage?"

"It should be in the storage cabinet."

Chayse crouched and pulled out a high powered penlight. The floor appeared smooth at first glance, but his sharp gaze caught what looked like brown paint caught in tiny nicks in the floor. He set down his shoulder bag and took out the luminal, a solution that reacted to blood when used with a black light. He sprayed the area liberally and reached into his bag for his black light.

"Can you turn off the lights for a moment?"

Aislynn nodded and moved to a switch hidden among the stones. When she flipped the switch, he turned on the blacklight. A great purplish blue swath filled the area below the pulley and individual sprays of more blue dots angled off in two directions.

"Well well. Definitely your murder scene."

"Sweet glory. Are the dots blood spatter?"

"Yes, looks like arterial spray from Johnson's thigh."

He pulled out a swab. It wasn't the most high-tech solution, but if he had a sample, he'd be better off than having nothing. He held the blacklight in one hand and dug in the cracks with the swab before he threw it into its container. He rose and looked for more. Brown flecks filled the crack in a roughly one meter circular pattern. He'd need photos.

"Please turn on the lights again." He switched off the blacklight and dropped it in his kit.

Even with the lights on, he needed better illumination. Holding the flashlight in his teeth, he dug out a small scale and set it on the floor for scale then grabbed his camera. Not the high-powered one they had at the lab, but still a pretty good point-and-shoot for emergencies.

"You still have some blood here."

"I don't know if I should feel shocked or relieved."

"Relieved?"

"Yes. If you find the killer, my club will be much safer."

Chayse snorted. "Highly doubt your club could be classified as 'safe.'"

"That's because you don't understand what it's truly about, Detective. But it's definitely not safe with a killer on the loose."

Chayse couldn't argue that. *Which means you better get back to work to find the killer rather than blabbering with the succubus.*

He scanned the floor in ever widening circles, but he found nothing else. They really had cleaned the room thoroughly.

"Which cabinet holds the cage?"

Aislynn skirted the center of the room to open a large upright metal cabinet. It reminded Chayse of the old paint cabinets in his father's garage. The double doors opened on silent hinges and he caught the scent of blood coated metal immediately. Aislynn backed out of the way and he swept the light over the surfaces. The metal strips hadn't been cleaned as thoroughly as the floor and he smelled several other substances including feces.

He grunted with disgust. "This is definitely where the victim was killed. I can smell that his bowels released. Did Felicia mention that?"

Aislynn wrinkled her nose. "No. She just said she'd cleaned up the mess."

"Lucky for all of us, she didn't do more than hose this thing off. Let's see if we get anything off it." He dragged the human shaped cage out to the floor, careful not to rip the thin gloves. He tipped it on its side and rolled it until the foot plates showed in the light.

Though the metal appeared clean, the stench wafting off it hurt Chayse's nose. A fetid mixture of blood, feces, sweat, and human musk became stronger the closer he got to the bars on the lower portion of the cage. His flashlight showed subtle stains and he took samples of each, but what most interested him was the skin flakes caught in a tiny crack in the metal. It appeared as if someone had reached through the bars and scraped themselves on it.

His gut clenched with excitement. If the skin belonged to the killer, he'd come that much closer to catching the bastard. *And I can see if it matches DNA from the jacket Nik recovered.* They'd matched the blood spatter to Mr. Johnson, but the hairs recovered off the fabric had come back as an unknown Caucasian male. Without a DNA sample from Nik's source, they couldn't rule him out, but they'd tested the hairs against Mrs. Johnson's DNA. The results hadn't come back yet, but now he had a new sample to test.

"I think I found skin."

"Really?" Her voice sounded curious and her scent pushed away some of the stink as she closed on him. "Do you think it belonged to the victim or the killer?"

"I won't know till I take it back to the lab and compare it to the sample we took from Mr. Johnson, but it's a start." Chayse bottled up his sample. "Do you have records of who was here in the Underground the night Mr. Johnson died?"

"Of course."

"I'd like to check them to see if we can narrow down the suspect pool."

Aislynn hesitated, her body stiffening. He tried not to notice how it pushed her breasts up or made his groin tighten.

"I already told you I'd protect my members."

He held up his hand. "I'm not asking for all your records, just the ones for the people who were there that night."

"That's quite a few considering there was an orgy."

He nodded and rubbed his forehead. "Maybe you can help me here. What if we looked at the records of the people who came into the strip club portion and matched them to the Underground? That way you could tell me who was in both places."

"How will that tell you who the murderer is?" She tipped her head.

"It won't, but it might narrow things down. Do you have surveillance in the club upstairs?"

"Yes. That's public and we have to keep track of anyone coming in."

Chayse zipped up his bag. "That's a place to start. If we're lucky, we won't have to look at more than a few members." Goddess knew he didn't really want to know what the prominent Vegas citizens did in Aislynn's Underground.

She eyed him for a moment, her expression guarded. "Very well. I have copies of the security footage from that night in my private office."

"Not in your business office?" He raised an eyebrow as he picked up his kit. "I thought you'd keep them there."

"I have them in that office as well, but backups are necessary and my private office is closer to where we are now. It will simply save time."

"Good plan. The sooner I get out of here, the better."

"I agree. Follow me." She turned on her heel, her back straight as she sauntered away.

Chayse rubbed his chest at the shot of hurt and disappointment her words engendered then anger smothered it. *You don't want her to want you. You don't care if she likes you. It's not important.* But the hard tone of her voice cut him anyway as he followed her out of the dungeon.

****

Aislynn's gut clenched. She shouldn't be alone with this man, especially after her fantasy. She'd told Felicia she wouldn't allow herself to be alone with him, not until they understood why he affected her so much. But he needed the information and they had to find the killer without involving human cops. She owed it to her clientele and to herself. Her clubs and brothels had always been safe places for people to experience their sexual needs. With a killer among her clients, no one was safe, and she'd be damned—well, again—before she'd allow the killing spree to continue in her club.

She led Detective Wolffe down the one "dead-end" hallway in the whole Underground. He'd seen it before, but a shiver of unease always followed her when she allowed anyone to see where her private quarters lay. The secret door stood flush with the stone walls and unless one knew what to look for, it remained indistinguishable. Some part of her loved the 'cloak-and-dagger' aspect of her home. *So why am I showing it to a cop, again?*

The rough-hewn stones hid the latch, one stone smaller and oddly shaped as compared to the rest, and the door swung inward on silent hinges. Aislynn stepped inside and waited for the cop to follow her before she pushed it closed again.

With the thick stone door closed, comfort and relief draped around her shoulders. This was her sanctuary, the one place she felt safest, with her few possessions and privacy around her. The oddness of allowing this man into it hit her again.

It's only to show him the security videos. Then he'll be gone to do his job and everything will be fine. It sounded good in principle, but even her mind didn't quite believe the words.

Neither of them said anything until they'd crossed the threshold into her office. She tried to take comfort in the homey furnishings and the familiar décor, but the sullen, wary presence of the man behind her ruined her ease. Aislynn dropped into her chair and keyed open the computer, trying to ignore the detective's brooding stance beyond her desk.

"Won't you sit down?" She didn't look at him. "Your hovering makes me uncomfortable."

"Does it? How inconvenient for you." He didn't move to sit. "Your very existence makes me uncomfortable."

"Yes, well, this is my home, like it or not, so please extend me the courtesy of having respect for it." Her voice had come out sharper than she'd intended, but she'd grown tired of his constant animosity. Yes, she was an 'evil' succubus, but he could at least try to be polite.

"I just need the videos and then I won't need to respect your home ever again. Hell, you can even email them to me."

"Wrong." She set up the video to stream to her monitor so they could watch visitors to Eve's the night of February sixth and rose from her chair. "You should always respect someone's home. I believe even the laws of Nevada state I have the right to shoot and kill you should you step across my threshold with nefarious intent."

"But I haven't done that, have I? And I'm a cop conducting an investigation in the *home* of someone who's naturally 'nefarious.'" Detective Wolffe's lip curled with derision and his fists balled at his sides, one tightening on the handle of his kit. "Are you threatening an officer of the law?"

"No, I'd never do anything so crass," she snapped, not sure why she baited him. Something about his anger excited her, made her push his limits to see how far he'd go.

Are you insane? Twenty thousand years and you've finally lost your mind. Leave him be.

"I just figured you'd have the same manners your brother displays when he's here. You had the same mother, after all." Aislynn raised her chin in challenge. "In fact, perhaps I'll only deal with him from now on. Your animosity and antagonism grow tiresome."

The thump of his bag against the floor presaged his movement, but Aislynn still squeaked when the man snarled and launched himself at her. He slammed her up against the wall, standing nose to nose as the computer sedately loaded the surveillance. The scents of his sweat, anger, and need flooded the air around them, and Aislynn's heart thundered with sexual excitement and predatory urges. She could feed from his energy and survive for weeks.

"Stay. Away. From. My. Brother."

Each word ripped him in a feral growl, fury, desperation, and desire burning in his steel-blue eyes. The emotions seduced her like a siren's call and all of her own anger melted away in the face of them. Before she could check her motion, she'd cradled his face in her palms and dragged it to her lips.

Detective Wolffe froze, his body as rigid as the hard length pressed against her belly. Tension and surprise sang almost as loudly as his desperation, and Aislynn yearned to soothe the powerfully negative emotions. She poured all her compassion, understanding, comfort, and love into her kiss.

Wait. Love?

He groaned and gave in, taking her kiss and nearly devouring her.

Hot, searing lust roared through her, burning away any fear or doubt about the rightness of their connection. While most of it belonged to him, some part of her answered with her own lust and desire, matching his need. He tasted of male, wolf, and desert nights under the stars, intoxicating. She'd never tasted scents or emotions before and each new flavor enticed her more and more.

I should stop. I'm becoming addicted.

The thoughts vaporized when he slid a hand up her thigh, hiking her skirt close to her waist. When she tried to pull away, he growled and shoved his hips against her, pinning her in place while his tongue ravaged her mouth. The enthralling emotions swarmed over her, sucking her down into their warm swirl, feeding the succubus part of her until she only wanted more.

Must resist. Can't kill him.

The howling maelstrom of desire and need drowned out the voice of reason and she kissed him back. Her hands gripped the hem of his shirt and worked it up his body until it exposed his abs and chest. She wanted to feel them against her bare breasts, but more importantly, she needed his cock in her pussy.

Wolffe pulled back and snarled, baring his extra-long canines. She responded with a hiss, daring him to fight her. His eyes flared with lust and challenge, and he used one hand to hold her in place while the other slid between her legs, palming her pussy. She gasped as his fingers probed her sensitive lips, and he held her gaze while he worked them into her slit.

"Is this what you wanted, demon?"

Lustful anger rose and she growled. "My name is Lady Aislynn."

He pulled his hand away and licked his fingers, his nostrils flaring over the scent and taste. "You're fucking wet, *Lady* Aislynn. Is this what you want? My hand in your cunt?"

She raised her chin. "No, Wolffe. I want your cock in my cunt."

His eyes widened as he pulled back from her, but left his hips spreading her thighs. She met his gaze, daring him to run. Daring him to fuck her. She wasn't sure which, but the lust burning through her veins seemed to arch to him and galvanize his motions.

He ripped the buckle of his belt open and shoved his jeans off his hips. His cock rose long, slender, and proud from a nest of golden curls and pre-cum beaded at the tip. Erotic joy surged in her chest as she dropped her gaze to the flared head of his dick and she licked her lips with hunger.

I want him. She shouldn't have him. She should push him away and let him go. But the lust and desire goaded her to reach out and slide her fingers over his sensitive tip rising between them.

Wolffe groaned as she rubbed the silken skin, wetting her finger tips, but he whimpered when she drew the hand to her lips and licked off his pre-cum. Smooth, tangy flavor reminiscent of a fine brandy hit her tongue and lit fires in places that hadn't seen flame in centuries.

Mine.

The thought seemed to belong to someone else, but she couldn't stop herself from grabbing his shaft and stroking him as if she owned him. She would've loved to bend down and suck on his straining cock, but he had her pressed too tightly against the wall. Instead, she tilted her head and pressed her lips to his throat, licking and sucking on his skin. She wanted to brand him as hers, to warn any other female or male off.

Her grip tightened on Wolffe's cock and he groaned as she licked his neck. Salty, male sweat hit her tongue and she echoed his moan, savoring his flavor. Her vocalization seemed to spark him into action and he thrust his fingers harder into her pussy, stalling her own grip on his flesh. His eyes glowed in the soft light of her office as he pulled his dick out of her hand.

"You're mine." The statement didn't seem to bring him joy, but he shoved her skirt out of the way and thrust his cock home.

Aislynn keened her pleasure at his hot, thick intrusion, and rainbow sparkles danced behind her closed lids. She dug her nails into his back to hold on as he pulled his cock out and thrust home again. Her inner muscles tried to hold him each time he slammed into her, but he jerked free with a grunt and bared teeth.

More. I want more.

She opened her eyes and met his gleaming cerulean gaze, raising her chin in challenge. He snarled at her and thrust faster, the slick slide of his flesh in hers building her orgasm faster than ever. Each thrust stroked her clit and each withdrawal teased her sheath. The sounds of wet flesh hitting hard echoed in the room and the scent of their arousal perfumed the air.

"That the best you can do, Wolffe? Fuck me harder. I can take it and I want it." She snarled back at him. "Fuck me out of your system."

His eyes widened and he paused, fear crowding some of the lust from his eyes, but she squeezed his cock with her inner muscles and the desire took over again. He grasped her hips and jack-hammered into her pussy with his cock. She whimpered and writhed on him, the pleasure increasing with each fevered thrust. He seemed to understand she'd come close but needed a little extra because he reached between them and strummed her clit.

"Oh, sweet Goddess!"

She keened her pleasure as her orgasm took her by surprise, but he didn't stop, his eyes glowing eerily blue as he watched her come. She didn't get much time to enjoy it before his thrusts built her arousal anew and this time she was determined to take him with her. She ignored the voice of reason warning against this action as she rocked her hips on him, her cum making them even slicker.

"Oh, Goddess, you feel divine, Wolffe, but you'll come with me now." She met his gaze and grinned in challenge. "Come with me now!" And she squeezed him hard.

Wolffe stiffened, his orgasm making him pound into her with two more hard thrusts. His emotional overload threw her into her own release, shooting her higher than she'd ever gone with any of her past lovers. Her scream blended with Chayse's into a cacophony of passion and release, probably heard throughout the entire Underground despite the soundproofing in the walls. Aislynn spread wings she never knew she had and sailed into the heavens. Just before she reached the peak of her flight, his teeth locked into her right shoulder and pure ecstasy exploded behind her eyes.

Joy, comfort, and a sense of 'coming home', of belonging, swirled through her, clicking into place like a missing puzzle piece. It fueled her flight and sent her higher. She'd never experienced such a connection before, or the urge to return the favor. The pleasure burned in her chest and she needed to give it back. She bent her head, laying a perfect *swak* on his left pectoral above his nipple. The quality of her kiss seemed different, even to her, and she pressed her lips against him harder.

The brush of her lips made him tremble and his cock flexed within her pussy. He seemed to come back to himself, releasing her shoulder with a gasp and ripping their contact apart. His eyes locked on hers and his expression filled with dawning horror, draining the euphoria from her faster than a syringe drew blood. A despairing groan tore from his chest and he pulled out of her with a jerk, taking his warmth and delicious scent with him. Aislynn dropped dazedly to the floor, her legs nearly buckling under her sudden weight.

Thank the Goddess for the wall.

"Holy First Canid, what have you done to me?"

Before she could respond to his horrified voice, a solid wall of despair and rage slammed into her mind. She tried to scream, but the juggernaut of negative emotions sucked her down into the black and she fell with it.

CHAPTER FOURTEEN

Nik stuffed his keys into his pocket as he stepped through the doors of Eve's Paradise, memories of being here with past lovers crowding his mind once again. Something about Aislynn's club settled his nerves and gave him comfort, stilling the nearly constant buzzing he'd noticed in the back of his mind for the last few months. He'd always experienced these emotions and he figured Lady Aislynn's presence had everything to do with it. Perhaps he'd always sensed his True Mate here.

His sister Cynthia mentioned something about the resonance of her True Mate, the complimentary hum that soothed and settled her. Her husband Steven had said something similar, but Nik didn't feel resonance. More like the absence of the annoying frequency of human energy.

Shaking his head, he glanced around the room for Felicia. The vampire stood beside the bar, her eyes on the tablet she held in her hands. He liked her in a distant way, like the sister of his best buddy or a casual acquaintance, but while she'd make an excellent Domme to the right submissive male, he didn't find that kind of connection with her.

"Good afternoon, Ms. Felicia."

"Ah yes, the other brother." Something in her voice told him she'd seen Chayse already and it hadn't been a pleasant experience. "Detective Wolffe said you'd be along. What can I do for you?"

"Actually, it's what I can do for you. One of the other executives attending the NMC conference had a lot of contact with the victim and I suspect he accompanied Johnson here to the club. I hoped it would be possible to check your security footage from that night here at Eve's to see if I'm right."

Felicia's tight expression eased a little. "That could be helpful, but I'll have to ask Lady Aislynn for her authorization."

"Good enough." Nik wanted to see Aislynn anyway. He wanted to make her a proposition, perhaps engaging her as his lover until he could convince her they were meant to be together in a more permanent capacity. She was his True Mate and he'd do his damnedest to make her understand it. He suspected Aislynn held herself separate from all others because of her species. Succubae were universally hated, but Nik had seen enough of her to know she had strength, character, honor, and compassion. And he knew she was his.

"I'll just let her know you're here and—"

A wall of emotion exploded through the room, slamming into them like a hurricane, rippling through the air of the club. Nik staggered beneath the onslaught, grabbing for the railing on the bar as Felicia shot ramrod straight.

"Mistress!"

Her shriek seared Nik's ears and she disappeared. *Holy shit, she can teleport.*

Rage and despair surged from his brother's link and nearly stopped Nik's heart. "Fuck!" He stumbled into a lumbering run toward the door to the Underground, hoping he'd be in time for whatever had happened.

The scents of human lust, love, and other bodily fluids assaulted his nose as he crashed down the stairs, nearly slamming his shoulder into the corner of the wall. He gasped in surprised pain, but kept going. The emotional scents of horror, fury, betrayal, and lupine misery overwhelmed everything else, and Nik ran blindly after them. His stomach threatened to vomit up his delicious lunch and he gritted his teeth against the urge.

He careened around a corner, dashed through a doorway, and skidded to a stop just inside Aislynn's personal office. Pure, unadulterated fear swarmed over him and froze his guts to ice.

Felicia sat on the floor cradling Aislynn's pale, limp body and rocked as she begged the succubus to come back to her. The scent of Felicia's terror swirled with a roiling stench of lupine horror and anger coming from the corner of the room. Nik's gaze found Chayse braced against a bookcase as far from the pair as he could go without leaving the room. He stared at the vampire holding the succubus with rage and disgust alternately flashing through his expression. Nik didn't understand why until he noticed Chayse's jeans open at his waist.

"What the hell happened, Chayse?" Nik barked.

Chayse's fiery gaze shifted to him. "I fucked her." The horror in his voice saturated the air of the room along with his agony.

"You bit her!" Felicia snarled. "And then you hit her."

"You *bit* her?" Nik's stomach rolled.

"I didn't hit her."

"What. Happened. Chayse?" Nik stalked to Chayse's side and grabbed his arm.

Chayse swore as he shook his head.

"Chayse?"

"She threatened you, so I told her to stay away from you." He shook off Nik's hand.

"By fucking her?"

"She kissed me and I'm an addict." Self-loathing burned down their twin-bond stronger than Nik had felt in years. It seared a blazing trail and made his guts clench against the pain. Something had broken the block on their emotional sharing and Nik could experience the brunt of them again. Too bad he couldn't avoid the roiling pain.

"Why is she unconscious? Did you cold-cock her?"

"No." Chayse grabbed his jeans and zipped them up, buttoning them closed.

At least that was a small favor. Nik couldn't imagine Chayse ever hitting a woman.

"He bit her." Felicia's fury drew Nik's gaze to Aislynn's still form. A bite mark completely different from a vampire's punctures marred the smooth, pale skin of the succubus's shoulder.

That looks like...

Nik's gut sank as he swung his gaze back to his brother. *He True-Mated her?* Aislynn was *his* True Mate. *Chewed bones, how can he True Mate my succubus?*

"You True-Mated her."

Chayse's lips tightened, but he said nothing.

"He what?" Felicia raised her eyebrows.

"He True-Mated Aislynn." Nik rounded on his brother. "Dammit, Chayse! How could you?"

"What the hell is 'true mating'?"

"I'm an addict! I couldn't resist her lure. Not this close." Chayse threw his hands out as his mouth pulled down, but Nik balled his hands into fists.

"By the Goddess, what are you talking about?" Felicia squeezed her Mistress. "Aislynn is out cold and he did something to her. I should never have left them alone."

"He True-Mated Aislynn," Nik growled. Fear and fury roiled in his belly. *How could he?* "Which means she's his 'one true love/soulmate', like humans call it. They're bound together forever, now."

"What?" Horror suffused Felicia's face and she

clutched Aislynn closer. "But she's a succubus, not a werewolf." Then she threw her rage at Chayse. "You werewolves always hit your soulmates?"

"I didn't hit her. And she's not my True Mate."

"No." Nik's outrage surged through him, tightening his chest. "She's mine." He swung with all his strength and slammed a fist into his brother's jaw.

****

Aislynn opened her eyes and looked for any familiar details around her. She lay on a patch of barren rock in the middle of a fire-burned forest, the scents of charred wood and grass filling the air. Pale sunlight filtered through the wisps of smoke shrouding the gaunt trees.

Testing her limbs for pain, she slowly sat up and scanned the nearly silent woods. Odd swaths of the forest remained verdant and untouched by the ravages of fire, but the rest stood scorched and blackened. Scents of new spring growth whispered past her nostrils showing hints of recovery, while the smoke choked her throat and stung her eyes. Below the natural forest scents, another familiar odor sat like a layer of decay affecting the world. She almost recognized it, but the soft breeze took it away before it made sense.

Where the hell am I?

The only sounds she heard beyond a breeze came from the crackling flames in some of the smoldering trees. Every now and again a branch would break and crash to the forest floor, echoing through the hollow world. No birds, insects, or animals broke the unhealthy silence.

This definitely isn't Vegas.

Aislynn pushed carefully to her feet and swung her gaze around the woods again. Small patches of pristine understory and new growth dotted the landscape, but much of the area wore the recent fire scar like a disease. While changes were apparent, the forest's health had yet to recover.

A keening wail of fear and despair split the air, making Aislynn's hair stand on end. She whirled around, searching for the source of the anguish. Everything inside her demanded she find the being crying out and offer succor. Gathering her strength, she tested her legs, hoping they'd carry her wherever she needed to go. The wail emerged again from behind a blackened pile of boulders to her right, and she picked her way around the charred stone, following the sound.

More oddly burned forest greeted her gaze behind the rocks and she stared in dismay. How would she find anyone in that? Another cry jerked her into motion among the scarred trees and she scanned the damaged landscape.

It took her a while to find the owner of the despair hidden in a small oasis of green in the ravaged forest. He sat with his legs drawn up to his chest and his arms wrapped around them. His blond head rested on his knees and he rocked a little, transmitting his distress. Despair filled the air with its noxious stench just before he threw his head back and bellowed another heart-rending cry.

Glory be, it's a little boy.

He couldn't be more than twelve human years old, tow-headed with vaguely familiar features twisted in misery. The pain broadcast from his whole body constricted her chest and Aislynn wanted to throw her arms around him and hold him close until it stopped.

"Are you all right?" she choked out.

She didn't who was more surprised. Her, at the youthful sound of her voice—*Goddess, I sound like a little girl*—or him at her presence. He gasped and jerked his head forward, his wide, frightened eyes locked on her face. Terror flooded out from him, inundating the air around them with its rancid smell.

"Who are you?"

His voice had qualities she'd heard before and it tickled her awareness with familiarity.

"Eva." Again, Aislynn's voice sounded strange to her ears. She'd never been a child, at least not physically, and it felt odd. That she'd offered her secret name for herself as an identity to this child made her stomach do flips in nervousness. She cleared her throat. "Who are you?"

"Chayser." He frowned and squeezed his knees. "What are you doing here?"

"I don't know." Aislynn/Eva hitched her shoulder in a shrug. "I don't know where I am."

"This is my forest." Chayser looked around. "Or it was before the monster came." Anger and pain flashed across his face. "The monster burned everything!"

"Is the monster still here?" The trepidation in her voice sparked surprise.

"I don't know. I hid here and I haven't looked for it."

Eva swung her gaze out of the oasis. "I saw patches of new growth in your forest as I walked through it. Maybe the monster is gone and your forest is starting to recover."

"It's never gone." The resignation in his voice made her heart bleed. "It's always there. It shows up if I ever forget to keep a look-out." Then suspicion suffused his features. "How did you get here?"

Eva bit her lip. "I don't really know. One minute I was in Las Vegas, and now I'm here. I was talking to…"

She trailed off as all the clues came together with a snap. The burnt forest smelling slightly diseased should have been the first sign, but his name, the "monster", and it 'always being there' clinched it for her.

She'd somehow gotten into Detective Chayse Wolffe's inner 'garden of the soul', his sanctuary ravaged by the succubus before her. Eva still had no idea how she'd gotten here, but she suspected it had something to do with the sex they'd had in her office.

She doubted Chayser would appreciate her presence if

he knew what kind of creature she was, but she didn't want to deceive him, not soul to soul. How could she portray her species as a positive thing to him after all this damage? She found herself wishing she could heal the pain, fear, and hurt she read in the landscape around her. Dammit, this was her werewolf! How dare someone else try to destroy him?

By the Goddess, I'll do my best to help him because he's worth it.

"I'm sorry, Chayser." Eva folded her legs under her, sitting on her heels. "I'm not sure how I got here, but I'm here to help you. I know what kind of monster was here before."

"You do? How?"

She took a deep breath against the fear threatening to strangle her. *Goddess, please don't let him hate me.*

"Because I'm one of them."

Chayser shrank from her as if she'd spat fire. His lips peeled back from his teeth as he bared his long canines in a feral snarl.

"Get away from me!" Even as young as he appeared, he had power and strength in his voice. Eva rocked backward until she sat on her butt in the ashy dirt. "You're evil. I will never be your friend. Get out!"

Her heart sank with sorrow and pain at his reaction, but she wasn't surprised. Still the hurt of his rejection tore through her like a knife and she swore she bled from the inside.

"Peace, Chayser." Eva didn't rise from where his energy had thrown her, though she ached to hold him. "I'm here to help you heal from my kind. I want nothing from you." *That's not entirely true. I want his heart.* "I only want you to be free of the taint. I want you to be strong again."

"Liar! That's what the last one said just so she could suck it all away again, making me want more of her nastiness. You're just the same."

"No, I'm not." Eva shook her head, trying to meet his

furious eyes. "No, I don't want to feed from you. I want you to be whole so you can be with your brother again."

His steel-blue eyes widened in panic. "How do you know my brother?"

"I saw him a few years ago when he came to my…" How did she explain the club to Chayse's inner little boy? "He came to my home because he missed his brother too much to be alone."

"Did you hurt him?" Rage flared.

"No, I only saw him. I didn't talk to him or hurt him. He's still strong and healthy." Eva found her heart warming with the thought of Nik Wolffe in her club. "He misses you, I think."

"I had to get away from him, to save him from the monster. Monsters like you."

"You did a good job. The monster didn't get to him."

"Because I saved him."

"Yes." Eva ran her hands through the new grass beside her, reveling in the soft feel of it. *Kind of like a wolf's pelt.* "But he needs you now. He needs you to come back and connect with him again."

"No. I can't. He won't be safe anymore." Chayser shook his head, his jaw clenching tight.

"He will be. I promise. And so will you. You're stronger together than apart." She nodded, knowing she could lose both these brothers forever. "Together, you'd be strong enough to keep out all the monsters from now on. You'd be able to recognize their energies and he'd be able to anchor you from falling into them. No one would ever pull you in again."

"That's not true." Tears slid down Chayser's cheeks. "I'm an addict. I'll always be an addict. I can't control the want for it. I can't stop it."

Eva's heart tore at his anguish and a little sob hitched her breath. "Yes, you'll always be an addict, but there's a way to change your addiction to something healthy rather than the pull of the monsters."

What was she doing? Why was she giving him the secrets to pull away from her completely? Eva mentally shook her head and pushed on, determined to help her werewolf, even against herself.

Chayser's eyes fixed on her face, his expression both suspicious and angry. "Oh yeah? How?"

Eva rubbed her hand over her knees in nervousness. "Your brother told me werewolves have true mates, the one person meant to be with them by the Goddess's design. Do you know about that?"

Chayser scoffed. "Of course."

She nodded. "If you find that one person, you can transfer your addiction to their energy rather than that of the monsters, of my kind. If you get your true mate's energy and bind yourself to it, not only will you heal faster, but you'll never be tempted by a suc–" She stopped before she said the word, not wanting to draw that kind of energy back here. "By a monster again."

He narrowed his eyes. "Wouldn't my True Mate be in danger because *I'm* the addict? Won't she be sucked in just like my brother would?"

"No, not with this kind of bond. It's too strong for monsters to break." *Oh please, Goddess, let me be right.*

"Why are you telling me this? You're one of them. This has to be a trap."

"No, Chayser, it's no trap. Once you find that perfect mate, you can't be corrupted. I promise." *I'd give my life to be right about this.* Eva tried to smile, but her uncertainty made it more of a grimace. "I'm telling you because you don't deserve what was done to you. No one does, it's true. I try not to do this to anyone."

"Why?" His question rang with doubt and accusation.

"Because I don't like hurting people. I never liked it, even when I had to do it to survive. It made me feel sick inside." She curled a hand into a fist and pressed it against her belly. "I couldn't do it anymore. I had to find some other way to live without hurting people."

"Why do you even care?"

Anger stirred and she raised her chin. "Not everyone is like the other monster. I care and it's important to me. You don't have to have my help. I can leave right now and you can suffer by yourself."

She gritted her teeth to stop her tears of frustration and lurched to her feet. He didn't want her help and it hurt, but she'd survive. She could let him go. She'd get over him like she had all the other males who'd come into her long, jaded lifetime. *It doesn't matter. He'd never trust me anyway.*

Eva wiped her eyes and turned away, trying to retrace her steps to where she'd started. The trees and blackened rocks blurred in her vision and pain tore through her chest. Why did this hurt so much? She'd only met Chayse Wolffe a few days earlier. How in the Goddess's name did they have this kind of connection?

"Wait!"

Eva ignored Chayser's voice as she kept walking, stumbling in a jagged line…somewhere. She didn't even know where she was going. The idea made her stop and look for an exit, but how did one exit a forest?

She swung around just as Chayser plowed into her, tackling her to the ashy ground. Eva shrieked in hurt surprise before struggling out from under his surprisingly heavy body.

"What are you doing? Get off me."

"Sorry." He backed away and wiped his face, leaving a streak of soot across his left cheek. "I tripped at the last minute. I didn't mean to knock you down."

She huffed and gave him a dubious look.

"Are you crying?" He cocked his head, trying to see her face clearly.

"No." Eva swiped at her tears.

"Yes, you are. Girls always cry."

"That's because we know it's better to cry than to hit. Boys always hit."

"Not all boys."

"Oh, yeah?"

"Yeah."

"You just knocked me down. What do you call that?"

"That was an accident." He stuck out his bottom lip and crossed his arms over his chest. "I'd never hit a girl."

"Only monsters."

"What?" Chayser's eyes opened wide.

"Only girl monsters. You'd hit them."

"No…"

"You just did."

"I told you it was an accident. I tripped." When she didn't say anything, he added, "And I'm sorry. I really didn't mean to."

Despite her frustration and hurt, Eva believed him. But she wasn't ready to forgive him quite yet. She rubbed her arm across her face and sniffled. "Why were you chasing me?"

To her surprise, mature amusement flashed through his expression, reminding her of the man he had become outside of his forest. "Because that's my name?"

"Very funny." But she did chuckle reluctantly. "But why, really?"

Chayser looked down and scuffed his hand through the detritus on the ground. "You were right. You're not like her, the other monster. You smell different and you're not…heavy."

"Heavy?"

"Yeah. You know…" He scrunched up his nose trying to find the right description. "Like gravity we learned about in school. Everything gets pulled into the heavier object, like meteors into the earth and stuff." He gestured at her. "You're not like that." Then he shrugged. "I feel better when I'm around you."

Eva's heart sank. Maybe she'd addicted him to her energy already. "Didn't you feel better when you were around the other monster?"

"Yeah. Well, no, not really." He rubbed his forehead, leaving more soot on his face like war paint. "It felt good and it didn't. I was always tired and she never wanted to be with me. She kept burning things and laughing at me. You're not like that." He grimaced. "You smell different."

"Good different or bad different?"

His expression turned mischievous. "Bad different?"

"Shut up." But she grinned when she said it.

He laughed and the sound shimmered through the air of the forest, snuffing some of the remaining flames licking the wretched trees. Eva enjoyed the laughter and wished she could make him do it again. *But I'm the monster he hates the most.*

"Can you really help me keep the monsters out? I mean, the other monsters."

Eva hitched a shoulder. "I think so. You already know what they smell like. And you know how you feel when one is around. Well, one other than me." She ran her hands through the grass and paused. Hadn't she been sitting on bare dirt and ash before?

"Do you really know my brother?"

"Yes. He seems nice."

"I miss him." Chayser brushed his hands on his knees.

"I think he misses you, too."

Chayser shook his head. "He's mad at me. I wouldn't share Celine with him."

Share? "Was that the other monster?"

"Yeah. It wasn't that I didn't want to share girls anymore, just not her. She would hurt him like she hurt me."

"You protected him." Eva recalled the conversation in her office and marveled again at Chayse's strength.

"Yeah, but he thinks I don't like sharing anymore. And I couldn't tell him why he had to stay away. So I told him I didn't want to do it ever again." His face crumpled. "Now he hates me."

"I don't think he does. Maybe you could tell him you still want to share." She hugged her knees as excitement shivered through her body. "What did you mean by sharing girls?"

Chayser blushed and wouldn't meet her eyes as he dug his toes into the new grass. The patch had grown around them to blanket everything almost up to the pile of boulders. The air smelled fresh as if the wind had blown away most of the smoke and fire scents.

"You *know...*"

Surprise mixed with delight at the thought of her two werewolf males sharing her. Would they still be interested? *When did I start thinking of both of them as mine?* But arousal shifted through her as she pictured herself between them, pleasuring and being pleasured by both of them.

Dear Goddess, I so wish.

"Oh." She smiled and tugged at her skirt, making sure it covered her legs all the way to her ankles. "I guess so. You'd have to ask him. But I know he's not mad at you."

"Really?"

She took a breath to answer when a blast of wind shook the trees, making them creak and groan under the onslaught. The scent filling the air reeked of fury and Chayser shrank from it as if the monster of his nightmares had returned. Eva gasped and jerked upright just as another blast of wind slammed into her, knocking her out of Chayser's forest and into the darkness.

CHAPTER FIFTEEN

"What the fuck is wrong with you, Nik?" Chayse had never seen his brother so angry before in his life and he scrambled away from him, rubbing his jaw.

"You stupid, selfish, greedy son of a prick!" Nik stalked him like they'd done as children, but this didn't feel very much like a game. "You already took everything with you when you left, but you had to take this too? I'm gonna kill you."

"What are you talking about? I didn't take anything from you."

Nik's eyes glowed with feverish fury. "Yes, you did, asshole. Aislynn is *my* True Mate."

"What? No fucking way, man. That's just the pheromones talking. She can't be your True Mate. She's a succubus."

"I *know* that, but it didn't stop her from being my True Mate. And you stole her from me!" Nik launched himself at Chayse and tackled him, crashing over one of the ornate chairs in Aislynn's office.

"That's enough! You can't fight here."

Felicia's voice disappeared beneath the snarls echoing through the room. Chayse's embarrassment shifted to anger as he caught his brother and twisted, trying to throw him down. Nik jabbed his fist into Chayse's gut, robbing him of breath, but Chayse head-butted his brother's nose. Nik roared and reared back long enough for Chayse to scramble up, but came back for another blow to Chayse's jaw.

Fuck, that hurts. What the hell is wrong with him?

Both of them flinched and pulled apart when a crystal glass shattered on the faux hearth beside their heads. Shards flew everywhere and Chayse turned his fury on the new assailant, only to stop when he saw Aislynn twitch. Felicia held another glass just in case they tried to resume negotiations.

"Take your fucking issues somewhere else." Felicia raised the glass. "Aislynn is coming around and I won't have her hurt because you're being assholes. Get over yourselves long enough to get out."

Nik immediately retreated to Aislynn's side, but Chayse's stomach cramped. He'd True Mated her, but the idea was so repugnant, he couldn't make his feet move. *I've done just fine up until now. What the fuck is wrong with me?*

Aislynn groaned and rubbed the heel of her palms against her eyes, her voice full of pain. Chayse resisted the urge to gather her into his arms and comfort her. *It's not real. It's just the addiction. I'm not really True-Mated to her.* He couldn't be. If he'd True Mated the succubus, he wouldn't be able to stand his brother being anywhere near her, but Nik's presence calmed Chayse and gave him the strength to maintain his distance.

"Are you all right, Mistress?"

Chayse thought it an inane question, but he found himself hoping Aislynn's answer would be yes.

"Both so angry." The succubus's voice both soothed and aroused Chayse, and he gripped the chair they'd knocked over during their fight. "Want to help, but don't know how."

"Sorry, Mistress?" Felicia glared first at Nik then Chayse, before returning her attention to Aislynn.

"Need him." Chayse's balls tightened against the base of his hardening cock and he took a step toward Aislynn before he could stop himself.

"I'm here, Lady Aislynn," Nik whispered, grasping one of her hands. Chayse wanted to be on her other side, offering comfort and support, but he held back.

It's just the addiction.

"Master Canin." Aislynn's relieved whisper made them both stiffen and Chayse's hard-on wilted.

"What did she say?" he growled.

"Master Canin." Felicia bored holes into Nik with her gaze. "Isn't that you?"

"That's the name I take here at the club." Nik dropped his gaze to Aislynn again and squeezed her hand. "I'm here. I've got you. You're safe now." Pain, anger, and regret coursed down the bond from him and Chayse rubbed his jaw again. Could his brother really be Aislynn's True Mate?

"Don't be mad at him, Master. Please." Why did Aislynn sound so subordinate to Nik?

"Why not, Aislynn?"

"Loves you. Misses you. Still wants to share."

"What the hell is she talking about?" Chayse barked, his guts tightening in fear.

"I don't know, but shut up so we can figure it out," Felicia snapped.

"Needs you, Master. Needs you more than me."

"Who does, Aislynn?" Nik's voice had softened.

"Chayser."

Panic blazed across Chayse's chest and he jerked upright. How the hell did she know his inner name for himself? Only Nik had known that name. *Oh, fuck, if she knows my inner name, she has the keys to the vault.* Somehow, she'd gotten in, just like Celine had. Despair surged and his stomach threatened to empty.

Aislynn groaned as if someone had stabbed her in the gut, but Chayse couldn't stay one moment longer. Everything screamed at him to run to Aislynn's side, but he gritted his teeth and pushed past them, striding for the door.

"Where the hell are you going?" Nik grabbed his arm and swung him around, but Chayse ripped free.

"Somewhere far away from *that*."

"She needs you, you idiot. You True-Mated her."

"No, it sounds as if she needs you, *Master Canin*." Derision dripped from his voice and he shoved his brother's shoulder, pain and frustration ripping through him.

"How did she know your name?"

"How the fuck should I know? But I'm not staying here any longer than I have to. I gotta get to a *Morukai* and shake this fucking addiction."

"Chayse, you have to stay—"

"No, I don't! Take her if you want her. True-Mate her if that's your thing, but leave me the fuck alone." He jerked away and headed for the door, his metaphorical tail clamped securely between his legs. Everything within him screamed for him to return to his Mate's side, hold her and comfort her, but he knew it wasn't real. He thrust the urges away and ran.

****

Aislynn opened her eyes as someone brushed her forehead with a gentle hand, and her gaze fell on Nik Wolffe. The PI looked as if he's survived a fight. Dried blood from his nose crusted his upper lip and his hair hung in disarray. The eyes looking back at her held a mixture of pain, yearning, and compassion, and she wished she could do something about all three.

"Mr. Wolffe? When did you get here?"

She grimaced when her voice squeaked at the end and he gave her a lopsided smile.

"Just about the time my brother bit you. How do you feel?"

"I've never experienced it personally, but I've heard it said 'I feel like I've been hit by a Mack truck'." A wave of remorse and dread washed over her, freezing her blood. "I think I may vomit."

"Easy, kit. Take it one breath at a time." Despite her greater age, the endearment and his voice helped her push back some of the distress. "Let's get you off the floor and onto the couch. Can you stand up?"

"I don't know…"

"I'm here, Mistress." Aislynn felt Felicia's arms around her, belatedly realizing the vampire had been holding her. "Please forgive me, Mistress. I never should have left you alone with that werewolf."

Nik grimaced at the remark as he offered her his hands. Aislynn picked up what 'smelled' like frustration and anger from him—*emotions have scents? When did that happen?*—but he only smiled at her and tugged her to her feet. Felicia's scent had soured as if she used herself as a whipping post, and in Aislynn's experience, that usually resulted in her assistant disappearing for a few days, mentally.

"That's enough, Felicia." Her voice cracked like a whip. "You will not take the blame for this, nor will you dwell on any mistakes you *think* you have made in the past twenty four hours. If so, I will have to revoke some of your privileges and require you to oversee the bar without feeding for several nights. Is this understood?"

Felicia sighed and her tension bled away. "Yes, Mistress. Thank you, Mistress."

"Very well. Now, I think I would like to rest in my room for a while."

"Of course, Mistress. Do you need to feed?"

"No…" Aislynn paused, assessing herself. She didn't feel hungry at all. In fact, she felt satiated for the first time in centuries. The only other times she'd experienced such well-being was when she'd drained someone dry of their life essence. *Dear Goddess, what have I done?*

"Where is your brother?" She locked gazes with Nik, panic building and cramping her stomach.

"Easy, Aislynn. Chayse is fine. Angry, confused, still a frustrating jackass, but fine." He grasped her hand and warm tingles ran up her arm. *That's odd.*

"I didn't drain him?"

"Drain him?" Felicia snorted. "He left here stronger and angrier than ever. And he bit you."

"What?" Aislynn pushed away from them and staggered toward the hallway.

"Whoa, where are you going?" Nik steadied her as he followed her out the door.

"I have to see." She stopped in front of her hall mirror over her favorite tiled mosaic table.

A puncture wound showed at the base of her neck on her right shoulder. While the skin showed red, it didn't look infected and the edges closed as she watched.

"What is that? Why did he bite me?"

Nik sighed and dropped his head in the mirror. Aislynn frowned and squeezed his hand.

"Nik?"

"Come. Let's get you to bed, kit, and I'll explain."

Aislynn allowed him to draw her down the hallway to her bedroom, her curiosity mixing with uncertainty. Why did he seem so sad? Was there more to this bite than just a flesh wound? *I didn't think it was like the movies and I'd turn into a fuzzy, ravening beast every full moon.* He drew her to the bed and pulled back the autumn leaves duvet. She loved the bold golds, oranges, and reds against black, but today it didn't offer her the comfort it usually did.

"What's going on, Nik?"

"Felicia, would you be willing to brew Lady Aislynn some tea?" His unusual courtesy to her assistant made her nervous, but Aislynn waited with ill-concealed impatience for him to turn back to her.

"It's time to be frank with me, Nik. What is the meaning of this bite mark on my shoulder?"

He sighed. "We're going to be family soon, like it or not."

"What? How will I be part of your family?" And why did that idea thrill her beyond everything?

"You know werewolves True Mate." His viridian eyes still held pain, but he kept it out of the rest of his expression.

"Yes, I do. What of it?"

"When they find their True Mate, werewolves are driven beyond all reason to make love to that one person, but while they make love, they bite their partners, sealing the Mating Bond." Nik brushed her hair away from her right shoulder. "My brother bit you."

"What? Wait." Aislynn shook her head and flipped through her memories. "But it was just sex. He didn't really want to be there and he certainly wants nothing to do with me. I'm a succubus." She knew it was a stupid thing to say, but nothing made sense. "He can't True Mate with a succubus. I'm not even his species."

"Ah, kit, the Goddess has Her own ideas of who can mate with whom, and it looks as though She chose you for Chayse." The sadness in Nik's voice and his body could have drowned an elephant. He truly believed in what he said, but it was impossible. She couldn't True Mate a werewolf. She was twenty thousand years old, for the Goddess's sake.

"No, that can't be."

"I can smell it. Your scent is changing to be a mixture of his and yours. It's a done deal."

She didn't smell any different to herself, but she *could*

smell Nik's emotions as if each one came in its own
jeweled bottle from the perfume counter. Sorrow smelled
like fermenting lilies, while anger had a vinegar-like
sourness. A tang of resignation like paint thinner underlay
the other scents. She'd never experienced it and she
wondered how the heck she'd be able to separate them all
in the future.

"Wait. Why are you so sad about it? Don't like the idea
of a succubus at the family reunion? Afraid I'll suck in
some other poor member of your family?"

She knew the questions were unfair and unkind, but she
desperately needed a dose of reality in the surreal events of
her day, and anger seemed the easiest way to find it. Nik
drew back from her as if she'd slapped him. His brows
lowered as the vinegar scent intensified.

"No, that's not why I'm disappointed." He bared his
teeth at her as he grasped her shoulders his hands. "I came
here tonight to tell you I figured out that you were
supposed to be *my* True Mate and to convince you to be
with me forever, but my fucking brother True-Mated you
first. Now I'm shit outta luck and you're gonna be part of
the family. I'll never be able to avoid you and I'll always
know I lost you to him!"

Aislynn gaped at him. "Wait, I'm supposedly *your* True
Mate? When did that happen?"

Nik grimaced and scanned her room as if searching for
answers in the leaf pattern on her bed. "I don't know, but I
figured it out when I saw you serving the forgotten folks.
And I got hints of it when I first came to the club." He
traced the outline of a brilliant red leaf with his finger.
"This club was different. It smelled good and the buzzing
in my head stopped."

"Buzzing in your head?"

"Yeah, the overall hum of human existence. You know,
the constant sounds of cars and electronic devices. It all
becomes an irritating drone that only quieted when I

stepped through your doors." He looked at her from the corner of his eye. "I thought it was the club and finally addressing my dominant needs. But now I think it's because you were here. You made all the other bullshit go away."

"But I never saw you before the murder. Well, I *saw* you, but I didn't meet you until then." She tried not to be elated he'd sensed her at the beginning. "What changed to make you think I'm your True Mate and not Chayse's?"

Instead of saying anything, he leaned forward and pressed his cheek against hers, inhaling deeply beside her ear. His scent filled her nose, teasing her with flavors of leather, vanilla oil, and fresh sand. He threaded his fingers through her hair at the back of her head and closed his hand into a fist, tugging her face up until she met his gaze. The power in the movement sent arousal flooding her pussy and she gasped in heated surprise.

"I know because I can scent your arousal when I pull your hair." His other hand slid over her hard nipples. "And your nipples are begging for my touch even now." He dropped his face to her shoulder and licked her throat, making her moan with the exquisite touch.

Pleasure swamped Aislynn as much as it had when Chayse pushed her up against the wall, and she squirmed, wishing he rested naked against her. He slid one hand down the front of her body until he reached the hem of her skirt. His fingers dug for the edge of the material then pulled upward, his breath tickling her neck.

Aislynn moaned when his palm rested on her mound, branding her with his heat and strength as he ground gently against her clit. He rotated his hand until his fingers caressed the flesh of her inner thighs and she drew them apart to allow him greater access.

"I know you're my Mate because you're already wet and I haven't done more than kiss you." He pressed another soft kiss against her skin. "Do you deny your reaction to me?"

"No." Her voice came out breathy. Where had the strong, take-no-lip Mistress gone? Why did she act like a damsel around Nik? "But I was already wet from Chayse's fucking before you, so..."

Nik growled and pulled back, his silver-green eyes furious. He jerked the bed clothes away and straddled her body before she could do more than squeak. Then he dropped his face to her groin, pushing her skirt to her hips as he inhaled the scents from her pussy.

"What are you doing?"

"I can smell my brother on you, but your own, new arousal, overlays his scent." Nik nuzzled her mound and Aislynn damn near lost track of the conversation. "You're wet for me, Aislynn. And I'm hard for you, harder than I've ever been for any woman."

The traditional line knocked away some of the lustful veneer. "I'm sure." She raised an eyebrow at him. "Harder than you've ever been? Forgive me, Nik, but I find it difficult to believe. I suspect the line has worked wonders on several of your partners in the past."

Nik sat up, his legs still bracketing hers. His jeans stretched tight over his thighs, showing the power of his muscles in the soft denim. She raised her gaze past the large bulge in front up his belly and chest to his face. His expression had become unreadable, but his eyes still glowed brilliant green.

"Do you doubt me, Aislynn?" He crossed his arms over his chest, making his black t-shirt stretch dangerously.

His question held more than just a simple request for information. Something underlay the words, something close to desperation and hurt, as if he needed her to need him. *But I don't need anyone. I'm my own mistress, I run this show.* But her heart said something else, something far more primal. She *wanted* his dominance, his protection, and his mastery. She wanted him to take control in the bedroom. He made her feel safe and protected for the first time in her ridiculously long life. *For the first time since Adam.*

"Do you doubt your master, Aislynn?"

"N-n-no." She shook her head as she met the fiery green gaze. "I don't doubt you."

"Sir."

"What?"

"You need to say 'I don't doubt you, *Sir*'."

She hesitated, wondering if she could be submissive. *I'm a succubus, I can be anything to anyone.* But while that would be an act, this felt different. She met his gaze and he raised an eyebrow in question.

"No, I don't doubt you, Sir."

"I will always tell you the truth, Aislynn, no matter how odd or difficult it seems to be. I only require that you do the same for me and believe me when I tell you something. If you don't trust me to be honest with you, I can't be your master."

Do I want him to be my 'master'? The simple answer was yes. She wanted him to take away all her choices and control, to allow her to let go for once. She felt feminine, delicate, in need of protection and strength when around him. In regular life, she had to stand on her own, fight her own battles, master the club and the Underground. But here, with Nik, she could be Aislynn, his lady to protect, his submissive to pleasure, his lover to...

Panic surged through her and she stiffened, her stomach trying to climb up her esophagus so hard she choked. Tears flooded her eyes and her jaw clenched so hard she thought her teeth would break.

"I can't. Dear Goddess, I can't!" She struggled to pull her legs out from under him, but he clamped down on her, bracing his hands against her shoulders to keep her still.

"Whoa, easy, kit." Nik's eyes lost their remote power and concern filled his features. "Slow down and breathe.

What can't you do?"

"I can't be your lover, I can't be…this." Aislynn struggled, but he only tightened his grip. "I'm a succubus. I kill my lovers, I drain their life forces. I won't kill again. I've given my word to myself and the Goddess. I won't destroy you or your brother or anyone."

Tears cascaded out of her eyes, sweeping her cheeks to pool at her throat. Aislynn continued to struggle, to writhe beneath him, but Nik held on. She caught the scents of patience and concern, an odd combination given her own ramped-up panic, but Nik's expression exuded confidence, determination, and calm.

"Easy, Aislynn. Settle a little." He released one shoulder to stroke her head with a gentle but firm hand. To her surprise, the panic receded with his touch as if he'd pulled the plug in the bathtub allowing the emotion to drain out of her. "That's it. Come back to me. Just breathe."

He continued to stroke her hair, tucking a few wayward strands behind her ear. She knew she must look like a mess what with Chayse fucking her and now the panic attack in bed, but he didn't seem to mind her state of disarray. His gaze held her captive as her heart slowed and her breathing evened out.

"There, that's better." Nik swung his leg over her and settled beside her on the bed. He gathered her into his arms, her back pressed against his chest. One hand glided over her arm in the same soothing motions he'd used on her head, while the other wrapped around her waist, pinning her to him.

"Now, tell me again why you're panicking." As she recalled what they'd talked about, the fear began to rise again, but Nik tightened his grip on her waist and his motions on her arm never stopped. "Focus on me now and we'll get through this, kit. What's wrong?"

"You know how succubae survive, yes?"

"Yes, they infiltrate sexual dreams and drain the

dreamer's life force."

"Sometimes it doesn't even need a dream. Most of them—us—can do it in person as well." Aislynn bit her lip. "I've sworn I'd never kill someone that way again. I feel dirty as if I've destroyed something so beautiful just to live another day. I can't do it again." She stopped his hand as she tipped her head to look up at him. "That's why I can't be your...your submissive, your lover. I don't want to kill you when we make love."

She expected him to laugh at her, to shrug it away like all the others had in her early years, but Nik gazed at her with patience and consideration, taking in her words. A part of her rejoiced in his understanding while the rest deteriorated into despair.

"Let's consider this from all angles." He trailed his fingers over the mounds of her breasts pushed up by the corset. "When I found you tonight, you'd just finished fucking Chayse." His jaw clenched and she could smell his frustration, but it quickly dissolved as if he'd forced himself to let it go. "You're the succubus, but Chayse remained on his feet and you were the one out cold on the floor. According to your experience, he should have been dead or drained as soon as you orgasmed. True?"

"Yes." But according to everyone in the room, Chayse had been strong enough to leave under his own power. *How does that work?*

"But he True Mated you." The growl returned to Nik's otherwise calm voice and the scent of his anger intensified, but his touch remained gentle as he wrapped his arms around her again. "And survived." Given Nik's thoughts on the matter, Chayse's lifespan might be severely shortened.

Nik tipped Aislynn's chin up so he could meet her eyes. "I *know* you're my True Mate. No one else has ever made me hunger or pine over them. Lately, when I'm away from you, I'm edgy and unsettled, unable to focus on anything. But it all goes away when I step into the club and smell your scent." He smiled slow and sexy, his fingers caressing her jaw.

The look he gave her became both possessive and tender. Thousands of men over the centuries had looked at her with yearning, a desperate infatuation care of the magic associated with her species, but none had ever offered her this look. *What makes it so different from him?*

"But I could kill you."

"I'd die with a smile on my face."

Her stomach curdled and she jerked her chin out of his hand. "That's what they've all said. It isn't funny when it's true."

"Aislynn, you have to trust in the Goddess."

An old hurt curled through her belly. Trusting the Goddess had never been easy after the initial indiscretion leading to her new 'life' as a succubus.

"Don't you trust the Goddess?" She heard the surprise in his voice.

"You make it sound so easy."

"It is—"

"It is not!" She tried to sit up away from his chest, but he held her down. His resistance both infuriated and aroused her. "The Goddess is the one who gave me this 'duty' to pay for my transgressions."

"You could look at it as a gift." Why did he sound so reasonable?

Aislynn froze, sure he'd gone mad. "A gift? I killed hundreds of people before I knew how to control the hunger. How is that a gift?"

How could he say such a thing? He had no understanding of what it felt like to watch a lover die in the throes of passion. She'd experienced pleasure only to end up coupled to a dead body. The physical sensation still haunted her nightmares.

"Without the Goddess' change, would you ever have learned to curb your appetites? Would you have learned control, or compassion for others?" Nik stroked her stiff shoulder. "Without this change, you'd never have lived this long or…" Now he pulled her head up to meet his silver-green eyes. "Met me, your True Mate."

The fairytale was always so much cleaner than reality. "Why would you want me after I've hurt so many?"

"We all have pasts. Some of us choose to make an effort to learn from them and grow, others just wallow in them." He paused and she waited for the other shoe to drop. "You have no idea how many people you've helped."

"Helped?" Aislynn laughed with derision.

"Yes, helped. You've built this place for those people who have sexual needs not acknowledged by mainstream society. Without you, they wouldn't have a safe playground in which to find satisfaction."

"It wasn't safe for Mr. Johnson." She grimaced.

"He was an anomaly and Chayse is closing in on his killer." Nik *tsked* and tapped her shoulder in mild rebuke. "Don't change the subject. This is about you and those you've saved by finding this solution to your needs."

"You don't know that."

"Neither do you. Now, it is time to stop wallowing in fear and take a chance."

"How can you say that? It's your life you're risking."

"Aislynn, to me, you are worth it. But it's your choice. Are you willing to trust the Goddess and take the chance?" Nik's heartbeat continued, steady, sure, strong beneath her back. "Would you trust me to know what's best for you?"

"But my experiences—" Twenty thousand years of them.

"Yes, they tell you we'll fail." He leaned forward until his lips brushed her ear and sent a sensual thrill through her. "But Aislynn, ask yourself what you truly want, what you truly need."

She wanted Nik, his strength, his confidence, his mastery. His dominant attitude had attracted her from the beginning and she longed to let him make the decisions, to take the reins, at least in bed. *What if he's wrong? What if I kill him?*

"What do you want, Aislynn?" he whispered.

"I…want you."

CHAPTER SIXTEEN

I want you.

The words damn near brought tears to his eyes. Nik gazed at the woman of his heart and shoved aside the hurt from the realization that Chayse Mated her first. *This is no time to hold on to the pain.* He should have been repulsed from her, the scent of her and his brother nauseating. But though her scent had changed, it only enticed and aroused him more.

"How do you want me, kit?" The new endearment had come out of nowhere, but now he couldn't imagine calling her anything else.

"I want you in my bed. But I'm afraid." She closed her eyes and shook her head.

"What are you afraid of?" He wanted to squeeze her tight and tell her everything would be all right, but she had to find the courage to see it herself.

"I'm afraid I'll take too much. I'm afraid I'll get out of control, that I'll kill you." Panic soured her scent and her heart thundered under his arms.

"Calm, kit. I trust the Goddess and She has told me you're mine." He smoothed her hair with his hands, the texture still smooth despite the sex she'd had. He swallowed the growl of frustration. "The question is do you want to be mine? Can you trust me to be your master? To know what's best for you, even in the face of your experience?"

Please let her see it. He rarely begged the Goddess for anything, but despite his brother's actions, he still wanted Aislynn. *She's still mine, dammit.* And Chayse had run. New anger kindled. No one ran from their True Mate, at least no one worth the connection. *What the fuck is wrong with him?*

"It's not about trust, Nik. Your life hangs in the balance. If you're wrong, you'll die, and I'll have killed you. The risk is too great." Her expression closed and his heart almost broke.

"It *is* about trust. Trust that I know what's best in this instance. Can you move beyond your fear, hand me control?"

"But what if—"

"No 'what ifs', Aislynn. No second guessing. Just yes or no."

She stopped talking, closed her mouth and her eyes, and Nik ignored the fear roaring through him. How could he show her that past events wouldn't be repeated? *The Goddess reveals our True Mates and Aislynn is mine.* Crimes long done had taught her to be afraid. He stood ready to show her she didn't have to give in to fear anymore, but she had to trust him. He could do it. His gut remained settled on that point. But would she see he could?

A painful chuckle shook her body and his gut sank. *Please, Goddess, don't let her say no.*

Aislynn opened her eyes, fear still lurking in their depths and took a deep breath.

"Yes."

Nik resisted the urge to launch himself off the bed and run around in happy circles. Instead, he made his expression impassive.

"Yes, what, Aislynn? Be specific."

"Yes, I trust you to be Master in the bedroom, to know best in this instance, to take care of my needs. To not die in the attempt." The last sentence squeezed through her clenched teeth, but she meant every word.

Nik laid a soft kiss above her ear and resumed stroking her arms, relief pouring through him. "Very good, kit."

She released some of the tension in her body and settled into his ministrations.

"Good. Relax more. Let it all go."

He used his best 'loving-master' voice to offer comfort and help her settle into the new way of being. He suspected the feeling would be both familiar and strange to someone used to giving orders, but the tension continued to leave her body without resistance.

"Well done, kit. You're looking better than when I brought you to bed. How do you feel?"

"Better."

"Better...?" His voice sharpened and she tensed.

"Better, Sir."

"Good."

Silence and relaxation followed his statement, but before he could get his thoughts in order, Felicia bustled into the room with a tray of tea and two crystal teacups held by sterling silver frames. Aislynn smiled and he thought he read wistful nostalgia in her expression.

"Thank you, Felicia."

"How are you feeling, Mistress?" Felicia eyed Nik narrowly while Aislynn resumed her leadership role.

"I'm fine. Please return to the Club and keep an eye on it for me tonight. I'm not to be disturbed unless there's an emergency." She reached for the teapot, but Nik grasped the handle and poured the tea into the mugs. "Thank you, Nik."

He nodded as if they hadn't established his dominance just moments earlier. Despite their agreement, he wouldn't dream of taking over Aislynn's position in the club. He'd only dominate her in private. Their bond was too sacred to show to others.

"Yes, Mistress." Felicia hesitated on her way out the door. "Is he treating you well, Mistress?"

"Yes, Felicia. He is." Aislynn paused, her expression turning thoughtful. "If Detective Wolffe returns to the club, please bring him down to my private apartment."

Felicia looked like she'd just been asked to give up blood as nourishment. "Sorry, Mistress? You want me to allow the man who bit you and knocked you unconscious close to you again?"

"Yes, Felicia. It's important that I talk to him if he comes back."

"I don't understand, Mistress."

Aislynn nodded, compassion softening her features. "I know, Felicia. But it will become clear in due time. Please bring the detective here if he returns tonight."

"Yes, Mistress. Is that all, Mistress?" The vampire turned cold.

Aislynn's chin rose. "Does your lack of understanding override your ability to address me with the respect I've earned, Felicia?"

Felicia immediately dropped her gaze and her head, her body language becoming submissive. "No, Mistress. Please forgive me. I had no right to question you."

"Very well. Please take care of the club tonight. I will check in with you closer to dawn."

"Yes, Mistress." Felicia bowed and backed out of the room, her energy contrite.

When she'd gone, Aislynn relaxed back against Nik's shoulder, her mantle of leadership weighing her down. "I don't remember leadership being so taxing."

Nik chuckled as he handed her a teacup, proud of the way she'd handled the insubordination. "I think it only gets bad when you never get a break from it." He cocked his head. "When was the last time you got a break, kit?"

She shook her head. "Never. Not since the beginning. I've always been dominant." She studied his face, a small line appearing between her brows. "Except with you."

"Then I think it's time for you to set your mantle aside and let me take care of you."

"Perhaps we should establish the rules of our relationship first."

Nik tipped his head, a smile curling his lips. "All right. Does that mean you're willing to admit we have a relationship?"

She eyed him thoughtfully. "What do you mean?"

He sighed and slid from behind her so she didn't have to stretch her neck at an odd angle. He settled beside her and took her hands. "I came here tonight to talk to you about the investigation, but also to tell you about my revelation. That you're my True Mate and I want only you."

"Oh. And your brother had mated me already."

Nik gritted his teeth to push back his fury. "Yes. But it doesn't change what I feel. I *know* you're my True Mate. It doesn't make any sense. Most of the time, when two people True Mate, the rest of us know it and smell it, almost like you wear a 'get away from me' scent." He squeezed her hands, enjoying her soft skin in his rougher palms. "But you don't smell repugnant at all. In fact, you smell better to me than you did before you mated my brother."

She searched his expression for several breaths. "That's strange, isn't it?"

He shrugged. "I don't know. I think so. My folks and the other mated pairs I've met all said so, but you don't smell bad to me. You smell fucking delicious."

"Maybe the succubus magic is overwhelming the werewolf mating."

He almost scoffed, but the resignation returning to her body language made him take his time answering as he sipped his tea.

"Maybe." He nodded. "But I don't feel drugged, or hazy, which as I understand it from Chayse, is how I'd feel if I was under a succubus's spell. I feel in complete control of my mind, my choices, and my heart. And my heart wants you, Aislynn."

She bit her bottom lip, her brow creasing with confusion. "And I want you, Sir. But I also want your brother." She shook her head. "None of this makes any sense." She closed her eyes, took a deep breath that pushed up her breasts and made his mouth water. He forced himself to keep his gaze on her face despite the allure.

"Okay." Aislynn squared her shoulders and opened her eyes. "It has been centuries since anyone has touched me the way you and your brother have."

Nik couldn't hold back his gape of surprise. "Are you serious?"

She raised her eyesbrows then laughed. "No, no, I meant my heart and my mind, not my body." Her grin warmed him and aroused him at the same time.

"Ah, okay. So let's do this, then." He met her gaze and waited for her to focus on him. "I'm going to blindfold you and tie your hands down. This will give you a chance to focus on you and your needs rather than that of your lover. And we'll start our relationship off the sensual way."

She frowned, a cute crease appearing between her eyes. "Isn't that unusual for a werewolf? Don't you mate in a fast and furious meeting of lust and desire?"

He smiled and shrugged. "Yes, that's what I understand. But Chayse already did that with you, and it's not what you need. So I'm suggesting a different tack." He scanned her bedroom, noting some silk scarves dangling from the hat tree in the corner before returning to her gaze. "What will your safeword be?"

She snorted. "I'm a succubus. I don't need a safeword."

"Oh, Aislynn, everyone needs a safeword." The growl

of possession came out of nowhere, but his Brother wolf echoed it.

Her eyes widened with surprise, and she licked her lips with arousal. He scented her shift in demeanor and interest, and his cock hardened in his jeans. *So my little succubus likes to be dominated.*

"Halo."

"Halo? As in the angelic accessory?" He almost smirked, but her expression remained earnest as she nodded. "Halo it is." He ran a hand over her hair. "Did you choose that because you figured you'd never have one?"

Aislynn never looked away, but her shoulders slumped and her eyes grew sad. "I'm afraid my purity has long since fled after all the deaths I caused."

"Stop." Anger and frustration rose in his chest and his voice came out sharper than he intended. "Here's my first directive as your Master. You'll never again wallow in guilt from the deaths of the past. You've done what you can to make amends and changed how you feed to keep from hurting others. From now on, you'll remember those losses can't be changed and you'll focus on the good you're doing with this club and the forgotten. Is that clear?"

She met his gaze steadily, her face unreadable. The sorrow and guilt radiating off her made his breath stall, but she neither nodded nor frowned. *Goddess, I hope she takes my direction.* If she didn't, he worried they'd have a much harder road ahead. She was his True Mate, but if she couldn't take his direction, he needed to find a way to reach her.

"When you speak badly of yourself, Aislynn, I hate it. I wish I could make you stop. But that needs to be your decision. And if you decide to ignore my directive, I will get up and leave right now." His heart squeezed in pain, but he couldn't listen to her demean herself anymore.

The silence stretched and his gut sank. He'd have to follow through and it would kill him, but he'd do it because he said he would. Sometimes it sucked being a Dom.

"Very well, Sir. I promise to focus on the good I've done and won't demean myself in front of you or others." Her voice rang clear and steady despite the expression of trepidation she wore, and Nik's shoulders relaxed.

"Very good, kit."

She frowned, but her lips curled into a half smile. "Kit?"

"My little fox, sweet submissive while we play."

Her brows lifted and the smile expanded. "Kit. I like it. Thank you, Sir."

Her acceptance of his pet name warmed his chest and he resisted the urge to wriggle like a puppy with his first full-sized bone. Instead, he shifted off the bed and set his tea aside before holding out his hand to her.

"Where are we going?" Despite her question, she reached for his hand.

"You need a shower and I intend to take care of you tonight." He pulled her to her feet and turned her until her back met his chest as he wrapped his arms around her waist. "It is my duty as your Dom and as your True Mate."

His Brother wolf rumbled a growl of agreement.

"I would like that very much, Sir."

"Very good, kit." Excitement rose in his chest and he had to take several deep breaths before he was calm enough not to tear her clothes.

****

Aislynn had never felt so cherished or wanted in her life. Nik only stood behind her and held her against his chest, but he laid a soft kiss on the back of her neck and she almost melted to the floor. The kiss was both proprietary and tender, a lovely mixture sending her heart racing. But while excitement made up the bulk of her emotions, trepidation blinked like a warning light in the corner.

"May I ask a question, Sir?"

"You may, kit." He pulled at the laces of her corset dress and she turned her head to gauge his demeanor. Nik's body flexed in the low lighting, glowing with health and virile strength as he worked to rid her of her clothes. She shivered with arousal and appreciation as he opened the corset bodice and unzipped the skirt.

A powerful surge of lust shot straight to her pussy and liquefied her core. She whimpered and caught his smile as arousal flared in his green eyes.

"I see that pleases you. What is your question?"

Aislynn shook herself back into the present. "I wanted to ask…" She trailed off as uncertainty surged. *Nothing to fear, I'm* Lady *Aislynn, a twenty thousand year old succubus, for Goddess's sake.* But with Nik, she wanted to be his lady, his submissive, there to listen, not demand.

"Yes?"

"Are you angry with me for being with Chayse?" The words came out in a jumbled mass. She hardly dared taste the spaces between them.

Nik's shoulders tensed and her heart sank, but his hands remained gentle as he slid her dress off her hips. She'd displeased him and she hadn't even been his submissive at the time. But the face he turned to her showed hot intensity rather than anger.

"No, kit, I'm not angry with you. I'm furious with my brother, not only for True Mating my Mate, but also for treating you so badly you blacked out." He tugged her to step out of her dress and led her across her room toward the bath. "But sharing you with him, that doesn't anger me. In fact, before he met the other succubus, we used to share all our women."

Vibrant jealousy rose through her and she actually growled before she could stop herself. Nik raised his eyebrows as he closed the bathroom door behind them, but she raised her chin. He and Chayse were hers, especially now. She might be submissive to Nik, but she'd be damned worse than she already was before she'd let another female touch either of them.

"What is that about, Aislynn?" Nik's voice sharpened.

"I do not share, Sir."

He stood in front of her and picked up one of her hands, caressing the palm as if each inch of skin provided a new puzzle to solve. "Explain, kit. You don't share what?"

"My mates, Sir. You and Chayse, Sir. You belong to me."

"I thought it's you who belong to me."

"I've given my word on that, Sir. But I cannot belong to you if you choose another submissive. In that way you've broken your word to me."

"Are you topping from the bottom, Aislynn?"

"No, Sir. I'm telling you my hard limits." *Take them or leave them, werewolf.* She might agree to be his submissive, but to be her mate would mean the only pussy he enjoyed was hers.

He gave her a half-smile as he stepped away long enough to turn on the spray in her stone-paneled shower. When he returned, he slid his hands down her sides and caressed her ass, his gaze hot and possessive. Cream slicked her nether lips.

"Fair enough." Nik unbuckled his belt and unbuttoned his pants before jerking his t-shirt over his head. "You'll be happy to know, once a werewolf has True Mated, he or she can't stand to make love to anyone else." He crouched to unlace his boots and laid small kisses on her knees in between loosening the laces. "That's why I'm so angry with Chayse. But for some reason you don't smell badly to me, and yet I know you've made the bond with him." Nik inhaled against her skin as he scanned the marks left on her neck.

"What if you're both my true mates?" The question came out of left field and made her heart flutter. Both of them? Was it even possible?

Nik stood and pulled off his boots, setting them to the side before adding his socks. She couldn't read his expression and wondered if she was simply chasing rainbows. To stave off her unease, she took pleasure in admiring the hard muscles of his back as he worked his jeans off his hips. When his ass came into view, she forgot to breathe.

Sweet Goddess, it's been so long since I've seen one so beautiful.

"Are you staring at my ass, kit?" He shot her a grin over his shoulder.

"Yes, Sir." She met his gaze with a guileless smile. She hadn't ever been a blushing virgin. Sex was nourishment as well as a pleasure, and she held no embarrassment in enjoying it openly.

"Nice to know." He stood and faced her, his thick cock rising.

She let her gaze slide over all of him, including his lovely cock and balls nestled in a thatch of dark hair at the juncture of his thighs. Her mouth watered at the thought of dropping to her knees and taking all that beautiful flesh into her mouth. *Goddess, I want to suck his cock.*

Nik laughed. "I know that look, but into the shower with you, my lovely Mate. A wash first, then you can do whatever is going through that devious mind of yours."

"Is that a promise, Sir?" She arched a brow as she sauntered to the shower in front of him, swaying her hips on purpose.

He inhaled sharply and she suspected his gaze had riveted to her ass. *You might be the Dom, Sir, but I know who's in control.* She pretended not to notice as she leaned over to test the water, spreading her legs just enough for her nether lips to show between them.

His hand landed on her left butt cheek and she squealed in surprise and delight.

"That's for teasing, kit. Into the shower with you."

Aislynn giggled for the first time in over a century and hopped into the tiled box behind the glass door. She stepped under the spray and closed her eyes as his warm body settled against her back. She moaned in delight, enjoying the simple contact under the hot water. He slid on hand down her hip while the other reached past her to grab a puff hanging from a bath hook.

The scent of body wash filled the small space as he thrust the soap-laden puff under the water. He pulled it back to lather it up, his gaze as hot as the steaming water.

"Face me and get your hair wet."

She turned around and tilted her head back to let the spray soak her hair. Her eyes closed as the water splashed into her face. Before she could wipe it away, Nik's soap-covered hands slid over her breasts, massaging the suds into her skin. Aislynn sighed, reveling in his deft and slick touches.

When he dropped his hands to her hips and groin, she whimpered as he rubbed her clit with slick fingers.

"Oh my sweet succubus, you're wet for me."

"Yes, Sir." She could barely form words through his ministrations. It had been so long since someone had lit her fires as well as Chayse and Nik Wolffe, but two in one night? She didn't know whether to be nervous or grateful.

Nik dropped to his knees and thrust his fingers into her pussy.

Grateful. Definitely, grateful.

"Oh, Sir, that feels so good." The last time she'd been this breathy, Jefferson had been in office.

He stroked her slow and deep, rubbing her thighs with his free hand still holding the puff. Between the hot water, his slick hand, and the fingers in her pussy, Aislynn closed in on her orgasm faster than expected. She rocked her hips on his hand, whimpering and whining for release. *By the Goddess, it feels so good.*

Before she could hit her peak, he withdrew his fingers and licked them with a sly grin.

"Oh, no, kit, there will be no coming until I say so."

She resisted the urge to stick her tongue out at him as he rose, his cock telling her he'd enjoyed teasing her as much as she did.

"Wash off your front while I clean your back."

He pushed her gently under the water and scrubbed her back side from her neck to her heels. He moved his hands in circles, massaging the muscles as well as stimulating the skin. Aislynn relaxed into his touches, letting go of some of her stress and fear.

How long had she been their marionette, dancing to their warning claxons? *Too many millennia.* The fear was based in terrible knowledge, but it had been centuries since she'd last killed someone through feeding and she longed to let go. She wanted to hand control to someone else, to experience blissful abandon once again.

Give me liberty or give me death. It wouldn't be her death, but Nik's. *But Chayse survived.* The little voice in her head lit a flame of hope and more of her fear drifted away.

"Very good, kit." Nik pulled her out of the water and rinsed out the puff, rivulets of suds sliding down his abs to split around his cock. "Now." He scrubbed his hands over his groin and the stiff flesh straining there. "Sit down on your very handy shower bench and let me feast on that pussy I've been stroking."

"Feast on it, Sir?" Aislynn settled on the bench she used for shaving and Nik crouched between her legs, pushing her thighs wide.

"That's right. Feast." He grinned as he stroked her inner thighs, sending shivers up her back. "You've aroused the big, bad wolf, and I've been smelling you since I brought you to bed. It's time to taste what I've scented."

"You mean this right here, Sir?" She slid her hands

between her thighs and opened her nether lips to him, smiling with smug amusement.

"Naughty minx." He chuckled.

"Not minx, succubus."

Her words ended in a gasp as Nik thrust his head between her legs and fastened his mouth on her pussy lips. His long tongue swiped through her folds, and they both moaned. Hot slick pleasure shot up her spine as he went to work on her pussy, licking and sucking the sensitive flesh.

His moans of appreciation carried over the sounds of the water and the steam brought the scent of her pleasure to her nose. Nik slid his hands along her wet thighs, stroking the skin with his rough palms as he massaged her folds with his nose. She grabbed his wet hair in her fists and held on while he worked on her pussy.

"Oh, Goddess, Sir. That feels so good." Better than it ever had in her long memory.

"It tastes even better, kit. But you can't come until I give you permission. Got it?"

Aislynn whimpered. "Yes, Sir."

"Good girl."

But he went to work on her sensitive flesh as if trying to drive her to completion early, and she tightened her grip on his hair, whimpering and squeaking in an effort to keep her orgasm at bay. Nik tortured her with soft swipes of his tongue then switched to sucking on her clit, alternating between sensual and erotic pleasure. She tried remembering all the countries she'd visited and the languages she'd mastered to keep the arousal from breaking her control. *I'm a twenty-thousand year old succubus. I should have the strongest willpower out there.*

By all rights, she should've had the most willpower, but Nik's sensual torture was relentless and the arousal built higher and higher. Aislynn held on by her fingernails, clenching her jaw so tight her canines elongated and scratched her lower gums. She rarely lost so much control as to shift into her demon shape, but Nik pushed her closer than anyone ever had.

"Sweet glory, Sir, I don't think I can hold back. Please let me come."

Nik growled against her clit and she fisted his hair as the vibrations nearly set her off.

"No coming until I say, kit."

It felt natural to bow to Nik in the bedroom, despite normally being in charge when it came to her business and the Club. *There has to be some sort of psychological diagnosis for that.* Whatever the reason for the dichotomy, she simply gave in to being submissive to Nik here in her bedroom.

She squealed as he inserted one finger into her clenching pussy and sucked on her clit. The pleasure coiled in her belly, ready to explode beyond her control. She tried to recapture the serenity she displayed to the outer world, but her mind couldn't focus on anything but the pleasure. When Nik inserted a second finger, a gut-level groan broke from her lips and she whimpered one word.

"Please."

"You may let go, kit."

He punctuated his words with deep and steady thrusts of his fingers then dropped his mouth to her clit. One swipe with his tongue shot her into the cosmos. Ecstasy washed over her in ever expanding ripples as he pumped his hand in and out of her clenching pussy. Nik hummed his own approval as he lapped up her release, but the humming only sent her higher. Her cares and worries slipped away, leaving calm contentment behind.

She didn't remember him moving or shutting off the water in the shower, but she came back to herself wrapped in one of her fluffy towels held against Nik's chest. He'd moved them to the bedroom again, cuddling and murmuring sweet nonsense in her ear. She floated on a cushion of pleasure and satisfaction unlike any she'd experienced before, even with Chayse.

Of course, she couldn't really remember what it'd been like with Chayse. *Hmm, need to change that next time...if there is a next time.*

"How do you feel, kit?" Nik's voice rumbled over her.

"Excellent." When had she ever been this breathy? She settled into her pleasure as her hand dropped to his groin and met hard flesh. She opened her eyes and looked down. "But I think I need to return the favor."

"It's not necessary. This was for you tonight—"

"Oh, no, it's not going to be like that, Sir." She hated to leave the euphoria behind, but her desire to pleasure her mate superseded her satisfaction as she squirmed off his lap.

"Are you topping from the bottom again, kit?" He didn't smile, but humor glinted in his gaze.

"No, Sir, but I won't be completely satisfied until you've reached your pleasure, too." She damn near fell off the bed because her knees resembled Jell-O too well. "Let me suck your cock, Sir, to show you my appreciation for your gifts."

"No, kit, not tonight."

She pouted and he smiled, his eyes crinkling at the corners. Despite their relative ages, and his significant youth as compared to her, she loved the experience told by his crow's feet. It warmed her despite her disappointment.

"Tonight, I want you to ride me and take your pleasure from my cock."

"But what about you, Sir?" She allowed him to lift her over him and she settled her sensitive pussy on the hard ridge of his dick.

"I plan on taking my own pleasure, but only after I've tired you out completely." He dipped his head to suckle on one of her breasts and the spike of pleasure made her grind her clit against his cock. "That's right. Soak my cock with your slick juices, kit."

He threw his head back, gritting his teeth as she slid her cleft over him. His hands gripped her hips, holding her steady in a path of maximum friction over the ridged head. She whimpered as her arousal built again.

"Oh, Goddess, you're so wet, Aislynn. Wetter than you were in my mouth." He met her gaze and his green eyes flared with lust. "I want you to ride me. Ride me slow and sensuous. I want to see the ecstasy take over your face and body before I give you my cum."

His words and the gravely growl in his voice made her pussy clench even before he slid into her. She'd been expecting it, but the hard, hot intrusion of his cock still made her gasp and groan with delight.

"That's it, kit. Take my cock and ride it slow."

Aislynn rocked her hips, rising and falling in a slow rhythm, and watched Nik's green eyes flare with lust and arousal. Her own desires urged her to move faster, to rev up her pleasure, but he held her hips with a strong grasp and she forced herself to keep to the same frequency as she started.

"Oh my glory, your cock is so thick, Nik."

He rumbled a strained chuckle. "All the better to fuck you with, my dear."

She leaned on her hands on either side of his head and ground her hips into his. His shaft slid between her nether lips with an irresistible friction, setting off small sparks of arousal within her as she moved. Her breath came in little gasps and she whimpered each time she came down on his thick flesh.

The pleasure built faster and soon she moaned and whimpered as she increased the tempo. This time Nik didn't make her slow, but thrust up harder, matching her downward grinding. The sounds of wet flesh slamming together filled her bedroom and she reveled in it. It pushed her mind out of her worries and sent her spinning directly into burning arousal.

Her orgasm built like an inexorable wave, but it seemed to be stuck at the crest, unable to break over into the cascade.

"Come for me, kit. Now." Nik reached between them and stroked his thumb over her clit.

Fireworks exploded behind her eyelids and her orgasm surged through her, making her scream out her pleasure. He answered her with his own roar as his cock hardened to silken stone. He thrust harder and faster, prolonging her release as he shot his hot cum into her pussy.

Before she'd come down, he sat up and latched onto her left shoulder with his jaws. A new blast of pleasure surged through her and she dropped her head against his arm, laying another perfect *swak* against his biceps like she had on Chayse's chest.

****

Nik came back to himself wrapped up in Aislynn's body and his jaws locked in her shoulder. His balls were spent, but energy coursed through him as if he could run for hours. *A good Dom takes care of his kit.* The reminder spurred him to gently slide out of her tight body and head to the bathroom to find cloths to tend her. He ran the water until it was hot then returned to the bed to tenderly wipe her clean. She smelled like satisfaction and he tossed the cloth aside before he crawled back into the bed to cuddle her against his chest.

His own satisfaction ricocheted through him as he gathered his Mate into his arms. Something had clicked into place, like a misaligned building block fitting securely at last, and he'd never experienced such 'rightness' before. He'd found his True Mate, the one woman who completed him in ways he'd never considered. Despite this, something seemed missing, just slightly off, as if he tried to tune into a radio station and it wasn't quite clear.

Aislynn snuggled up to him like a contented kitten, warm, sleepy, and relaxed. He ran his hands over her back and ass, just stroking to remind her he hadn't gone anywhere, and it didn't take her long to drop into sleep. Too bad he was too wound up to sleep with her.

His Brother wolf urged him to stay with his Mate, but the feeling that he'd fallen short of the mark wouldn't go away. *Actually, it's not me who's fallen short of the mark.* Anger over Chayse's rejection of Aislynn churned in his gut and he slowly slid out from under her body to keep from waking her. Once he was free, he threw himself into the shower and tried to wash away his fury, but it kept showing him an image of Chayse tucking tail and running.

I gotta get out of here before Aislynn thinks I'm mad at her.

He suspected she still worried his anger came from his brother Mating her first, and initially, that had been the case. But after spending time with Aislynn, he'd realized he and his brother complimented each other in more ways than their coloring. They both belonged with Aislynn, and Chayse had abandoned her.

A growl erupted between his lips and he shut off the shower and dressed in haste. He had to get out before he did something stupid like hunt his brother down and beat the shit out of him.

Nik left the bedroom and searched Aislynn's office across the hall for pen and paper. He had to leave her a note so she wouldn't think he'd abandoned her as well.

Dearest Aislynn,

Thank you so much for the glorious night of your submission. I've never been so satisfied or contented in all of my forty-six years. You're my True Mate and I'm so blessed to have found you.

That said, I must take some time away to get my head on straight. I'm afraid I'm liable to kick Chayse's ass for abandoning you, for running from the most important person in his life. Damn, even writing about it makes me furious. So I'm headed out for a day or two. Maybe I'll go up to Ely or visit my older brother in Hershel. He has a spread where it's good to run as my Brother self.

Know that you are my heart and soul, Aislynn, and I'm hoping my time away will cool my anger and allow Chayse to have some sense knocked into him without it having to be my hand. Because if it's me, he might not be able to walk or talk for a week.

I will return in a couple of days and hopefully Chayse will be with you and apologize for being an unmitigated jackass. I'll take my phone with me so you can contact me if needed.

All my love, kit.

Nik

He added his cell number at the bottom and took the note back to Aislynn's room, setting it on the table beside the bed. He paused long enough to stroke a lock of hair away from her face and lay a soft kiss on her forehead. She sighed in her sleep and burrowed deeper into the pillow.

Nik smiled and forced himself to retreat to the club aboveground. His phone showed the time to be just after four a.m. The large room sat silent and empty, and it occurred to him to suggest they put a guard on the door to the Underground. Nik closed it behind him and headed out to the main parking lot just as the moon rose above the Strip casinos to the east. It was nearly full and underscored another reason why he needed to get out of town. When the moon sat full, he wouldn't be able to control the need to shift and fight his brother. Emotions would ride too close to the surface and his Brother wolf wouldn't hold back.

Nik unlocked the door of his truck and slid in behind the wheel. With his need to shift too close, he wondered if visiting his elder brother Thio in Hershel was a good idea. As far as Nik knew, Thio didn't have a mate and sometimes running with family gave him the support he needed when he wanted to rip Chayse's throat out. *And Hershel's not too far from my Mate.* He could get back fairly quickly if needed.

That seemed like the best solution. It'd give him some space from his delinquent twin and yet kept him in proximity to Aislynn. He threw the truck into gear and headed out toward I-15. It was a two hour drive to Thio's place, but he could use the time to think of what to say to his older brother. It had been months since they'd seen each other, but he'd get texts from Thio from time to time. *Give me a place to crash, brother. I could use the perspective.*

He just hoped Thio had some.

CHAPTER SEVENTEEN

Chayse snarled as he threw himself out of the car and stomped up to Master Kindle's Reiki Garden. Despite the late hour, the Master kept the Garden open for any visitors in need of succor and sanctuary. *And this is Vegas, the city that never sleeps.* The *Morukai* shaman had helped Chayse detox from the last succubus attack and he hoped the man would be able to help with his connection to Aislynn now.

"Be welcome, Detective Wolffe. It has been many months since you visited. Are you well?" The man's voice could soothe a rabid wolverine into complacency. His deep brown gaze scanned Chayse from head to toe.

"No. I need your help, Master Kindle."

"Yes, I see. You're energy is...intriguing." The *Morukai* tapped the corner of his mouth, a small smile curling his lips. "Please, have a seat in the serenity garden until I call for you."

"But—"

"Trust me, Detective. It is as much for your benefit as mine."

Chayse's fury, fear, and impatience surged and Master Kindle's expression became stoic. Before Chayse could protest, the man held up his hand.

"These are the conditions that must be met before I can help you. Take them or leave them."

Chayse knew that tone of voice and swallowed his protest. The master wouldn't be moved until he'd calmed down. He removed his shoes and socks, and strode across the sandy floor to one of the meditation pillows, his fists in tight balls.

"Focus on this candle. When it goes out, you may see me." Master Kindle placed a little tealight candle in the sand before the pillow and left Chayse to his thoughts.

Despite his fears, the energy in the room quieted Chayse's mind and relaxed his body. His breathing evened out and he closed his eyes, trying to find the measure of calm Master Kindle required.

His mind still raced, but he let the thoughts slide past his awareness like leaves on a river. With his breath steady and his heartbeat at a resting rhythm, Chayse's shoulders relaxed and his mind slowed. Images of more pleasant things appeared before his mind's eye and he let them flow like the thoughts.

Until Aislynn appeared.

Chayse inhaled a sharp breath and held it, a moan trapped in his throat. Arousal and yearning hit him along with his anger and his fists clenched. *Get the fuck outta my head, bitch!* His heartbeat sped up and his cock hardened. *No, no, no! Leave me alone.* He didn't want to see the succubus's face or remember her scent or the feel of her pussy wrapped around his dick.

True Mate, his Brother wolf whispered.

Chayse groaned and opened his eyes to see the candle sputter out. He prepared to jump up when a hand on his shoulder held him still.

"Be still, Detective Wolffe." Master Kindle laid his other hand on Chayse's opposite shoulder. "Just breathe for a bit while I take a look."

Chayse forced himself to sit still while the *Morukai* hummed below his breath. The sound reverberated through him and stole some of his anger, leaving the arousal and yearning behind. Tears formed behind his lids and spilled down his cheeks. Goddess, he wanted the pain and addiction to stop. He wanted to feel normal again.

"Very good and very interesting, Detective Wolffe." Master Kindle trailed his hand over Chayse's shoulders as he shifted to sit in front of him. "Things are progressing better than I'd hoped for you. The damage done by your encounter with the succubus has almost completely healed."

"Please, Master Kindle, you must help me." He shook his head and opened his eyes, ignoring his tears. "I've met another succubus and I can't shake my interest or need for her." His fists tightened. "Goddess help me, I had sex with her and….and bit her."

Master Kindle's gaze sharpened. "How recently have you done this?"

Chayse shrugged miserably. "Two hours ago."

Master Kindle blinked, surprise flitting across his face before the serenity returned. "Take a deep breath in and let it out slow while I look you over again."

Chayse tried to relax, but the tears kept flowing and his yearning increased the longer the *Morukai* worked on him. *Goddess, I'd like to get out of here in one piece. I can't do this anymore.*

A dry chuckle full of humor and joy flooded over Chayse and he jerked his gaze back to Master Kindle. The man smiled with mild delight and patted Chayse's shoulders.

"Well done, Detective Wolffe. You've found your True Mate." Master Kindle inclined his head in a bow. "I am pleased for you."

"No, that's not possible." Chayse shook his head. "Please, Master Kindle. Tell me what I need to do. I can't stop thinking about this demon and yearning for her."

"I suspect that's because you've forged an unbreakable mating bond with her, and you're feeling the pull of your True Mate."

Chayse's breath froze in his chest and he gaped at the *Morukai.* "That's not possible. I can't True Mate a succubus."

"The Goddess makes the rules, Detective. We don't get to choose them ourselves." Master Kindle shrugged, his serene mask back in place. "The damage you suffered from the previous succubus is almost completely healed and you're stronger than you've been in years. Don't you feel it?"

Chayse shook his head again, wanting to deny what the shaman said. "No, you have to break me of this bond. You have to help me. Please."

Master Kindle frowned. "Even if I had the inclination to go against the Goddess's work, I cannot break the bonds She forges between Her children. This is Her doing and it would kill you, and most likely your True Mate if I should try."

Chayse considered the *Morukai*'s words. He'd damn near died trying to escape the addiction to Celine. Was he willing to die to kill Aislynn and free himself from her forever? *What about Nik?* Could he leave his twin permanently?

"The bond appears to be missing something." Master Kindle took a deep breath and closed his eyes, pressing one hand to Chayse's chest over his heart. "As it stands now, it will heal you and make you stronger, but there's a piece missing, like an unfinished puzzle." He nodded sharply. "Go home, Detective, get some rest, and find a way to get more of the energy that has improved your heart. Go back to your True Mate."

"The succubus?" Revulsion rose in the back of Chayse's throat.

"Yes. She isn't poisoning you. She is the cure."

Master Kindle rose and reached out a hand to help Chayse up. He took it, his amazement weakening his legs.

"She's the cure? How can she be the cure?"

"She's part of the cure, most of it. There's a piece missing. Search your heart, find the piece, and you will be healed, Detective Wolffe." Master Kindle patted his chest again. "Blessings go with you."

Chayse blinked twice before he gathered up his socks and shoes, and retreated to the foyer. He sat on the bamboo bench and redressed his feet, his mind whirling. *Aislynn is the cure? How can that be?* He still didn't understand any better when he stood up and walked out to his car.

Master Kindle said go home and rest. But he didn't want to go home to an empty apartment filled with ghosts and nightmares. It had become just a place to sleep, not a place to live. The cold February wind pulled at his jacket and he climbed into his car to escape its grasping fingers.

Go to your True Mate. His Brother wolf whimpered in supplication, begging him to listen. *True Mate needs us. We need her.*

Chayse sighed and leaned his head against the steering wheel, moaning. *I'm so messed up.* He didn't know what to believe or where to go.

Go to your True Mate.

He turned the ignition before he realized he'd moved and the heater blasted cool air into his face until he switched it off.

"I'm going insane." He took a deep breath and sat back in his seat. "I'm gonna take Master Kindle's advice and go home." And maybe he'd be able to find the courage to face Aislynn again, especially after running from his True Mate.

****

Morning came with no less confusion than the night

before, but Chayse rose, showered, shaved, and tried to focus on police work. His Brother wolf growled and sulked, but Chayse felt no closer to understanding Master Kindle's words than he had the night before.

The sun rose in a glorious spring display and the wind had calmed overnight. The air smelled fresh with a hint of moisture and new buds appeared on the flowering trees as he pulled onto the freeway. He had to admit, the Mojave in the spring made everything seem better.

He drove to work, his mind going over anything to distract him from the memory of fucking Aislynn up against the wall of her office. Old fear surged and he gritted his teeth against the anger that followed. His Brother wolf whined and snapped at him, reminding him he needed to see her, but he resolutely parked in his space in the underground parking lot at the Fremont station.

The offices remained relatively empty this early in the morning and he found himself grateful for the silence. He focused on the progress of the Johnson case. Mrs. Johnson had stopped by and offered her DNA to compare against that which was found on the jacket Nik brought in. She'd been surprised they'd asked for it, but had acquiesced despite her understanding that her brother could be implicated. His respect for her had grown, and he realized Mr. Johnson may have done her a disservice not telling her about his needs. She was stronger than anyone supposed.

Shows what we know about our loved ones.

The thought came out of nowhere and made his stomach drop. Had he made the right decision to keep his brother away from Celine? *Absolutely.* But he wondered if he'd sabotaged his own healing by hiding from Nik during his long road to recovery. The thing was, he hadn't wanted Nik to know just how badly damaged he'd become, and figured he'd come back to his brother when he'd fully recovered. Unfortunately, he hadn't gotten there.

Until now. At least according to Master Kindle.

How can Aislynn be the cure? The question had plagued him all morning and he didn't like the answers his Brother wolf kept throwing up. *True Mate.* He scowled at the papers stacked on his desk and threw his light jacket into the corner of his office with more force than necessary.

"Rough night?"

Chayse looked up as he dropped himself into his chair. Jamison stood at the door of his office, eyebrows raised and papers in his hands.

"Something like that. Please tell me you have some good news to offset the shit."

"Something like that." Jamison's lips quirked. "We got the results on the DNA from Mrs. Johnson. Eighteen shared markers. Whoever had the jacket first is a sibling to her."

"Hot damn." A grin stretched Chayse's stiff facial muscles. "DNA off the jacket was male, right?"

"Yep. Male and Caucasian." Jamison matched his smile as he handed the results to Chayse.

"Well, hell, I think we have a reason to bring in Mr. Hemmings for questioning." Chayse read over the data on the page. "Which reminds me." He rose and pulled out his kit. "I was shown the original crime scene. I have blood and tissue samples from the floor and cage of the dungeon."

"There's a dungeon with a cage?" Jamison's eyes widened.

"Yeah. But we need to test this blood to see if it matches Johnson's, and the tissue to Mrs. Johnson. I suspect it belongs to our killer."

"Whoa." Jamison ran his hands through his whiskey-colored hair before taking the samples. "I'll jump on these, but wow. Dungeon with a cage, really?"

Chayse snorted, some of his old humor coming back. "I told you Eve's Paradise was more than just a pretty strip club. Put a call in to the judge to issue a material witness warrant for Mr. Hemmings. I'd love to arrest him for murder, but the data isn't clear yet. If that doesn't work, we can always convince Mrs. Johnson to call her brother back to Vegas to help her with arranging transport for her husband's body. It'll give us a chance to talk to him about his afterhours activities. Because what happens in Vegas stays in Vegas, and that includes his arrest for murder."

"You don't know if he's guilty, do you?" Jamison headed toward the door.

"Nope, but the evidence of the security video from the Desert Oasis, the witness reports, and now this point a damning arrow straight to him." Chayse shrugged. "I'd like to talk to him and see what he has to say about everything. I'm gonna go back to the strip club and get their security videos to put him at the scene."

Jamison raised his eyebrows. "Wait, didn't you do that last night?"

Chayse's gut sank and he thought fast. "Yeah, well, things didn't go as planned." *Understatement of the century.* "I had another relapse."

Jamison had been present for Chayse's slow, painful recovery from the withdrawals of Celine's company. The man thought it had been alcoholism and Chayse hadn't corrected him.

Jamison grimaced. "Shit. Did you fall off the wagon?"

Chayse took a deep breath. "I came *this* close, but ended up talking to my sponsor instead. Took me over three hours to calm down." Thank the First Canid Master Kindle had seen him, but his answers still freaked him out. "So that means I have to go back to get what I should've gotten yesterday."

"You want me to go with you this time?"

Chayse shook his head. "No, thanks. I think I'll be okay. The club is closed so I should be able to focus on the goal rather than the temptation." *Let's hope so.* Except the person he really needed to see and talk to was the biggest temptation of all. "Just make sure Hemmings gets his ass back to Vegas."

"Will do."

Chayse took a deep breath and prepared to get up, but realized the morning hadn't advanced to normal banking hours. Relief flooded his system as his breath rushed out. Aislynn wouldn't even be awake yet given her usual late night schedule. *It'd be rude to barge in now.* He'd been given a reprieve and forced himself to get done some of the other paperwork lying around his desk.

CHAPTER EIGHTEEN

Chayse sighed and glanced at the clock. Quarter to three in the afternoon and he couldn't put off seeing Aislynn any longer. He couldn't even claim a late lunch break. He logged out of his computer and made sure he still had the warrant in case Felicia wanted to see it again. Goddess knew she might not even let him in the doors after last night.

He ducked his head in the door of Maxine's office and found her tapping away at her keyboard.

"I'm headed back to Eve's Paradise to get the security vids for the Johnson case. I figure I'll make it the last call of the day."

Maxine raised her gaze to him and bit her lip in consternation. "Jamison told me you had a close call last night. You sure this is a good idea right now?"

"Yeah." Chayse nodded. "I'm good. My sponsor really helped and set me straight. Besides, the videos will place the suspect at the scene right in the middle of the timeline. That should nail the evidence coffin shut."

"Maybe you should take Jamison with you."

"Come on, Lieutenant. They're just security videos. You don't need two guys to get and check them." He shot her a half-smile. "Watching TV is like a guy skill. I think they give honorary degrees in it now."

She snorted and smirked like he'd hoped she would. "Yeah, I think my brothers have their masters' in it by now. Go on, then. But if you need help or backup, text either me or Jamison. We'll be there. We look after our own."

"Will do. Thanks, Lieutenant." Chayse waved and headed out to the parking lot, surprised at the warmth and gratitude filling his chest. Both Maxine and Jamison had stuck by him when he'd crashed after he'd walked away from Celine, but he'd never really considered how much a part of his family they'd become. Both were human so he couldn't tell them everything, but he valued them as much as he could without revealing his true nature.

Like the fact I'm a Moon Singer and I'm going to talk to another succubus.

He grumbled as he climbed into his car and hit the power button. The last place he really wanted to go was back to the strip club, but he had to get the videos, and he had to talk to Aislynn. He tried to shrug away the unease building in his gut as he pulled out of the parking lot and headed straight for Eve's Paradise.

Traffic remained light in the middle of the day, and Chayse reached the strip club in less time than he hoped. He parked his car near the front door and shook his head. *I'm only here to get answers, both in digital and in person.*

Aislynn is True Mate, his Brother wolf whined, ears flat.

Chayse wanted to question the veracity of his Brother wolf, but Master Kindle had backed him up. He sighed and pushed open his car door. The cold wind urged him across the few feet to the front doors, chuckling at his hesitancy. He took a deep breath and stepped inside.

To his surprise, the fear and unease faded a bit, allowing his shoulders to relax. He closed his eyes for a moment, taking in the scents around him. Old smells of sexual arousal, desperation, sharp alcohol, and sweat filled his nose in a pungent morass, but under it lay the scent of *her*, the succubus and, apparently, his True Mate. *That just can't be right.*

He opened his eyes and damn near stood nose to nose with Felicia. The vampire's eyes narrowed and she looked like she stood ready to haul off and deck him.

"What are you doing here, Wolffe?" Her lip curled and one long canine showed.

"I'm here to see the security videos Aislynn offered me last night." When she raised her chin, he dropped his head a bit. "And to apologize to her."

Her eyebrows rose. "You? An Alpha werewolf? Apologize?"

"Yes, ma'am. It seems I made a mistake and need to make amends."

"Oh, you definitely made a mistake, Wolffe."

He nodded. "I know. May I please see the security videos? I do have the warrant." He held it up.

"Fine. I'll let you into the office."

"Thank you. I appreciate the cooperation."

Felicia snorted, but led the way up to the office behind the bar. He studied her lithe form, but while she held a great deal of beauty with her lush curves and graceful walk, she didn't stir his interest beyond appreciation. *Aislynn True Mate.* His Brother wolf's assurance poked him again and he almost growled "I know" aloud.

Felicia let him into the office and cued up the videos he needed on the computer.

"There. As noted in the warrant, you're only allowed to look at the surveillance of the night in question and we have a counter that lets us know which videos have been accessed in the archives." She shot him a withering glare. "I have work to do to get the club ready for the night. Don't screw this up, Wolffe. I'm meaner than I look."

He had no doubt about that. Vampires rarely looked as

dangerous as Hollywood made them out to be. *Hollywood at least made them seem scary, if sexy.* Real vampires were never so obvious unless they wanted to be.

"Yes, ma'am. I'll remember and stick to the rules."

"Good."

Felicia swept out of the room and Chayse breathed a sigh of relief. He'd have to work hard to get on her good side if he actually hoped to stay around Aislynn. The question was, did he?

Yes, yes, yes!

He ignored his Brother wolf and focused on the video in front of him. He took a deep breath and closed his eyes as Aislynn's scent filled his nose. Despite the knowledge of who it belonged to, Chayse settled more, pleasure and contentment relaxing his shoulders. He sat in her chair behind her desk and it seemed like the most natural thing in his world.

Better than the running away you've been doing. Rarely did his Brother wolf speak in complete sentences, but he couldn't argue with the statement.

"Get to work, Wolffe." He opened his eyes and hit play.

The view on the screen showed the door to the Underground despite its rather recessed location as compared to the rest of the club. Chayse checked the time stamp. It read 19:30. *Before they could have arrived if they went straight there from the hotel.* It took only about twenty minutes to get from the Desert Oasis to Eve's Paradise. Thirty if traffic proved heavy.

He watched on fast forward, but no one approached the door until around 21:00. He slowed the video down and watched a large group of people enter the Underground. Most were men leading women, either by leashes or with a proprietary hand on their arms or backs, but no one matching Hemmings's or Johnson's descriptions. *They must be the orgy participants.*

Chayse gritted his teeth and watched a few more

minutes before hitting fast forward again. Three more times he had to slow down, but again, no one in the video matched either of the men he sought. *Maybe they hadn't gone to this club for dinner.* But Aislynn had assured him they'd been there that night, so he throttled his impatience and kept the video moving.

His persistence paid off at 21:48.

A woman with Asian features wearing a short leather corset dress and thick-heeled platform boots over fishnets stopped at the door, waiting for someone. Johnson appeared behind her, his face toward the camera. His head dropped in submission to the woman as she gestured for him to trail her. When he hesitated, glancing away, she gripped his chin and jerked his face back to her. Whatever she said made him dip his head in acknowledgement before he followed her through the door like a dog on a leash.

"So Johnson goes downstairs with his Domme at ten to ten." Apparently, he still had almost two more hours of life left if the ME had the time of death right. "So was Hemmings with him until then or did he go somewhere else?"

Chayse let the video play out for a few minutes without fast forwarding, but no one else seemed to have booked the Underground for the next five minutes. He sped the recording until he found more people visiting the door at 22:26. A man dressed in jeans with rolled cuffs, white t-shirt, and leather biker jacket followed two women through the door, each dressed as buttoned-up librarians with thick 1950's style glasses.

Chayse snorted. *Gotta love role-players.*

No one else neared the door for the next half an hour. Chayse frowned and opened his cell phone to check his notes. According to the security video at the Desert Oasis, Hemmings had left again at 22:53. But he hadn't come near the door to the Underground at 23:00.

Chayse swallowed a growl of frustration and fast

forwarded the video again. Nothing but shadows passed the door until the time stamp read 23:17.

Bingo!

A man in a windbreaker, baggy overalls and a baseball cap strode to the door and paused, glancing warily from side to side. When his face turned toward the camera, Chayse stopped the feed and stared hard at the image. Paul Hemmings wasn't looking at the camera, but it caught his features clearly in the lights from the club.

"Gotcha." Chayse studied the image for any other details. The bottoms of Hemmings's jeans were clean. "What's this, no spots?"

He laughed at himself and resumed play on the security video. The door closed behind Hemmings's heels and nothing happened. Chayse waited a few minutes, but couldn't stand to let the clock just run, so he hit fast forward again.

The seconds and minutes ticked steadily by and he had to throttle his impatience. *I know he's the killer, I just have to wait for him to prove it.* But waiting was a pain in the ass.

When the time stamp read 23:45, Hemmings reappeared coming out of the Underground and Chayse paused the image again to study it. The man had the windbreaker balled up around his right hand and the spots had appeared on his pant legs. A smirk curled Chayse's lips. He took a still of the image and opened a browser to send it in an email to himself. *I've got you, you stupid bastard.*

Chayse watched a few more minutes of the video, but Hemmings never returned after 23:45. Chayse reversed to 23:17 and took another still of Hemmings entering the Underground to send to his email, but he would ask to have the hour from 23:00 to 24:00 sent to Metro as evidence. He closed the browser and opened a blank page in his cell note taker, satisfaction settling into his gut.

When they brought Hemmings in, they'd put him away for a long time. Chayse wrote down all the time stamps he'd seen with Johnson and Hemmings so he could keep the timeline straight, and added the ones they'd gotten from the Desert Oasis. If he had to guess, he'd bet Johnson revealed something to his brother-in-law that didn't sit well with Hemmings. It must have been bad enough to get the guy to commit murder, even one from passionate rage. *Maybe Hemmings saw Johnson following the Domme and figured he was cheating on Mrs. Johnson.* Nothing pissed off a brother more than a man cheating on his sister.

Or his brother abandoning him.

The tap of his fingers against the cell screen paused as the words sunk into his consciousness. Nik thought he'd abandoned him, when all Chayse had tried to do was protect him. He dropped his chin to his chest. *Fuck.* He needed to apologize to Nik, but he didn't know how. So much time had passed, he wasn't sure he could unknot all the tangled garbage between them. *I'm sorry, Nik. I should've been smarter.* Bad enough he'd fallen for Celine's toxic sweetness, but to avoid his twin pretty much assured he'd win dumbshit of the year.

He sighed and finished his notes before tucking the cell back into his jacket pocket. Nik wasn't the only one to whom he needed to apologize. Chayse swung his gaze around the office and nodded. Aislynn kept a comfortable and elegant workspace in which to meet clients. He only hoped she'd be willing to meet with him somewhere more private when he offered his contrition.

Chayse left the office and returned to the club floor, scanning the room for Felicia. Three hours had passed since he'd arrived and they'd been busy. The walls and light fixtures were festooned with pink, red, and white streamers, and festive red, white and pearlescent pink helium balloons rose in merry clumps from silver and red Mylar wrapped anchors on the tables. It looked like a birthday party and he shook his head in bemusement. *What the hell are they celebrating tonight?*

Felicia appeared beside him, her face a stoic mask. "Did you find everything you needed, Detective?"

"Yes, ma'am. Looks like the camera caught the suspect going in and coming out right around the time of the murder." He waved at the balloons and streamers. "What are you celebrating tonight?"

She shot him a look of surprise, transforming her face from elegant marble into surprisingly youthful beauty. "Love, Wolffe. Valentine's Day is tomorrow."

Chayse blinked. With the case and all his personal shit, he'd totally forgotten about the holiday of love. He'd always considered it a Hallmark holiday, a gimmick to get people to spend a ton of money on candy and flowers, but tonight it seemed apropos to what he had to do.

"Oh, right. I'd forgotten. May I see Aislynn now?"

Felicia raised an eyebrow. "You still want to visit with evil?"

"No, I want to apologize to someone for my inconsideration."

The second eyebrow joined the first. "You don't think she's evil?"

"I...no, I don't." It was harder to admit that than it had been to realize he'd been wrong about avoiding his brother.

Felicia opened her mouth to harangue him, but something must have changed her mind because she nodded with a thoughtful look. "Lady Aislynn is down in her personal apartments. I'll let the bouncer know you're allowed below."

"Bouncer?" He hadn't seen one on the security video. Chayse followed her through the club while a woman in a clear PVC nurse's outfit with white stockings gyrated on stage. "When did you install the bouncer?"

"Tonight. There have been too many people just wandering downstairs." She shot him a significant look.

He couldn't argue with that. He was surprised they hadn't done it earlier. Felicia led him to the familiar door and whispered in the ear of an older-looking man with black eyes and a turban. While he didn't appear imposing, Chayse caught his energy signature as the man nodded and waved him through the door. *Holy First Canid, he's a djinn.*

"Remember, Wolffe, do anything stupid and I'm coming after you."

The urge to draw himself up and snap at Felicia about being an officer of the law surged, but he closed his lips and nodded. "I wouldn't expect anything else."

Again, surprise flashed across Felicia's face before he stepped through the door.

The noise of the club cut off immediately when the door closed behind him and he breathed a sigh of relief at the silence. Torch-like lights came on just ahead of him then shut off a few steps behind. Smart use of electricity in a town that used too much. When he reached the lowest level, he retraced the path he'd taken before straight to the unassuming door in a dead-end hallway.

This is it. Was Master Kindle right? Could Aislynn truly be the cure? Chayse knuckled his eyes and sighed. He couldn't argue with a *Morukai* healer, but how did one succubus cure another's damage? He shook his head and pushed opened the suite's door.

Night noises consistent with a desert oasis filled the veranda beyond Aislynn's apartments in the Underground. Chayse paused just outside the sliding glass doors and inhaled the scents. Grass, water, flowering plants, and serenity filled his nose, creating a balm against his concerns. His shoulders loosened and he exhaled.

Master Kindle said I need more of what I'd been getting. Still, standing here in Aislynn's world gave him the jitters.

"Can I help you, Detective?"

A small pool of light attracted his attention, as well as the large expanses of creamy coffee skin flashing as Aislynn moved. A gaping silk shirt offered superficial cover on her shoulders. The succubus pressed an open book over her chest and fixed him with curious eyes.

"What are you doing?" Somehow the sound managed to get past his dry throat.

"Reading. What are you doing?" Aislynn tipped her head, a small smile curling her lips as his gaze slid down to her neatly trimmed mound. His mouth watered. *Goddess, I want her.*

"It looks like you're doing more than reading.

She laughed. "Actually, I'm NETing."

"What?"

Aislynn held up a steaming mug. "Naked Evening Tea. It's a good way to unwind after the stresses of the day." The book slid to the side, exposing her luscious breasts.

He damn near swallowed his tongue. "Got any more tea?"

Aislynn raised her eyebrows. "Is this the beginning of a courteous conversation between you and me, Detective?"

Chayse grimaced, but his gaze flicked shamelessly over her body, drinking in the long, luscious curves in the soft light. "I came to apologize for my earlier behavior."

She tilted her head, her expression thoughtful, before gesturing to the lounge chair beside her. "Come, join me. There is a mug in the wet bar behind me and extra tea in the teapot."

He retrieved a cup and sat facing her with his elbows on his knees. Sitting so close to the succubus made his fears scream in warning, but he forced himself to relax. The *Morukai* shaman said he'd True Mated her and her energy helped with his healing. *And I have felt better since spending the afternoon in her upstairs office.*

He looked up at last, trying not to drool over the full swells of her breasts as she folded the book she'd been reading closed and set it aside. Two bite marks, one on either side of her neck, marred the smooth skin. From what he'd been told, he'd made one of them.

"I understand from Felicia you finally got to look at the security videos in accordance to your warrant. Did you find what you needed?"

He nodded. "I did, actually. The suspect entered the Underground and exited in a time frame right around the murder. No one else came in or out in the bracket of time. I'm pretty sure we've got him."

"I'm relieved to hear that." Her smile remained cool and professional despite her state of relative undress. "So you won't have to return to Eve's again. I bet that's a relief to you."

Was it?

NO! Chayse's Brother snarled in the back of his mind and his shoulders slumped.

"No, ma'am. It's not."

Her elegant eyebrows went up. "It's not?"

"No, ma'am. But first let me say I'm very sorry for taking advantage of you and fucking you in your office." It didn't sound the way he'd hoped, nor did it convey his true contrition.

She nodded, her expression still polite. "Apology accepted. But do you really regret it? Your brother said we True Mated because you bit me. He said it only happens once in the lifetime of a werewolf. Can you truly regret that?"

"I don't understand how I can True Mate you. You're not even my species." He shook his head. "I don't regret the Mating, and my *Morukai* healer says it was good for me despite....my hang-ups. But I do regret how it happened and how I ran after. I've been taught you never leave your Mate to be cared for by others. And I left you." He tightened his hand into a fist around his mug and fought back the disgust at himself.

Cool fingers grasped his chin and lifted his face as Aislynn met his gaze. "Neither of us understood what was happening at the time. I bear you no ill will." She released him and sat back, her eyes narrowing. "But I won't tolerate pity or moping. If you'd like to indulge, please take your time elsewhere."

Chayse blinked. Where had the polite succubus gone? This sounded more like a werewolf alpha female. Despite her nakedness, Aislynn wore her authority like a coat of armor, impenetrable and durable.

"Are you saying I should just get over it and let it go?"

"Is that so difficult? You made a mistake and you're sorry for it. Regret only hampers the joy of the present. The past cannot be changed, only learned from." She picked up her mug and sipped her tea. "So you can wallow if you choose, but not here."

Anger surged. Where did this bitch get off? He'd come to apologize and she told him to move on. "Go to hell."

"I'll see you there, darling."

The anger coalesced into fury in his chest and he stood, his hands fisting at his sides. "Listen—"

"Sit."

The snapped command did something odd inside him and he dropped to the seat like a well-trained dog. *What the*— His throat dried and his cock hardened as Aislynn swung her feet to bracket his knees. The scent of her woman's musk slid over him, filling his nose with a tantalizing fragrance.

"Listen to me very closely, Detective Wolffe. You will let go of your regret and focus on the now. Do you understand?"

Aislynn held his gaze without a smile, her expression serious. Everything inside him wanted to bow at her feet and agree to her command. *What the hell is wrong with me?* He'd never bowed to anyone in his life. *Is this the addiction talking?* But the *Morukai* said he'd recovered too much to allow the sickness to take over his decisions. And this felt different, more empowering, as if she offered him a freedom he'd never had.

"I understand, Lady Aislynn." Whoa! Who was using his voice?

"Very good, my lovely wolf. Now." She picked up his mug and handed it to him. "Drink your tea and talk to me. What do you fear most about what happened in my office?"

Images of taking Aislynn hard against the wall rose in his mind and self-loathing bounded after, pulling down the corners of his mouth. How could he have let anger take over when having sex with a woman? Chayse clenched his jaw and shook his head, his gut churning.

"Look at me."

Aislynn's command made him open his eyes—when had he closed them?—and lift his gaze to her clear silver-gray one.

"Are you breaking your promise to me?"

"What?" What promise?

"Are you wallowing in regret when you promised to let it go?"

How did she know he'd been walking that road? "I'm sorry, ma'am. It's a familiar place I've been."

"Then we'll have to give you new travel destinations. And you may call me Aislynn."

He jerked a little. "Why?"

"You said we'd True Mated. If that's the case, shouldn't we be beyond formalities?"

Fear surged, but he gritted his teeth against spitting out vitriol. "Yes, ma'am. I'm sorry. It's going to take me a little while to trust a succubus." His voice sounded bleak even to him.

Her expression softened. "You don't have to trust a succubus. You've True Mated me, so the relationship we have to work on is ours. May I call you Chayse?"

He nodded. "How can we work on this?"

"Do you want to?"

He nodded again.

Aislynn grew thoughtful. "I think it's recognizing past experiences aren't representative of the now. Not all succubae are the same, and I should know. I'm the first."

"The first succubus?" He blinked, searching his memories. "You mean...Lilith?"

She nodded.

His jaw dropped to his lap. "How old are you?"

"Old enough to know how not to hurt those I care for or even those I don't." She gave him a half-smile. "I told you the reason I have the Underground, Chayse. Instead of killing being after being, I just take a little of the sexual energy others generate, and I can survive without causing death. Not all succubae have discovered this secret, or care enough to do so."

"Why do you?" He hoped he didn't sound belligerent.

"Because I'm lonely." She shrugged at his confused frown. "It's hard to have long term relationships of any kind when my sustenance comes from the sexual life energy of anyone around me. Intimacy is out of the question entirely. But with the sex club, I can feed without killing anyone, and I can have a few companions who don't have to fear death."

"What about addiction?" Chayse swallowed back bile at the thought of how badly he'd deteriorated with Celine. "I have an addiction to the allure of succubae. Celine taught me my strength and species didn't matter. I will always have the addictive personality."

Aislynn nodded. "Perhaps we have to make sure your addictive personality is always fed by what it needs rather than what will destroy you."

"How do you propose we do that? I'd have to be shut up—"

"That's not true, Chayse. We will protect you and stand with you, and give you what you need."

"We?" Why did hope curl through his chest and out his mouth?

"Your brother Nik and I."

Chayse stared at her a long time, trying to find coherency in a vast sea of overwhelming emotion. He wanted to belong, and he missed his brother. They'd shared more than just women until Celine. But he wanted Aislynn with an intensity greater than what he'd felt for the other succubus. *Not addiction. True Mate.*

His Brother wolf's voice had been silent for years after Celine, but since meeting Aislynn, the wolf had been returning in strength. *It's not a fluke? Aislynn is my True Mate?*

Yes. The answer brought both relief and amazement.

"Are you True Mated to Nik, too?"

"Yes." Aislynn tilted her head. "Is that a problem?"

He shook his head. "No. Nik and I used to share our lovers. But after I became addicted to the other succubus, I had to protect him from her, and we stopped."

"Then let us protect you now, Chayse. Let Nik and I be the guardians of your heart and spirit." She flashed him a dark grin. "Believe me, I won't tolerate any other succubus trying to take what's mine. And you and Nik are mine."

Fierce yearning exploded within his chest and he resisted the urge to drop to his knees and lay his head in her lap. *I've lost my mind.* He'd always been alpha, never bowed to anyone, always protected those he loved. But he wanted to belong to someone and have someone protect him for once.

"Will you accept me as your Mate, the guardian of your heart and soul, who takes care of you, protects you, and stands with you, Chayse?"

The little boy within him screamed *"YEEESSSSSS"*, but Chayse held still, sorting through the emotions rattling against his mind. "What does that really mean? You're not going to whip me or tie me up, are you?"

"I will only ever give you what you need." She studied his face. "You have to trust me to know exactly what that is."

He reared back, anger and fear making his heart pound. "Trust you to know what *I* need? How would you know what I need?"

"Peace, Chayse." Aislynn laid her hand over one of his fists and some of his tension melted away. *How does she do that?* "It's my job as your Luna to know."

He frowned. "How do you know about the Luna?"

She gave him a one-shouldered shrug. "I did some research. I didn't know enough about werewolves, but I figured if I'd True Mated with two of them, I better brush up on my facts. Since the Luna is the Alpha female of the pack, she's the one who watches out for the lower ranking members. Isn't that the case?"

Chayse nodded, thinking of his mother. "When there's a big enough pack, yes."

"I don't think the number of members is important. The Luna must lead with experience and wisdom from paying attention to the pack's needs." She unfurled his hand and matched her palm to his.

"You just think you can do anything you want to me."

"Can a Luna do anything she wants? Doesn't she have rules she must follow, lines she can't cross?" She unfurled his other hand and held it between her own. "In this lifestyle, there are rules that dictate what can and cannot happen. And they're agreed upon by all partners before anything starts between them."

"You mean the sub agrees to do anything the Dominant says, right?"

"Maybe. It depends on the relationship. Each one is different and has different rules. Some exist in this lifestyle 24/7. The submissive is always submissive, even in public."

"I don't want that. I'm not a submissive."

Aislynn nodded. "No, I don't think that would work for or benefit you. Others find their needs met by what could be termed as "bedroom bdsm." The power exchange only happens in private between the partners." She slid her hands up to his wrists and closed her fingers around them. "That is what you need." She paused, her brow creasing. "Or what you need from time to time. As I said, the rules for our relationship are ours to determine."

He wanted to believe her and bow to her confidence and strength. He was so tired of making many decisions and fighting just to stay ahead of his addiction. He just wanted someone else to take the reins for once.

"I don't…"

"You don't what, Chayse?"

"I don't know if I can let go of control." *I'm scared.*

"A valid fear." Aislynn nodded. "It comes down to trust. Can you trust me to take care of you and keep you safe?"

I want to. He groaned, fear warring with desire, and all his muscles tightened up. "I don't know."

She rose and he found himself nose to pussy with her, surprise taking away most of his fear. She held out her hand.

"Come with me."

"Where?"

"Trust me."

"Why?"

"Because you want to." Her voice held confidence, but no arrogance. She waited with her hand out, meeting his gaze with steady patience.

How can she know that? How could she know when he didn't? *Because she's my Luna.* The voice of his Brother wolf came from somewhere deep inside and he saw his hand close over hers as he stood.

"Very good." She pulled him after her and his eyes found her naked ass. Each step flexed the delicious mounds and he followed them, grateful he didn't wear his natural form. *Cause I'd be panting like a dog.*

Aislynn closed the sliding glass door behind him and the silence deepened. She led him through the apartment to a doorway across the hall from the office. The bedroom beyond looked like an autumn bower. Gold, burgundy, and rust décor matched the autumn leaf bedspread and more of Chayse's concerns dropped from his shoulders. Smells of vanilla orchids and jasmine spiced with her natural musk, filled his nose with the emotional scent of "sanctuary". He wanted to wrap himself up in it and stay forever.

She stopped him beside the bed, shrugging out of her shirt. "Now, I want you to take off your jacket and belt, and undo your jeans, but leave them on. Then sit between my legs with your back to my chest. Do you understand?"

Honestly, no, he didn't. But he nodded and pulled his shirt out of his jeans as Aislynn crawled onto the bed and sat with her legs demurely folded. How she managed to look regal and in control while naked he couldn't fathom, but he found himself desperate to please her.

He jerked his jacket off his shoulders, tugged the belt from his jeans, and unbuttoned the fly, dragging the zipper down until the waistband hung loose on his hips. *What am I supposed to do now?* His memory foundered for a moment as he took in the visage of her perfect breasts rising and falling with her breath. She raised a warning eyebrow. *Oh, right. Sit between her legs with my back to her.*

Chayse turned and sat down on the bed, his eyes falling to the floor between his feet. The hiss of skin over the coverlet tightened his shoulders as she settled in behind him, one silken leg on either side of him.

She rested her warm breasts on his back and wrapped her arms around his waist. The heat from her nipples burned straight through his cotton shirt. He sighed, inhaling her scent and absorbing the sense of completion with her body against his. Tension sang along his shoulders, but when she did nothing else, he slowly relaxed.

"That's it. Just relax for me." Her voice caressed his ears and made him think of home. "Now as I understand it, once you have True Mated with someone, you'll be able to smell emotions and lies. Is that right?"

"Yes. At least, that's what my parents told me and Nik."

"So you'll be able to tell when I say something untrue?"

"Yes."

"Good." Aislynn tightened her arms around his waist. "Listen carefully, then. I will never hurt you on purpose, Chayse. When I become your Luna, my job will be to give you pleasure, release, and protection. Am I speaking the truth?"

He inhaled a deep breath, sifting through the scents in the room. Lies often smelled like rancid meat or vinegar, but her words contained no rot.

"Yes, you're telling the truth."

"When I become your Luna, it will be my job to give you what you need and serve you with all that I am. True?"

He blinked. She meant her words, but he didn't understand. "How are you serving me if you're the dominant one?"

"Oh, Chayse." Her hands unbuttoned his shirt and cupped his pectorals as she laid her head between his shoulder blades. "That's the unspoken secret in a D/s relationship. The Domme is the true servant to the submissive's needs. A Domme needs to be needed, and She cannot help but serve Her submissive in every way that's required. The submissive has all the control."

He digested her words, smelling the truth of them, and his fear evaporated a little at a time. "How? If I'm tied up, where is the control?"

"Being tied up only restricts your body, not your person. You will have a safeword, and nothing can go beyond it." Aislynn stroked his chest with soft fingers. "It is stronger than ropes, or leather, or steel. It stops everything, no questions. The Domme is bound by your safeword, and by your trust."

He swallowed hard, desperate to give it to her, but fear stalked him. "How can I believe you?"

She caressed his belly and ribs. "I can only show you. If there's a better way, I don't know it."

His heart thundered in his chest, warring between fear and excitement. If she meant what she said, he'd be free of the fear. Forever.

"Bones. That's my safeword."

"Are you sure, Chayse? You don't want anything you might say by mistake, because I'll abide by your statement and will stop all play." She cupped his shoulders with her hands as she leaned against his back. "I've heard your brother say 'chewed bones', and I don't want to be confused."

He inhaled a calming breath as he nestled into her chest. Her warm breasts pressed on his shoulder blades through his shirt and his cock hardened with arousal.

"I—I don't know what to use, then." He gritted his teeth against the uncertainty and wobble in his voice.

"Easy, now. Let's find something simple to remember, yet uncommon in your daily speech." She ran her hand over his head, calming him more. "What is something you find easy to remember, but don't say often?"

He closed his eyes and settled into her ministrations as his mind roamed memories, flipping through them like pages in the dictionary.

"Bandicoot."

"What?" Aislynn's hand paused.

"Bandicoot is my safeword."

She snorted softly behind him and he reveled in the tickle of her breath. "You'll remember that?"

"Yeah. It was something we'd yell when we discovered each other while playing hide-n-seek as kids." He chuckled at the memory of playing with his brothers Thio, Nik, and Jayson. "We saw this show on TV about Australia and how they had these little critters called bandicoots. We thought it was the funniest word, and it stuck." He shrugged. "Bandicoot."

"Very good. Bandicoot. I'll remember that, and the story that goes with it."

He nodded and some of his nervousness returned. "Uh, so what happens now? Am I going to be strapped down to something, or chained, or tied up in some other way?" He swallowed hard and his heartbeat ramped up.

"Peace, Chayse. We haven't gone over all the rules yet." She continued to run her hands over his head, her breathing steady. "We're agreeing to a private D/s relationship, where it's only when we're in our own playspace, rather than in public. Is that right?"

He inhaled deeply, her scent filling his nose with heaven and his mind settled down. "Yes."

"And we agree that the playtime isn't every time we're intimate, but only when we both feel we need it. Is that correct?

More of his tension bled away. "Yes."

"And when you respond to me while we're playing, you'll refer to me as Luna, right?"

He nodded. "Yes."

"While we're playing, you'll trust I know what you need and how far to push you. If I ever hit a hard limit or something that is beyond you at the moment, you will safeword out of play and we'll stop. After I release you, we'll talk and find out what triggered you. Do you understand?"

"Yes." He relaxed completely against her chest, his eyes closed and his fear fading fast. "Yes, Luna."

"Excellent. So are you ready to start?"

Chayse had never been so relaxed before in his life, and never so ready to find peace. "Yes, Luna."

CHAPTER NINETEEN

Aislynn reached around him and pulled his shirt over his shoulders and down his arms. Uncertainty reared its ugly head and he tensed. "What are you doing?"

"It'll be difficult to play if you're dressed, Chayse." Her voice held warm amusement. "Let's get you out of these clothes."

"I'll do it." He made a move to stand up, but she tightened her arms around him.

"No. I need you to relax and breathe, and hold still. Is that clear?"

He took a deep breath. "Yes."

"Yes, what?"

What had he missed? "Yes, Luna."

"Very good, Chayse."

Aislynn removed his shirt and folded it neatly over her arm. She slid out from behind him and set the garment on a nearby chair. He watched her, his heart still hammering in anxiety even as her naked beauty hardened his cock. She smiled as she returned to stand in front of him, his eyes level with her nipples.

"I like that color on you."

Chayse blinked. "What?"

"The color." She ran her hand down his arm as she pointed at his folded button down shirt. "Dark teal looks lovely on you. Matches your eyes. But I prefer your shirt off."

Me, too. She ran her hands over his chest again, but when he tried touch her in return, she pushed his hands away. "What did I tell you about moving?"

"You told me to hold still…Luna."

"That's right. So let me take care of you, Chayse." Aislynn leaned forward and pressed a kiss to his sternum, her breath tickling the hair on his chest. "My my my, aren't you lovely under those clothes."

She dropped to her knees between his legs and strummed her fingers over his nipples. His belly contracted as his cock filled, and he swore his heart would explode out of his ribcage. Holy First Canid, just her simple touches set him on fire. Her full breasts rested against his thighs, but he knew better than to caress them. She'd said not to move and he'd stay still, even if it killed him.

"I like how soft the hair is on your chest and belly." She leaned forward and pressed her nose between his pectorals, inhaling deeply. "And it smells so good. I bet your balls smell even better."

Chayse blinked. "My balls?"

"Mm-hmm." She leaned back and pushed his jeans wider. "Let's find out, shall we?"

Her words set him on fire and his cock took the opportunity to fill even more. By the time she pulled back his underwear, his cock pushed its way out to greet her, the slit leaking with aroused abandon. She didn't raise her gaze to him, but tugged down the waistband of his briefs to expose his shaft.

"That is a lovely cock." Rolling back on her heels, she shoved her hands into his clothes at the hips. "Let's make sure I can see all of it."

He obligingly lifted his ass and she worked his pants

and underwear off his legs, gently lifting each foot to free him. She rose and set his clothes to the side before pausing to look him over. Despite the vulnerability of wearing nothing, he felt cherished, valued, and wanted.

"You're beautiful, Chayse."

He snorted. "I'm sure I look exactly like my brother."

Aislynn took a step forward and grasped his chin, forcing him to meet her gaze. "No, you don't. You're an original, and I love that about you. You're brother isn't here and doesn't need to be. It's just you and me. Are we clear?" She didn't smile.

He swallowed hard. "Yes, Luna."

Her lips curled in satisfaction and she stroked his cheek with her thumb. "Very good. Now, I want to smell your balls. Spread your legs, please."

He swallowed hard again and opened his thighs as she dropped to her knees between them. Her smile warmed him from the inside out, but he almost scooted away from her when she dropped her nose to nuzzle his cock and balls. He tightened his hands into fists in the bedding and gritted his teeth as her breath warmed the skin of his scrotum.

"Holy First Canid." He'd never heard his voice sound so rough, even with other lovers, and his cock jerked with anticipation.

"I'm sure the First Canid approves of our playing together."

He latched onto the first word he could to keep his arousal from breaking his hold on it. "Playing?"

"Yes, playing." She dragged her nose over his balls and up the length of his shaft. "We all need to relax, even when we don't have time to play. That's why these rooms in the Underground are called "playrooms" and what we do is "playtime". Because it's not day-to-day life, it's the time to reconnect to who we are on the inside, beyond what we show the world."

Aislynn raised her gaze to meet his. "I want to know the

real you, Chayse. I want to see beyond the anger, fear, and armor. Will you let me in?"

He wanted to. He needed to, but the fear rose despite his arousal and his cock deflated. His gut sank as she sat back on her heels and regarded him thoughtfully. He dropped his gaze, unable to face her disappointment and anger.

"Hmm, I think this calls for more drastic measures."

He swallowed hard. "What did you have in mind?"

"Ropes."

"What?"

She rose and retreated from him, her lovely ass swaying as she strode across her room to the old fashioned wardrobe standing against the wall. She opened the ornate doors and reached into the interior beyond his view. To calm some of his trepidation, he watched the muscles of her back flex above her rounded ass, and his cock perked up. What would it be liked to have her sitting on his thighs, her ass bouncing on his lap? He shivered with pleasure.

She closed the doors and turned to face him. Golden satiny rope hung in a neat coil from her hands and his throat dried up as she advanced on him. It looked soft and strong, and a part of him wanted to run his hands over the length to test the texture. But another part made his stomach drop and his breath catch.

"What are you going to do with that?"

Aislynn slid the coils of rope over his thighs, the cool, slick loops leaving goose bumps in their wake. He hissed in surprise at both the sensation and the arousal rising once more.

"I'm going to tie your hands behind your back to give you the illusion of immobility." She watched his face without making a move. "I want you to open to me and simply feel. Binding your hands will allow you to let go. It's symbolic because we both know you could snap this rope with your strength or simply shift out of it." She dragged the rope back down to his knees. "Will you let me give you that freedom?"

Chayse gulped and met her gaze. "I really don't understand how tying me up is freedom."

"It's the freedom to not be in control, to allow someone to serve and pleasure you. To let go." She met his gaze without a smile. "And to know someone will catch you and keep you safe at your most vulnerable." She cupped his cheek and tenderness slid over her expression. "Do you trust me to keep you safe, Chayse?"

He wanted to trust her, and his Brother wolf insisted he do so, but his old fears screamed a warning. *Chewed Bones, I'm so fucking tired of being afraid.*

His face crumpled and tears started from his eyes. "Please, Luna, help me escape from the fear. I'm so tired."

"I know, sweet wolf. I will. I promise." She laid a chaste kiss on his forehead. "Give me your hands."

He held them out and ignored the panicked warnings of his mind as she looped the soft rope around one wrist and guided his hand behind his back to add rope to the other. She worked without hurry, testing the pull of his shoulders as she connected his wrists across his back.

"How are your shoulders?" She tugged on the ropes between his wrists. "Not too tight?"

"No, Luna."

"Good. Please stand up." She helped him to his feet then turned him to face the bed. "I want you to lay belly down on the bed while I finish. I'm not going to blindfold or gag you, because I want you to see what I'm doing and I need to learn your reactions. Crawl onto the bed using your legs." She helped him by supporting his chest while he moved.

When he'd settled onto his belly, his hands lay against his back at the level of his kidneys, the ropes stretched between them. While it wasn't the most comfortable position for his arms, he didn't feel any pain.

"How are your shoulders now?" Aislynn knelt beside him, her breasts hanging off her chest as she leaned over him. He suddenly wanted to suckle on them, rolling the turgid nipples over his tongue, but she gently slapped his ass and he blinked.

"What?"

"You need to focus a little better, Chayse. How are your shoulders?"

"Oh. Good, Luna."

"I need you to tell me where you are by using traffic lights. Green means you're fine and feeling nothing beyond your limits. Yellow means you're closing on your limit and something needs to change to continue play. And red means it's too much and play needs to stop. Do you understand?"

"Yes, Luna. Why do I need the safeword then if 'red' stops play?"

"Your safeword stops everything, not just play."

"You mean, if I say my safeword, we won't play anymore?"

"Not for that day or until we can talk about it, negotiate, and find our footing." She ran her hands over his back in a soothing caress. "Your safeword keeps us both safe."

"How does it keep you safe?"

"It keeps me from losing your trust. I'm your servant, Chayse, but if I lose your trust, I lose everything." She patted his ass cheek. "So are you ready?"

He swallowed hard against the surge of unease, but nodded. "Yes, Luna."

"Very good."

She leaned over him and continued working on the ropes between his wrists. He couldn't see, but it felt as if she wound them around and around, strengthening the lines connecting his hands. At last she finished and sat back, surveying him.

"How are your shoulders and arms, Chayse?"

He pulled on them a little. "Good. Secured."

She sighed. "What color?"

"Oh. Green, Luna. My shoulders are green."

"Very good, my lovely wolf." Satisfaction warmed her voice. "Now, rest a moment while I get some toys for play."

Toys? What kind of toys did she have in mind? *I don't want anything in my ass!* He'd heard about women wanting to fuck a man's ass and Celine had hinted at her interest years ago. He'd almost capitulated to please her because of his addiction, but he'd stepped back just in time.

Chayse jerked on the rope binding his wrists, but only succeeded in rubbing it into his naked back. Panic rose and he opened his mouth, trying to pull in as much air as he could. *Can't breathe!*

He fought against the fear, rage swelling in its place, but his breathing only quickened more. Sweat broke out on his skin and he moaned in fury, writhing against the smooth cotton sheets of the bed.

"Peace, Chayse." Aislynn's voice flowed over him like silk, soothing some of the fury, but none of the fear. "Breathe easy. You are safe."

Ha! Safe with a succubus who wants to use 'toys'? Not fucking likely.

He gritted his teeth and squeezed his eyes tight, reaching for calm, but the panic surged, and Goddess help him, he whimpered.

Aislynn's weight hit the bed and she grasped his face between her hands, forcing his head up.

"Open your eyes, Chayse."

I can't. I won't fall again.

"Chayse, trust me. Let me help and protect you." Her thumbs caressed his cheeks and temples, wiping away the tears. "Let me be your strength, your solace, the guardian of your heart and soul. Give me your faith and I will set you free."

The panic slowly bled away and he opened his eyes. "I don't know if I can."

She offered him a compassionate smile. "I can't make this choice for you. I'm a succubus, I can't change that, but I won't coerce you in this. Your trust is either freely given or I release you from your bonds and we end this now. The decision is yours alone. Just say the word."

The word, his safeword. Did he really want this? Could he trust Aislynn, a succubus, the oldest succubus, to hold him sacred? *Can I handle my addiction if I'm with her?* He flexed his arms and the rope hissed over his skin. *Who am I kidding? I've come this far and let her bind me.* But Aislynn still offered him a choice, an out, even now.

"I want to be healed. I want to be whole, but I don't want to be fucked anally. Can you give me that?" His voice sounded bleak even to his ears.

"We'll do nothing you don't want, but I can't do anything without your trust. We must be in this together or not at all." Aislynn studied him as she tipped her head. "We are connected now, so your pain hurts me. But if you can't trust me to protect and love you, Chayse, I will somehow let you go. Even if it breaks me. This can't be one-sided."

He read the truth in her eyes, and felt it in the energy coming from their bond, but the fear tried to drown them out with words like 'addiction', 'despair', 'craving', and 'sickness'. He shuddered with each new onslaught. The little boy inside him screamed with frustration and Chayse wanted to yell back at him for not understanding. *I'll be bound to a succubus!*

You already are, moron.

Like an icy bucket of water, the realization hit him with shocking intensity. He'd already bound himself to her and lived to tell the tale. In fact, his previous addiction mellowed into the ache of an old injury from years past with every moment he spent with Aislynn. She'd done as she promised, protecting him from the old hurts.

But was it really true? Had he only substituted one addiction with another? While he did want to be around her, to bask in her physical radiance like he had Celine, the energy he picked up from Aislynn made him feel neither sick nor jonesing. It recharged his batteries and rejuvenated him, even when not around her. He hadn't felt so healthy since before he'd met Celine.

"Give me your trust, Chayse, and I will be your servant."

He snorted with mild derision. "*You'll* be *my* servant?" He rattled the chains. "Right."

She chuckled and caressed his shoulders with light fingers. Arousal surged and he squirmed.

"Remember, the sub always has control. The Domme is only serving his needs. In truth, you own me."

"I own you?"

"Yes, by paying me with your trust, I become your slave."

Chayse raised his gaze to Aislynn, studying her beautiful face. Her expression filled with honesty, strength and compassion, and his skepticism turned to belief.

"Goddess help me, I believe you." He took a deep breath. "I will submit to you."

"Luna," she prompted.

"Luna."

The brilliance of her smile hardened his cock and she patted his ass before her fingers slid between his cheeks and stroked his balls. Electric pleasure flooded his brain and made him gasp, tightening all the muscles of his body.

"Tonight you're mine, Chayse. I will cherish your gift of trust by serving your needs and proving you need no other. Do you understand?"

"Yes, Luna."

"Very well. Do you remember your safeword?"

"Bandicoot, Luna."

"Very good. And what will happen if you say that

word?"

"You will stop whatever you're doing."

"Not just what I'm doing, but the whole game. You have control, Chayse. Remember, if we hit a hard limit, say the safeword, and everything will stop." She trailed her fingers over his back, raising goose bumps in their wake. "Do you understand?"

"Yes, I understand."

Aislynn *tsked* and he added, "Luna."

"Very well." Her whispered words tickled his buttocks just before she licked his sac between his spread legs.

Wet heat wrapped around his balls and shot arousal straight to the back of his head. He moaned, he couldn't help it, and closed his eyes to keep his focus on the pleasure. She didn't say a word, just kept teasing and tasting the soft skin between his legs. His cock hardened like magic and he had to shift his hips to give it space under him.

"I was right. You smell divine, sweet wolf." She inhaled deeply and ran her hands down his thighs as she licked his balls again. "I think I need to tease you a little more. You're still too much in your head."

She moved from the bed and cooler air swept over his damp balls, making him shiver. *What does she mean I'm still too much in my head?* The idea seemed ludicrous and he opened his mouth to ask when something soft and ticklish swept over one calf.

All questions died as the erotic sensation moved up one leg, across his ass, and down the other. When it reached the opposite heel, Aislynn paused and knelt between his legs, blowing on his cooling balls. The skin tightened up and he groaned, which turned into a gasp when her hot tongue hit his scrotum.

"Dear Goddess."

She chuckled. "Not for centuries, but I'll take that as a compliment."

The tickling returned up his right leg while she licked and fondled the sensitive skin of his testicles. Chayse lost track of his worries with each new assault on his senses. Whatever she brushed his skin with played a sexy counterpoint to her hot, wet tongue between his legs. His cock grew taut beneath him and soon he squirmed with each touch, a whimper working its way out of his throat.

"Oh yes, my sweet wolf. That's it. I'm going to devour you and set you free. Do you understand?"

"Yes, Luna." He hadn't expected his voice to be filled with such entreaty, but he didn't want her to stop.

"Roll over for me, little wolf."

It took a few seconds for him to understand what she wanted, but with his hands secured behind his back, he had no leverage. She straightened one arm and bent the other before helping roll his body over. She'd given him enough play in the ropes to allow his hands to rest on either side of the narrowest point of his waist while still leaving him bound.

He took a deep breath and her gaze sharpened on his face.

"Color?"

The word made no sense until he replayed their conversation in his mind. "Green, Luna."

Her intensity softened and she smiled, running her hands over his chest and shoulders. "Good."

She plucked his nipples, making him grunt with pleasure. She followed that with a kiss to his breastbone and trailed more down his belly until she reached his cock straining above his balls. *Oh, please, suck my cock. Please.* His shaft flexed as if trying to get her attention, and she smiled her sultry smile as she skirted around it to the sensitive skin on his inner thighs.

"Your cock is flexing like an exclamation point. Should I heed its imperative?"

Please, please, please. "Yes, Luna."

"As you command, my little wolf." And she slid her mouth over his shaft.

Stars exploded behind his closed lids as soft, slick pleasure swamped his mind. Chayse succumbed to her seductive magic, gasping and trying not to writhe under her glorious torture. Her hot mouth worked over his shaft and his arousal increased, sending him racing for the pleasurable finish.

But the more turned on he became, the more strident the voice of panic. Aislynn's ministrations on his hard cock brought him so close to orgasm several times. But each time he closed in on the release, Celine would appear in his mind, grinning with maniacal avarice, and the pleasure died. *I can't do this again. I'll never get out.*

After the fifth time, Aislynn raised her head and stroked his cock with her hand. "Tell me what's going on, my little wolf. You're distressed."

He moaned and tears started behind his eyes, but the words wouldn't come.

"Chayse, you must tell me what's going on. I'm your Luna, I'm here to give you everything. What do you need?"

Chayse squeezed his eyes tight and shook his head hard. He wanted to believe it wouldn't be the same this time, but experience shook his resolve. Fear stole his voice, tucking it deeply into his chest and constricting his throat. His body hummed with exquisite pleasure, but panic pushed tears from his eyes and only a sob escaped his lips.

"You must tell me what you need or I can't help you, my little wolf." Aislynn's voice remained calm and coaxing. "I can only help if you tell me."

"I need…" The words stuck in his throat as fear pinched them off and he jerked against the ropes binding him.

"Deep breaths, Chayse." She stroked his chest with light fingers and his nipples hardened to sharp points. Her scent changed from desire to compassionate arousal.

"Calm. Find your center and tell your Luna your desires."

Pleasure ramped up as she grasped his sagging erection and slid her hand along its length. Breathing deeply helped him focus on that instead of the screaming panic. When her hot mouth settled over the head of his cock again, he moaned as the panic receded and his shaft stiffened.

"I need…you to take away everything."

"I will do that for you, I promise, Chayse." Before he could say more, a new, tighter heat engulfed his cock and he gasped again, jerking his eyes open.

Aislynn sighed with pleasure as she seated herself on his hips, her pussy snug around his shaft. "Give me your fear, little wolf. Give me your dread. I will take everything away and replace it with love and pleasure."

Chayse groaned and thrust into Aislynn, his body taking what it needed before he could stop it. His hands clenched into fists beside his hips, but he couldn't reach her with the binding ropes.

"You are going to come, my little wolf, and when you do, you will release all the fear keeping us apart. You will give it to me to keep. It's no longer yours. Do you understand?"

Aislynn's voice held a note of command even as she rode him hard, her pussy clamping down on his cock and driving his arousal higher. He writhed and moaned, giving himself up to the pleasure she gave.

"Do you understand?"

He'd lost track of the conversation until Aislynn asked her question again.

"Yes, yes, I understand, Luna."

"Good, then keep your eyes on me so you know who's fucking you, and come for me, Chayse." And she clamped down hard with her inner muscles.

The orgasm crashing over him set him free as he sailed through the stars cascading across his vision. In the distance he heard himself cry out and Aislynn's more musical voice joining his, but he remained in the glory and peace where he floated.

After a few moments, the world around him seemed to settle into familiar lines. Great tree trunks and soft moss grew amongst lush understory like something out of a children's book. Chayse found himself in the guise of his mental child. He stood in his favorite clearing with the stream chuckling in its rocky bed. The forest used to look desiccated and sickly, but now the trees rose tall and straight, and every bush held full, leafy foliage.

"Wow. It looks a lot better here."

Chayse spun and found Eva standing in his glade, wearing a delighted smile and Aislynn's eyes. "I like what you've done with your soul garden." She wore a "trust me…I'm Irish" t-shirt and a pair of denim Capri pants.

"Eva? What are you doing here?"

Eva blinked and tilted her head. "You brought me here. You've asked me to be your guardian, the sentinel for your soul garden, so here I am."

Chayse frowned, sifting through his memories, but he couldn't remember asking her that. "When?"

Her smile turned kind. "When you gave me your fear and dread. When you submitted to me, and freed yourself. I'm the one who will stand beside you and defend you with all that I am."

"Why?"

"Because I love you, Chayser."

He brushed his hands through the fronds of a bracken fern waving gently in the soft breeze. The scent of his mother's jasmine bush drifted through the tree trunks and shadows danced with the sway of branches overhead.

"But I'm not who I thought I was. What if my addiction comes back?" His biggest fear made his voice break as if he'd returned to his teenaged years.

"Your addiction is to a succubus's energies, but you're now True Mated to one." She gave him a big smile. "Any time you need such energy, I'm here for you."

"What if another succubus comes? What if she tries to take me away?"

Eva changed in a blink of an eye from a fresh-faced, happy-go-lucky teenager into the demon she truly was. Gnarled horns rose from her forehead into twisted spires and great leathery wings stretched behind her back. Claws reminiscent of a golden eagle sprouted from her fingertips and her eyes glowed with brilliant fire.

"No one takes what's mine and survives. Any succubus who comes after you will deal with me, and I'm the oldest." She tilted her head and winked. "I've been there, done that, and gotten the t-shirt, corset, and cravat." Her form shifted back into the teenager with capris and t-shirt. "It's all good."

"Whoa. You're really scary when you want to be."

She grinned and winked. "Come on and fight like a girl." But she sobered and folded her legs under her as she rested in the grass. "Being the first succubus has given me a little bit of experience and ability."

"Just a little." Chayse snorted and sat down, draping his arms over his knees as he fingered a piece of grass. "How did you become the first succubus? Is the story about Adam and the apple the real deal?"

"It's not like the stories say, and yet it is." She shrugged. "There were rules to follow and choices to be made, but the knowledge tree with the apple is just a metaphor. What it came down to is Adam and I chose to have sex with someone other than each other. Demons as it turned out. With that choice, the Goddess cursed us to need sex to survive."

"I'm sorry."

Eva nodded. "Don't be. It was a choice, and at first neither of us understood what it meant. Sex for survival? Awesome, right?" She shook her head with a rueful smile. "It took me several times to realize my survival meant the death of others. Then it wasn't so fun. I had to be careful not to orgasm with my partners, because if I did, I'd take too much of them and they'd be left to sicken and die."

"Did you stay with Adam?"

Eva smiled thoughtfully. "No, he and I went different directions when thrown into the world at large. I didn't see him for centuries, but I caught up with him in the late 1600s in St. Petersburg, Russia, and we had tea in the Hermitage."

Chayse laughed. "You're the founding pair of most creation stories and you had tea in the Czar's palace?"

"*Da, eta pravda.*" *Yes, it's the truth.* She smiled at him and picked a dandelion flower from the ground. "He'd changed, become wiser and sadder. We both had. I think he'd figured out how to break the curse. I remember he tried to tell me, but we were interrupted and I had to leave." She sighed, a little sadness in her expression. "I haven't seen him since, so I never found out." She offered Chayse a brighter smile. "But maybe it has something to do with you and Nik. I've had sex with both of you, and orgasmed hard, and neither of you died. Perhaps finding one's true mate means I no longer have to worry about killing anyone."

He tipped his head. "Or worrying about getting fed."

"Yeah, or that."

They lapsed into silence for a moment and he let his gaze rest on the healthy trees around them. "Is this all from you?"

Eva shook her head. "I think it's from you. Or rather from your recovery around me. I don't think I'm the one doing this. See over there?" She pointed to a particularly sickly looking oak standing in blackened grass. "There are still places that need help and recovery."

Chayse surveyed the damaged foliage and nodded slowly. "Yeah. I have a lot of work ahead of me."

She shrugged one shoulder. "Maybe, maybe not. Have you talked to Nik yet?"

He sighed and shook his head. "No, not yet."

She scooted over next to him and wrapped an arm around his shoulders. "You should. He's a big part of you. Of your healing. Haven't you been alone long enough? Nik needs you as much as you need him."

Chayse leaned into her embrace and let his thoughts wander to his twin. He'd cut Nik off to save him, but he suspected the reason he hadn't gotten better was because his brother was missing. He'd shared so much of his life with Nik—love, triumph, loss, and now Aislynn—to be without him stunted his own growth.

"Yeah. Brothers need each other."

"And I need you both. You're the other two quarters of my soul."

He blinked. "Not Adam?"

She shook her head with a nostalgic smile. "No. We started out together, but we weren't right for each other, which is why we didn't end up together. Still friends, but not True Mates."

Warmth filled his chest as he rested his head on her shoulder. "I'm kinda glad. Because I, uh, love you lots, Eva."

She laughed and his nervousness melted away. "That's good, 'cause I love you, too, Chayser."

They sat together in silence and Chayse let himself sink into her. He didn't want to go anywhere or be anything else. He just wanted to rest with Eva. He closed his eyes and wrapped an arm around her waist, holding on. And for the first time, he felt safe.

****

Aislynn came back to herself, her heart thundering and her body satisfied. She glanced down at Chayse between her legs and for a moment worried she'd killed him. But his chest rose and fell in an even rhythm and her fear slithered away. She gently climbed off him and strode to the bathroom to find a warm towel to clean them both, her mind reveling in her new found freedom. She'd visited Chayse's soul garden again, and he'd accepted her. Her, the baddest succubus ever known. She couldn't quite stifle the giggle of excited pleasure as she returned to the bed.

Chayse lay where she'd left him, his cock still at half-mast, and her heart did a little flip of pleasure. He was hers, now, and she'd never had such a wonderful responsibility. She crept up beside him and lovingly cleaned his cock and balls of their mixed releases. She loved touching him and he sighed with contentment at her ministrations.

Tossing the towel aside, she took her time to unwind the golden rope from his wrists. His eyes remained closed as she pulled the loops free and gently rubbed the skin. A contented sigh told her she'd done right. She took the time to turn out the lights and crawled up to the head of the bed. She gathered her sleepy werewolf into her arms and snuggled down into the pillows with her own sigh.

"I have you, Chayse. I won't let you fall. You're safe and you're mine. I'll protect you because you're my little wolf."

He gave a sleepy growl-yip, and rolled over to lay his head on her chest and wrap an arm around her waist. "Love you, Aislynn."

"I love you, too, Chayse." Truer words had never been spoken.

CHAPTER TWENTY

Chayse woke to the unfamiliar sense of contentment and damn near complete darkness. Despite the odd occurrence, panic didn't come. Instead, he felt safe, warm, and secure, as if no danger threatened him in this place. *Where the hell am I?*

A soft snort and matching sigh clued him in to the presence of company in the bed with him. *Did I spend the night with Aislynn?* The idea shocked him enough he didn't even move when she cuddled up next to him, her arm curling over his chest. He hadn't slept in anyone's bed in over five years. The only bed he'd visited was the pitiful excuse for a sleeping place in his empty one-bedroom apartment. He'd had sex, but never stayed. Especially after Celine.

But lying there with Aislynn wrapped around him, he found himself content, settled. Love had pushed out the fear and he lay there listening to the echoes of it in the halls of his heart. It bounced off the walls, rebounding and growing with every passing minute. Only one dark corner reminded him something needed to change.

He had to talk to and reconcile with his brother.

He didn't know how he'd do that yet, but being

snuggled with Aislynn kept the unease at bay.

"I can hear you thinking all the way over here in my own head." Her sleepy voice made him smile.

"Oh yeah? That's pretty good. What am I thinking?"

"I don't know, but it's loud. Why don't you tell me and I'll think about getting up to really talk to you."

He chuckled. "I was thinking about Nik and what I have to say to him."

"Mm-hmm. What do you have to say, Chayse?" She propped her head on one hand and surveyed him with her silver-gray eyes.

He took a deep breath. "I have to apologize for not coming to him for help when I'd finally gotten away from Celine, and for not explaining why I'd cut him off in the first place."

"That sounds like a good thing to do, especially since you've both True Mated me and I've true mated you."

He nodded. *Yeah, things have gotten complicated.* "Hopefully, it shows how strong I am. The hungry part of me wanted Celine all to myself, but the other part knew I had to shield Nik from her or risk losing everything, including my soul. I didn't want to hurt him, but she was toxic."

"And now she's gone."

"Thank the Goddess."

Aislynn nodded. "So what now? You go to work, apologize to your brother, and then what?"

"I haven't gotten that far yet."

She didn't say anything for a moment, just traced imaginary lines through the hair on his chest with one finger. "Would you…come back here with Nik after work?"

He took his own moment to organize his thoughts. "Do you want me to?"

"Yes, very much." She sounded remarkably vulnerable. "If I could have my way, I'd have a room waiting for you to move in." She hid her face against his pectoral as if embarrassed with her admission.

"You want me to move in here?" He let the idea bounce around inside him for a few moments, liking it more with every passing second.

"Yes, more than I've ever wanted anything." She peeked up at him. "Nik, too."

The idea was growing on him, but he had one concern. "What about sleeping here with you? I don't want to sleep alone anymore."

"Oh, no, I want you in my bed." She smiled shyly. "I just thought having your own space would make it more attractive for you to move in. I don't want to push too hard too fast." She ducked her head again. "But I want you here where I can see you as much as possible."

Her admission warmed him more than her body against him. "You really want me and Nik here in your sanctuary?"

"Yes." She raised her head to meet his gaze guilelessly. "You're my mates and I want you here with me, where I can keep you safe."

He snorted. "You know I'm a cop, right?"

She gave him a half smile. "Yes, I know, but not when you're off duty. Then you're mine to protect, body and soul."

Somehow, he really liked that idea. The fear of addiction tried to push past his contentment, but he shoved it into a box and locked it. *I'm done with that. I have my Mate and my brother.* Or he would, just as soon as he gave Nik a call.

"I'll move in here if it's what you want, Aislynn."

"Today?"

He snorted again. "Well, I do need to stop at my apartment for some clothes."

"Not on my account." He could hear the grin in her voice and laughed with her. Goddess, it felt good to do that.

"No, not for you, but for the humans I work with. I'm

not sure they could handle this much werewolf wandering around in the buff."

She laughed and something clicked into place. He wanted to hear that from her all the time. It sounded lighthearted, something he suspected she didn't get to be very often. *I will serve her to the best of my ability, if only to make her laugh.* Damn, one night with his True Mate and he was becoming a romantic.

"Speaking of which, I do need to head to work. My boss will be looking for the results of your security videos."

Aislynn stiffened. "You said you found something helpful, right?"

"Yes. I have the suspect coming and going at times bracketing the murder." Satisfaction bloomed again. "We'll nail him for it. All the evidence points straight to him."

"More than just the videos?" She sounded curious.

"Yep." He sat up, dislodging her arm. He missed it immediately. "But if I'm going to finish processing it all, I need to get going."

"But you're coming back, right?"

"I promised I would."

"I know." She switched on a lamp and the glow gilded her sexy, naked form. His cock saluted, but he controlled it before it grew too large. "But a lot can happen between now and then. Doubts, fears, insidious memories."

"Aislynn." He rose and walked around the bed to kneel in front of her. He loved being between her legs. "I promise I'm done running away from you. You're my True Mate, and whatever else is wrong with me, I believe in that from the bottom of my soul. I'm done running."

She stared at him a long time, searching his expression for any hint of mockery, but he meant every word. "I believe you. Just come back to me safe, Chayse."

"I promise, Luna."

****

Leaving Aislynn had been one of the hardest things he'd done since he'd ripped his way out of Celine's hold. Chayse reluctantly climbed into his car and made the drive through the early morning streets of Vegas without too much trouble. *Sure is nice not having to take the 15 today.* Using the freeways was always a pain in the ass at rush hour. His usual forty-five minute commute had dropped to fifteen minutes. *I could definitely get used to this.* And to waking up beside his sexy mate.

He pulled into his usual parking spot and turned off the car before reaching for his phone. He held it in his hand for a few moments, trying to think if he should text or call his brother. The coward in him won and he texted Nik to meet him at the precinct to discuss the case. He sent the text and shoved the phone in his pocket as he headed into the building. He had no idea if his brother would respond. Hell, his jaw still ached from the right hook Nik nailed him with.

Well-deserved, too.

Chayse made it to his office without being stopped. *Of course, it could be the 'early-morning-no-coffee-yet' glare I've got going.* Still, he didn't expect it to take too long before Maxine or Jamison appeared to check up on him.

While he waited, he opened his email and checked to be sure the stills he'd taken from the Eve's Paradise security videos had made it through. Luck was with him and he found them. He printed them to add to the file before his phone dinged with an incoming text message. Taking a deep breath, he opened the message.

Be there in twenty.

That was it. Chayse grimaced. He hadn't expected more from Nik, but he'd hoped.

"Well, you at least look better this morning. How'd it go at the strip club yesterday?"

Jamison stepped into Chayse's office and slumped his lanky frame into the wood chair on the other side.

"Better than I'd hoped. The security vids showed Hemmings going in before the murder and coming out after with his windbreaker balled up and his pants spotted." Chayse nodded with a satisfied smile. "If I was a betting man I'd say it was blood spatter. Any more DNA on that jacket?"

"Yeah." Jamison nodded. "The blood on it was a positive match for Johnson. With the epithelial DNA match with the Mrs., I'd say Hemmings is our guy."

"And the skin sample?"

"Still running, but it should be done late this morning."

"Goddess, I hope it belongs to Hemmings. That would definitely nail him to the wall."

Jamison nodded his whiskey-colored head. "Don't worry. Between the two security videos, the epithelial DNA, and blood on the windbreaker, we got him."

"Yeah." Chayse rubbed his face with his hands. They still smelled like Aislynn despite the shower he'd taken that morning. "Finally things are going well with this case. Is Hemmings on his way here?"

"Yeah, we got the material witness warrant. The guy should be here around one o'clock this afternoon." Jamison tipped his head. "Was it bad going to Eve's and being in the presence of all that temptation?"

You have no idea. But Chayse sat back in his chair and gave it serious thought. "Yes, and no. It hits me at odd times. But this last visit was easier, as if it didn't have the usual grip on me." Giving into his need to be with Aislynn helped, too. "I think it had to do with my focus. I needed those videos for the case and the only way to get them was to go back there. But the staff didn't fight the warrant at all and it went off without at hitch."

"And then you went home and got a full night's rest." It wasn't really a question.

Something like that. He'd definitely found a home with Aislynn, and slept better than he had in over five years.

"Yeah, I did."

"That's good. Maxine had me on stand-by all last night in case something happened."

Chayse blinked at his partner. "Are you serious?"

"Yeah. She didn't like you going to that place all alone after your relapse." Jamison gave a one-shouldered shrug. "Neither one of us wants to see you get fucked up again."

Chayse sighed with a grimace. "Yeah, I don't want to go there either." He met Jamison's gaze. "Thanks. And sorry."

Jamison shrugged again. "No worries. Turns out my plans fell through so I just sat on my couch and watched the game on TV."

"You had plans?" Chayse groaned. "I'm sorry, man."

"Don't worry about it. I told you they fell through." Jamison nodded, but Chayse caught some regret in the man's scent.

"You found yourself a sexy, new girl after Lindy?" Chayse frowned in concentration. "Wasn't she a hot porn star or something?"

Jamison shrugged. "Yeah, but the thing is after having sex all day the last thing she wanted to do was more of it when I got off work. It didn't work out."

"I'm sorry. That sucks. Were you going to go out with her last night?"

"No, it was with someone else, but she had something come up at work." Jamison dismissed it with a wave. "Not a problem." He stood up. "I gotta get some paperwork done, but I'll be prepped to go at Hemmings whenever he gets here. You ready for this dog-and-pony show?"

"Hell, yeah."

"Oh, one last thing. We may have the murder weapon."

Chayse's ears perked up. "Oh yeah?"

"Yeah. We found a ball point pen with the ink cartridge removed in the inner pocket of the windbreaker. It was covered in blood with skin stuffed up the cartridge hole.

We're running DNA on the blood and skin."

"Hot damn."

"And we also got the weapon used to knock out Johnson's lady friend. We ran fingerprints and compared them to prints the company has on file. Hemmings's prints were all over it."

Chayse blinked. "How did you get that?"

Jamison's expression remained remarkably blank. "Lady Aislynn's assistant gave it to me. She said she found it next to the woman the night of the murder."

Chayse raised his eyebrows. *Nice of her to share that info with me when I served the warrant.* "Well, that's quite helpful. At least we know how he incapacitated Johnson's partner. Let me know what shows up with the DNA. Think it'll be done in time for the interrogation?"

"We can only hope." Jamison grinned, relief in the set of his shoulders. "But my money's on Dick Johnson's DNA in the pen."

"That's a smart bet. I hope the skin sample from the cage belongs to Hemmings, though. Let me know what comes of it and I'll see you later."

"Will do."

Chayse smiled to himself. He hoped Jamison had found the murder weapon. Talk about the nail in the coffin of evidence. He knew Hemmings had killed his brother-in-law, but this would definitely hang him.

Chayse also hoped Jamison had found someone better than the porn star. Lindy had been nice enough and seemed to like Jamison, but she'd smelled off to Chayse. *It could be the scents of all the other people she'd been with at work all day.* He didn't think he could stand smelling all those other men and women on his mate day after day. *Thank the Goddess humans don't have an overdeveloped sense of smell.*

He pulled out his phone and started to transcribe his notes on Eve's Paradise for the case. He wanted to have everything where everyone could see it if they looked. Especially because he'd become involved with the owner of the club. He had to get this one done before someone discovered he'd mated Aislynn.

Yeah, maybe a slight conflict of interest. He was very interested in catching this killer, despite it affecting Aislynn's home. *No one endangers my town.*

"You had a breakthrough in the case?"

Nik's flat voice made him look up. His brother wore an expression of indifference, but it didn't hide the anger in his eyes.

"Yeah. Come in and shut the door, would you?" Chayse took a deep breath and did his best to dismantle his alpha tendencies while his brother closed the door and stood in front of the desk. "Would you sit down? Standing over me with a scowl doesn't make this any easier."

"I'm not scowling and I'm not in the mood to make this easy. You fucked up." Nik crossed his arms over his chest.

"I know. Would you just sit down so we can talk about it?"

Nik did a slow blink, but sat down with ill-grace, his arms still crossed. "I'm sitting."

Chayse resisted the urge to say, "Good dog."

"First, I want to say I'm sorry. I'm sorry for True Mating Aislynn before you. I had no idea she was your True Mate. Hell, I didn't even know she was mine."

"She's your True Mate?" One eyebrow went up. "And you know this, how?"

He almost shot his brother a smart-ass look of his own. "First, the *Morukai* verified it for me. But then I went and talked to Aislynn."

"You talked to Aislynn? Did you hurt her?" A low growl filled the office.

"No, you fucking moron, I didn't hurt her. I acknowledged the bond and spent the night with her."

Nik gaped. "Wait, you spent the night? In her bed?"

"Yeah. Last night. It's what mates do." Chayse frowned. "Speaking of which, where the hell were you? Isn't she your True Mate, too?"

"Of course she is. Wait, did you say 'too'?"

"Yep." Chayse waited as emotions rolled over Nik's face. "You surprised?"

"Aren't you?"

Chayse shook his head. "Every damn day on this case. But when it comes to this succubus being my True Mate, I guess I shouldn't be surprised that she's yours, too." He stopped and eyed his brother. "This going to be a problem?"

"I don't know, Chayse. You used to share with me all the time, then you fucking ran because of Celine. What's to say you won't do it again?"

His Brother wolf whined at the pain in Nik's voice.

"That's a fair question, but the answer is simple. I'm bound to Aislynn now, and so are you. There's nowhere I can go. Not without her or you." He ducked his head. "I'm sorry, Nik. I'm sorry I had to push you away, but I'm even sorrier I didn't come to you when I finally kicked Celine to the curb. I just thought you'd tell me I was stupid to have fallen for her and I couldn't face you until I'd healed from her influence. The problem was I didn't understand I needed you to help me heal."

Nik scowled. "You're a jackass."

"I know."

Nik sighed and rubbed a hand over his face. "So now what? What do you want from me?"

"Nothing. Well, that's not true." Chayse took a deep breath. "I want us to be a family again, to fix what I fucked up. And I want to share again, but only Aislynn. You and I are meant to be her True Mates, and that means we're meant to share. Like we did before." He hated feeling vulnerable and uncertain, but it seemed to be happening a lot more often lately. "Can we do that again? Share our lover?"

Nik didn't say anything for a long time and Chayse had the feeling the decision could go either way with his brother. *Chewed bones, I hope he doesn't make me eat too much crow. The damn feathers get caught in my gut.*

When Nik finally spoke, anger underlay the calm words. "I could forgive you for cutting me off to protect me from Celine. I could even forgive you for True Mating Aislynn before me because you weren't paying attention given your addiction. But what I'm having trouble with is your fucking cowardice and leaving Aislynn to be comforted by someone else after you True Mated her. What the fuck was that, Chayse? You left your Mate when she needed you most. You know better. We both do."

Anger of his own kindled, but he clenched his teeth together and focused on the questions rather than the accusations.

"I had to get away before I did something I'd really regret." He shrugged although he felt anything but ambivalence. "I had to get to the *Morukai* to find out if I was still caught in the addiction loop. I was so fucked up I didn't know if what I felt was the return of my addiction or something real. I couldn't tell and I couldn't fall again." He sighed. "Turns out, I didn't. Aislynn's the cure."

"The cure. To your addiction?" Nik's eyebrows rose, and the oddest feeling of hope came from him.

"Yeah."

"That's what the *Morukai* said?"

"Yeah."

"So you're not going to run away again?" Nik raised his chin.

"No. In fact, Aislynn wants me to move in to her underground place so she can be around and protect me more often."

"Does she? Wonder why she didn't ask me that." A frown creased Nik's brow.

"Maybe because you weren't there to ask, Smudge. So where the hell were you?"

Nik glowered. "Giving you time to hopefully come to your senses, jackass. And getting my head on straight before I kicked the shit outta you for being stupid." He took a deep breath and blew it out slow. "I went to see Thio in Hershel. He's got a big spread up there for letting my Brother wolf run. You've only pissed me off this badly one other time in our lives and that was when you disappeared with Celine. But this time…Hoo-boy, I was ready to do you bodily harm. I needed the time away." He shook his head. "But if I'm absolutely honest, after you disappeared, I didn't make nearly enough effort to find you and corner you. I wallowed in my own self-pity for a long time and took up the Dominant side of BDSM to distract myself from not tracking you down and having it out with you. You're my twin brother, and I was avoiding you as much as you were avoiding me. Kinda fucking pathetic."

"So much for being badass alpha werewolves, eh?" Chayse snorted.

"Yeah. I think we tied for loser of the year this time."

"At least we're in it together."

Nik snorted, humor curling his lips. "Shit, we were always in it together, no matter what it was. And this time is no different." He raised his gaze to meet Chayse's, his expression contrite. "I'm sorry I didn't hunt you down and find out what was really wrong. I should've done that, if for no other reason than to be your meddlesome older brother."

Chayse rolled his eyes. "You're only older by fifteen minutes."

"Hey, that means I have fifteen minutes more experience than you."

"Shut up." Chayse laughed as Nik grinned. "So are you gonna move in with Aislynn, too?"

"If she invites me." Nik nodded.

Chayse scoffed. "She'll invite you. She doesn't want to

be without either of us I'm pretty sure."

"What about you, Chayse? You want your brother in your home, too?"

Despite the sarcastic tone to Nik's voice, Chayse thought he heard some yearning under it. *Time to bare it all for my brother.*

"Yeah, I do. I want you there, Nik. I want us to share like we used to." Then he stuck his tongue out to kill the emotional overload. "But I still get my own room."

Nik blinked then laughed. "Fine. I'll just sleep with Aislynn by myself."

"Aw, hell no. I didn't say I'd sleep in my own room, just that I wanted one to myself." He rose from his chair and walked around the desk to stand beside Nik. "I'm sorry, brother."

Nik stood up. "Me, too." He opened his arms and Chayse threw his around him, squeezing tight. *Goddess, I've missed him.*

At last they stood back and smiled at each other. A weight had lifted from Chayse's shoulders he hadn't even realized he'd been carrying. He loved his brother and had missed him more than he knew.

"So you said you had something new on the case?" Nik gestured to Chayse's desk.

"Yeah. We got Hemmings dead to rights. Wanna stay for the interrogation?"

"He's here?" Nik grinned a feral smile. "Fuck yeah. I wanna watch you and Jamison roast the bastard."

CHAPTER TWENTY-ONE

Nik couldn't be more proud of his brother. Chayse might be a part-time idiot when it came to matters of the heart, but he could make a suspect quake in his boots. Paul Hemmings didn't have a chance. Not only did Chayse have all the damning electronic evidence from the Desert Oasis and Eve's Paradise, but he had the bloody windbreaker and a skin sample with Hemmings's DNA on it. But the best part was when Jamison pulled out photographs of the murder weapon, a ball point pen Hemmings had used to stab Johnson in the leg, puncturing the femoral artery.

Game. Set. Match. Nicely done, Chayse.

At that point, Hemmings turned into a raving ball of confession, snarling about his brother-in-law being an abomination with unnatural desires who cheated on his wife with a harlot. Apparently, on the night of the murder, Hemmings had come back into Eve's at the last moment, and saw Johnson as he went through the door to the Underground with the Domme. He made the assumption Johnson was cheating and came back later to confront him. He'd originally planned to beat the living daylights out of Johnson for adultery. But when he found the man suspended from the ceiling in a cage, he'd lost all control and knocked the woman unconscious before stabbing Johnson with the only weapon he had. A pen.

"So it was the salesman, in the dungeon, with the ball point pen." Jamison's quip brought a grin to Nik's face. "I don't think he'll find it nearly as funny as I do."

"Nah, probably not." Chayse shook his head as he signed the last of the paperwork and stuck it in the files with the evidence. "It's up to the lawyers now, but the evidence is pretty damning along with that raving confession he made today." He closed his eyes and rolled his head on his shoulders. "Shit, I'm tired. I'm so glad this case is done."

"Yeah, me too." Jamison nodded. "You guys headed back over to Eve's tonight?"

Nik shared a look with Chayse. "Why do you ask, Jamison?"

The younger detective cast a look behind him before he closed the office door. "You know the owner's assistant, Felicia Amberhall?"

Nik nodded slowly. "Yeah. What about her?"

Jamison blushed, the red glow contrasting starkly with his whiskey-blond hair. "We, uh, kinda hit it off when I was interviewing the staff at the strip club. I'm damn glad this case is over." He shot a guilty look at Chayse. "She was the one I had plans with last night."

"Felicia." Nik's jaw dropped. "You're seeing Lady Aislynn's assistant? The Domme—er, woman who oversees the strip club?"

"Yeah." Jamison frowned. "Why? What's wrong with her?"

"Nothing." Chayse shook his head. "We just didn't think you went for that kind of woman."

"And what kind of woman is she, Wolffe?"

"Hey, not our place to say. If you hit it off with her, go for it." Nik somehow crawled out of his amazement. "I will say this. She's been hurt pretty bad before, so be honest with her from the get-go. Some guys like to hide their shit from her and it doesn't go well. If you're honest, you'll be fine."

"Yeah, okay. That makes sense. So are you going there tonight? Wanna meet for a celebratory beer?"

"Yeah, sounds good, Jamison." Chayse nodded. "We'll meet you there around seven. That work?"

"Yeah. See you there, Wolffes." The younger man grinned and left the office.

"Well, hell." Nik shook his head.

"Yeah, no shit." Chayse shot him a look. "Think he knows she's a vampire?"

"No, I'm pretty sure he doesn't. Think he knows she's a Domme?"

Chayse rubbed his bottom lip with his hand and shrugged. "I didn't know she was a Domme. Guess they'll just have to figure each other out."

"Yeah, I guess so."

"You don't sound convinced." Chayse logged out of his computer.

"Don't you think we should warn him? At least about the Domme aspect?" Nik looked uncharacteristically nervous.

"What good would a warning do? It'd just piss him off and he'd still have to find out for himself, but this time, he'd be angry." Chayse shook his head as he walked around the desk. "Let him find out on his own. Felicia doesn't strike me as a woman who pussyfoots around. They're both adults. Don't be a matchmaking-mama."

"Shut up." But Nik still looked worried.

"I'm headed to my place to pack a bag and pick up my mail. You wanna come with or just meet me at Eve's?" Chayse switched off the light in the office and ushered his brother out the door.

"I'll meet you there. I need to check my messages at my office and get my own clothes." Nik paused, relief showing in his posture. "I'm glad you're done being a jackass. I've missed you, brother."

Chayse snorted to dispel the intense emotion swarming in his chest. "I don't know about being done at jackassery, but I'm done pushing you away. I'll try to remember that the next time the shit hits the fan." He grabbed Nik in a man-hug, slapping his back.

Nik squeezed him tight for a moment then released him, and rubbed his eyes with the back of his hand. Surprise hit Chayse just before the elevator dinged to let them on. *Was he tearing up?* His own throat closed at the rueful smile his brother shot at him and warmth flooded his chest from the renewed twin bond they shared. Damn, it felt good to have it back.

They rode down to the parking garage in companionable silence

"So I'll see you at Eve's." Nik clapped him on the shoulder as the doors opened.

"Yeah, see you there."

Chayse allowed himself to smile as he strode to his car. Things had shifted. The world didn't seem so dark or dangerous. He felt protected and strong for the first time in over five years. Which had everything to do with reconnecting with his brother and bonding to Aislynn. *I'm definitely a jackass.* Understatement of the year.

He braved the Vegas rush hour traffic to get to his apartment and parked outside on the street rather than in his assigned spot. He wouldn't be there long enough to make a difference. When he unlocked his door and let himself into the space, he stopped and looked around.

Pale white walls with no adornment greeted him and brought home exactly how much he'd been only surviving, not living. The rooms held the minimum furniture, most of which had come with the place, and nothing personal. Hell, he didn't even have much dirty laundry to cart off to the laundromat this week.

His life had been pathetic. It wouldn't take much to leave it all behind.

Chayse shook his head and strode to his bedroom to pack most of his clothes in a suitcase. He'd have to see what Aislynn had in mind before he moved everything out and cancelled his lease, but a suitcase full of clothes would do for now. And his Monster High werewolf doll. That went with him everywhere.

He tucked the doll in with his clothes and zipped up the bag, grinning. Jamison had given him such shit for going into the "girls' doll section" of the local store and buying it, but he'd liked the hip look to the doll. And the humans' fascination with werewolves in high school cracked him up. He'd never been so cool in high school.

Chayse took one more look around before he locked the door behind him and headed for the area where they kept the mailboxes. He'd go online and stop or forward the mail as soon as he got settled. *Am I really thinking of making this move permanent?* He didn't know the answer as he pulled the envelopes and junk mail out of his box, but something about it felt right.

He took a cursory glance through the mail, tossing most of the junk offering him new credit cards or payday loans, but his gaze stopped on a cream-colored square envelope. *That looks like a wedding invite.* He frowned and slid open the flap with his finger.

The honor of your presence is requested on May Twentieth at 4:30 pm in the afternoon for the wedding reception of Jayson Guardian Wolffe and Kate Bright Sky Blackamber at the Gitchiegummee Inn in Three Lakes, Michigan.

Chayse damn near dropped the card and all the extra bits of paper accompanying it. *Holy First Canid! Jayson's getting married.*

****

Nik laughed when he saw the incoming call from Chayse. *He must have gotten an invitation, too.*

"Hello?"

"Did you get the invitation?"

"Yep." Nik chuckled. "I guess little brother found himself a mate like we did."

"When was the last time you heard from him?"

"Not since last fall when he said he was bringing a woman home to meet Mom and Dad for Thanksgiving." Nik locked his office and picked up his duffel bag.

Chayse paused on the other end. "Did you go home for that?"

Nik sighed. "No. I was kinda hoping to get in touch with you and didn't want to leave the state in case you called."

"I'm really sorry, Nik."

"Hey, it's in the past. And we got a whole new future to look forward to now." Nik climbed into his truck. "We'll have our own Thanksgiving this year with Aislynn."

"Yeah. Where are you?"

"Just leaving my place, why? Where are you?"

"I'm at the Eve's parking lot. Want me to wait on you?"

Nik considered. It had been five long years since Chayse had even spoken to him before a few days ago. Now he called or texted daily. *Can I afford to be cavalier?*

"Yeah, would you mind? I should be there in about ten minutes max."

"Not a problem. I don't think Jamison is here yet. I'll wait on you both."

"Great. Talk to you in ten."

"Will do."

Nik clicked off his phone and threw his truck in gear. His heart rate jumped with excitement, but he didn't know what he was more excited for; seeing Aislynn or seeing Chayse without them fighting like dogs over a bone. *Maybe a bit of both*. It was good to have his brother back.

He made it to Eve's Paradise in only nine minutes despite the Friday night traffic, and found Chayse parked near the back of the lot with Jamison next to him. The evening's weather had turned mild with the winds down to a soft breeze. The scents of fried food and a hint of rain filled the air as he parked beside Chayse's car and got out.

Jamison had changed from his daily suit to a black fitted t-shirt with a large red heart on the breast pocket, and black jeans under a leather jacket. Chayse wore faded blue jeans and an untucked red button-down shirt under his leather coat. His brother had filled out in the last five years, his shoulders broadening and his arms bulking up. They almost looked like mirror images of each other now.

"Glad you made it. Ready?" Chayse waved at the doors, but the look in his eyes asked a far deeper question.

Nik settled his shoulders in his own leather jacket and nodded. "Yeah. You?"

Chayse nodded. Jamison eyed the two of them thoughtfully, but said nothing as he reached back to grab a bouquet of roses and baby's breath. Nik had to hand it to the guy. He made a damn good detective and knew when to keep his mouth shut.

"Let's do this."

Nik led the way to the doors, keeping an eye out for those patrons rushing to get in for the evening strip shows. Not everyone thought clearly when getting to their visual fix. Once they stepped inside the doors, slow and sultry music thumped through the air as several women on various stages bumped and ground against poles. Nik appreciated their athletic prowess as well as the festive décor filled with balloons and hearts in red and pink.

"Wow."

"Yeah, Felicia did a nice job, didn't she?" Chayse waved them toward the bar.

"Yeah, she did." Jamison scanned the people in the

club, looking for the vampire among them. He held the flowers tightly in his fist.

Nik still wondered if the detective and the vampire were heading for disaster, but Chayse had reminded him it really wasn't his business. Still, he hated to see friends hurt if he could prevent it. He opened his mouth to say something, but Chayse caught his eye and gave a quick shake of his head.

Damn, how does he know what I'm thinking? Chayse's look turned dry as he dropped his chin and raised an eyebrow. *Humph.*

"There she is." Jamison's voice held a note of excitement and they followed his gaze to the door to the upstairs office.

Nik's dick rose in salute and his mouth went dry.

Aislynn stood beside Felicia in a glorious red lace dress. A black satin waist cincher corset gave her the perfect hourglass shape to compliment her lovely breasts. A ruby and diamond necklace dipped between her cleavage damn near making him swallow his tongue. Matching earrings dripped off her lobes beneath the artful up-do of her hair. Tendrils hung on either side of her face and he wanted to tangle his fingers in them.

"Holy shit." Chayse's exclamation mirrored his own feelings.

Both women noticed them at the same time and Nik held back from puffing out his chest and beating it as Aislynn smiled in greeting. She didn't do that enough. *Note to self: encourage her to smile more.*

"You should roll those wolf's tongues back into your mouths, gentlemen, before you come across more like hound dogs." Jamison's remark set off an explosion of surprise and chagrin as the man handed them each a beer. "I propose a toast. To new love and case closed."

"Fuck yeah." Nik clinked bottles with the others, but his gaze never strayed from his Mate as she sauntered across the room to him.

"Love?" Chayse raised an eyebrow at Jamison.

"Yeah, well, it's Valentine's Day, right?" The man shrugged with a little of the red tingeing his cheeks. "Seems like a good time to celebrate love."

Valentine's Day. Nik's eyes widened and he met Chayse's. *Did you get Aislynn a gift?*

Chayse swallowed hard and shook his head. *Fuck.* No wonder Jamison held flowers.

"Good evening, gentlemen. What can we do for Las Vegas's finest?" Aislynn paused beside them and Nik's body came alive. Ever since they'd mated, he knew when she was close enough to fuck and his cock wasn't arguing. "Are there more questions we can answer or are you just having a night out?"

Nik grinned. "I'm not one of Las Vegas's finest, but I'm related to one. Does that count?"

Aislynn hit him with her silver-gray gaze and his cock flexed. "Oh, I'd say you're one of Las Vegas's finest, Mr. Wolffe." Her gaze did the slow meander down his body and back up. "Certainly one of the finest I've seen in a while." Then she fixed her gaze on Jamison. "Detective Jamison, so nice to see you again. Has your case concluded successfully?"

"Yes, ma'am. It has. We caught the man responsible and he'll be going away for a long time."

"That is excellent news. Thank you for all your help."

Jamison smiled and nodded, but blushed when his gaze landed on Felicia. "You're welcome, ma'am. These are for you, Ms. Amberhall."

"Thank you, Detective Jamison." Her sultry smile made the man blush deeper.

Aislynn didn't miss a thing, but she laid a hand on both Nik's and Chayse's arms, squeezing gently as she nodded. The zing of awareness shot to screaming level and Nik's cock insisted on getting some attention.

"I must make the rounds tonight as it's a holiday and I need to be sociable for a short time. Perhaps you gentlemen will join me for a nightcap in a couple of hours." Aislynn switched her gaze between Nik and Chayse.

"Yes, ma'am. We'd be happy to join you." Chayse covered her hand on his arm with his own.

Nik could only nod.

"Excellent. Until then, gentlemen, enjoy your night at Eve's Paradise."

Felicia gave her sultry smile and stopped beside Jamison to whisper something in his ear. Whatever it was made the man shiver and nod with a goofy grin. She patted the flowers and sauntered away with a definite swing in her hips. *Aw hell, the man is caught, hook, line, and sinker.*

Which wasn't too different from how he felt about his Mate.

"Lady Aislynn."

She paused and turned. "Yes?"

"Happy Valentine's Day."

The smile she gave him warmed him from the inside out. "Thank you, Mr. Wolffe." She walked away with an extra sway to her hips, too, and he almost let out a triumphant howl. That woman belonged to him and his brother, and he couldn't be happier.

Well, he could be happier when buried balls-deep in her sweet pussy, but that would come later tonight when they celebrated their love in high style.

Aw, yeah. It's gonna be hot in Vegas tonight.

CHAPTER TWENTY-TWO

Chayse watched his Mate saunter away and mentally smacked himself. How could he have forgotten Valentine's day? *It's not like I didn't see the balloons and streamers the last time I was here.* His mother would be appalled. While he'd never really considered it much of a holiday, especially after Celine, he really wanted to acknowledge the connection he'd made with Aislynn in a tangible way.

He sat back and enjoyed the atmosphere with his brother and his partner for the better part of two hours, but he still hadn't come up with an answer by the time Felicia came back for Jamison.

"Well, gentlemen, I'll bid you good night. I'm going to spend some time with my girl." Jamison set his beer on the bar and stood, shaking Chayse's hand and then his brother's. "Thanks for hanging out and you both have a good night."

"Night, Jamison." Chayse waved.

"Night, Jamison, Felicia." Nik nodded to the lovely vampire and she narrowed her eyes at him, but managed a smile.

"Hey, give her a break, Nik." Chayse punched his arm. "She's a big girl and Jamison is a big boy. They can work it out on their own. No need to play 'big bad guard dog' on this one. Let it go."

"I don't want either of them hurt." Nik shrugged, but Chayse suspected he worried more than he'd admit.

"It's not your call, Nik." Chayse stood up. "What is your call is what we're gonna give Aislynn for Valentine's Day."

"You wanna give her something?" Nik looked like a deer caught in headlights.

"Well, yeah. It's Valentine's Day, jackass."

Nik's brows lowered. "I know that. I'm just wondering what you think you can give a twenty-thousand year old succubus that she doesn't already have."

Chayse opened his mouth to reply, but nothing came out. *What do you give a twenty-thousand year old succubus for Valentine's Day?* Somehow, chocolates and flowers didn't seem to cover it.

"Why don't you try good old fashioned love, gentlemen?" Aislynn appeared at their sides and beamed at them. "Trust me as someone who knows. Love isn't as easy to find as the songs and stories make it out to be."

"I think most humans would agree with you." Nik raised her hand to his lips and kissed it. "My brother and I have a slightly different opinion."

"Oh?" Aislynn raised an eyebrow. "Do tell."

"No, ma'am. I think we should show you." Chayse flipped her other hand over and kissed the palm. "Tonight. Right now, even."

She grinned. "Fortunately for you two, Felicia has agreed to watch the club until midnight, but I promised her she could have some time with her beau after that. Would that be amenable to you?"

Chayse checked his watch and raised his eyebrows at his brother. "That gives us about three hours. That long enough for you, Nik?"

"Not by half." His brother winked. "But I guess for

tonight it'll have to do and we'll make it up tomorrow and the next night and the night after that."

She laughed. "If you can keep that kind of schedule up."

"Is that a challenge, sweetheart?" Chayse wrapped an arm around her waist and tugged her against his side.

"Maybe." She winked and his heart fluttered with joy. He'd never seen Aislynn so playful and he liked this side of her a lot. Her energy seemed lighter and he reveled in it.

"Maybe you'll let us walk you home, Lady Aislynn." Nik held out his arm for her to tuck it through.

She grinned. "Like an old fashioned date?"

"It is Valentine's Day."

She blinked and lost a little of her smile. "I don't think I've been on a date in centuries."

The regret in her voice boosted Chayse's need to pamper her a little. "Then let us take care of you tonight, Luna. Let us show you all the love you deserve."

Her gaze met his and something within them softened with gratitude. Chayse's heart swelled and he resisted the urge to strut around like the Alpha. Instead, he waited for her to nod and gestured for his brother to lead her toward the Underground door with the djinn bouncer.

At the door, the turbaned man bowed low. "Good evening, Lady Aislynn."

"Good evening, Suresh. These two gentlemen are my lovers, Nik and Chayse. They are free to come and go at any time. Is that clear?" Aislynn's voice remained light and polite, but a core of steel ran underneath.

The djinn's gaze met Chayse's then moved to Nik's, and his chin rose and fell in understanding. "Of course, Lady Aislynn. It is my honor to meet such worthy gentlemen." And he gave an elegant sweeping bow.

Chayse resisted the urge to bow in return, but he inclined his head instead. Nik did the same. Neither of them wanted to piss off a djinn. Touching, even a handshake without being invited, was a huge no-no.

"Excellent. Thank you again for your service. Your efforts keep us all safe." She nodded as he opened the door for her, and he blushed a little under his rich skin.

"Again, it's my honor, Lady Aislynn."

They filed past him and Chayse hid a smile. Djinn were proud beings, easily offended and had long memories, but they also had large egos. Aislynn may or may not have meant her compliment, but it would ensure the djinn's service for as long as she needed it.

"Nice choice in bouncer, kit." Nik's voice held admiration and amusement. "Unassuming, yet powerful."

She gave him a smug smile. "I like to keep a low profile. We haven't had any problems yet, but tonight is Friday and some of the young cocks think the whole place is open to them when they get a little alcohol into them."

Chayse snorted. "Yeah, that happens a lot around Vegas on Fridays and Saturdays."

"I imagine the police are extra busy on those nights." She opened the door to her apartments and strode through, Chayse and Nik hanging back just enough to watch her ass in her lacy dress.

"Holy shit, I don't think she's wearing anything under it." Chayse almost swallowed his tongue.

"I'm pretty sure she's not." Nik shook his head before leaning closer. "Did I hear you call her 'Luna'?"

"Yeah." He swallowed against his unease. "She's, uh, well, she's the Alpha female of my heart. It seemed to fit."

"Yeah, I guess it does." Nik nodded as he strode beside Chayse into the apartments. "I got to say, it's good to see you over your addiction."

Chayse shook his head. "I'm not over my addiction, I just trust Aislynn. I'll always be uneasy around other succubae."

Aislynn paused beside a door he'd never seen before and waited for them to catch up. She brushed a hand over

Chayse's chest before sliding it down the door.

"This is your room to do with as you please, Chayse."
She gave him a warm smile. "When I had this place built, I
didn't know why it seemed so necessary to have two more
rooms attached to my bedroom, but I had a gut feeling I'd
need them. Now I know why. This one is for you. There is
a connecting door that can only be locked from my side."

She opened the door and flipped on the lights. The
scent of lavender-flavored cleaner hit Chayse's nose as he
took in the room. Simply furnished with a desk, chair, and a
queen-sized bed without coverings met his gaze. The head
and footboards had been made out of pine boles, giving the
bed a rustic look.

"So you were serious about me staying." It wasn't
really a question.

"Yes. I want you close." She shot a look at Nik. "Both
of you. There's another room on the other side for you,
Nik. It's the mirror image of this one and has even less
décor. I wasn't sure you'd want to move in because I know
you have your own place, but nevertheless…"

She looked so uncertain, Chayse almost gathered her
into his arms, but Nik made the first move.

"I want the space, kit. It's perfect for me. We'll move
some of my things into it this weekend." He squeezed her,
the love they shared visible in their embrace. "Thank you."

Chayse's throat closed at the ease of their affection, and
he rubbed the back of his neck as he stepped deeper into the
room, ostensibly to look around. Maybe someday he'd be
able to have the same easy connection his brother and mate
shared. *Damn you, Celine, to hell and back.*

He almost jumped when arms wrapped around his waist
from behind and Aislynn's warm body pressed against his
back. He stiffened at first, unprepared for the intimacy, but
slowly relaxed into her embrace.

"You're not second-best to me, Chayse."

Her quiet words eased some of his fears. "I'm the

broken one, though."

"No, not broken, just wounded. Trust doesn't come overnight."

"It should." He buried the growl as his hands fisted. "You're my Mate, the one person beyond my twin who I should trust more than anyone. But past experience—"

"Has taught you to be wary." Aislynn pulled back and turned him to face her. Her silver-gray eyes showed tenderness and patience. "These rooms are mostly for you so I can earn your trust, but you still have a place to escape to. Like I told you when you first visited me here, this is a sanctuary, a place for retreat and recuperation. What was done to you is inexcusable, but my goal is to help you out of that place, and give you safety and love."

Chayse swallowed hard. "I definitely don't want to be there anymore."

"Hey, remember what I said? New travel destinations."

He opened his mouth to ask what she was talking about when it clicked. *No wallowing in self-pity.* He huffed a rueful laugh and nodded. "Right. I'll work on my itinerary."

The brilliant smile she gave him warmed his heart. "Very good. Now." She turned and gestured for Nik to precede them out of the room. "I'm very interested in enjoying my mates to celebrate Valentine's Day. So gentlemen, let's go to bed."

CHAPTER TWENTY-THREE

Aislynn breathed an internal sigh of relief. She didn't want Chayse revisiting his old regrets and fears. Not tonight. Not when she had both of her wolves with her. Granted, she'd be working on restoring Chayse's faith and truth for a long time, but tonight she didn't want to master him. She just wanted to share in their love and feel their mutual connection.

Let's hope it's not too much to ask for.

They left Chayse's personal space behind and retreated to her bedroom. She'd prepared all afternoon to make it welcoming to her wolves. Candles flickered like twinkling stars and a bucket full of chilled bottles of water sat beside a table covered in rose petals and chocolates. Both wolves paused to take in the warm lighting and romantic atmosphere, and she watched them, trying to guess their reactions.

"Wow." Nik stopped just inside her bedroom, his eyes wide. "This place looks great."

Chayse pushed past him, inhaling deeply. "I love the smell of roses." He shivered and Aislynn mentally fist-pumped. "How did you know?"

She shook her head as she closed the door. "I didn't,

but I had the strongest gut feeling to make sure we had roses tonight. I'm glad I listened."

Nik rumbled a sexy laugh. "You do know roses are a werewolf aphrodisiac, right?"

"They are?" Now she grinned. "I didn't, but I'll remember from now on."

"Good." He wrapped his arms around her and nuzzled her neck. "Because now I want to show you just how hot they make me."

Aislynn wanted to melt into his embrace as he licked the skin below her ear, spearing his hands in to her hair. *No, I gotta resist or I won't get what I want tonight.* She groaned in protest when his hands slid down her back and grabbed her ass through the lacy skirt. Each touch was designed to break her resolve, but she wouldn't be deterred.

"You're a very sneaky man, Nik Wolffe, but I'm not falling for this." She stepped back and gestured imperiously. "On the bed with you. Now."

He chuckled and headed for the bed while Chayse grinned impishly.

"Don't laugh at him, Chayse. You, too. Sit on the bed. I want to see you two side-by-side."

Her blond lover grinned, but joined Nik on the bed. Both crossed their arms over their chests and raised damn near identical eyebrows at her. She gave them her best serene smile to hide her amusement over their similarities.

"Gentlemen, how am I to truly appreciate you when you're still dressed?" She *tsked* and shook her head. "Clothing. Off. Now."

While they laughed and stood, she retrieved a chair to seat herself in front of the bed and watch her men disrobe. She settled herself primly, employing all her Domme abilities to keep the delighted grin off her face as she wove her fingers together and set them on her knees.

Nik and Chayse assessed her as much as she did them, but they didn't fight her command. Their shirts came off first and Aislynn almost forgot to breathe.

Both men had the same broad shoulders and tall frames, but where Nik was barrel-chested, Chayse was lithe and lean. Both men had chest and belly hair which made her mouth water. Goddess, she loved hair on men and how it outlined the lovely muscles gracing their bodies.

When their pants came off, her excitement rose and she had to take some calming breaths. She'd seen both men naked, but having them side by side to enjoy made her heart flutter.

"Oh, my."

Nik's lips curled into a half-smile. "See something you like, Aislynn?"

"Oh, yes, my dear dark wolf. Please sit on the bed beside your brother. Hip to shoulder."

Chayse's brows went up, but he tossed his pants onto another chair and settled on the bed next to Nik. "Like this?"

"Yes, perfect."

She stood and paced toward them, her gaze studying their forms. Both their cocks rose to point at her as if begging for her to taste them. *And taste them I shall.* Both of them reached nearly to their navels, but Nik's was thicker, and had a delightful curve. Chayse's shaft stood straight and slender like the man himself.

She stopped in front of them and knelt down. "Absolutely perfect." She smiled and glanced up at them as she took a cock in each hand. "I'm of the mind to suck cock, gentlemen. Both of you at the same time. It's been a fantasy of mine and I've never been able to fulfill it."

Chayse shuddered as she stroked him, but still managed to find his voice. "Why never?"

She shrugged, focusing on the hot, smooth texture of his shaft. "Too dangerous. It was hard enough to keep my focus with only one partner. Having two at once would've ensured their deaths."

The edges of her mouth turned down as the ancient guilt and sorrow rose, but before it could take over, Nik had grasped her chin and turned her head to him.

"We're not like them, Aislynn." He rubbed her cheek with his thumb. "We're your mates, and are bound to you. We won't die from making love with you."

"I know. I remember. Thank you, Nik." She smiled at him.

"Sounds like I'm not the only one who needs new destinations." Chayse leaned forward and kissed her forehead. "We'll find new places to go together, okay?"

"Yes, okay, Chayse."

Their concern and determination touched her heart, but she didn't want to be mushy tonight. Or at least not until much later. She wanted to be sultry, sexy, and lustful. She wanted sensation rather than sentiment. Shoving her concerns into a box, she smiled at them both as she tightened her grips on their cocks.

Both men moaned in concert.

"Tonight, my dear wolves, I'm going to enjoy your hard cocks and sexy bodies. You're mine, and as such, I will pleasure you as much as I can."

She met Nik's gaze as she fitted her mouth over the head of his cock, her left hand still stroking Chayse. Nik's green eyes blazed with feral lust and he inhaled deeply as she sank down on the shaft. His thick dick filled her mouth, tantalizing her with his musky taste. His pre-cum had a sharp tang, like Mexican beer with lime, yet it went down smooth and tempted her for more.

"Oh, fuck, yeah, kit. Suck my cock." Nik threw his head back and growled deep in his throat. It electrified her, but she couldn't neglect her other lovely mate.

She slowly pulled off Nik's shaft and replaced her mouth with her hand as she shifted her stance to lean over Chayse's lap. His cock stood rock-hard in her hand, pre-cum leaking from the tip each time she massaged up its length. She shot him an anticipatory smile and licked her lips.

"I need to taste your cock, Chayse."

"Chewed bones, it's yours, Aislynn." Intensity tightened his expression and his voice betrayed his strain. "Suck my dick like you did my brother's."

She didn't need to be asked twice. But she wouldn't suck him like Nik. Each man was different and she'd treat them accordingly. Instead of sliding his shaft into her mouth, she sipped the tip, trailing her tongue over the head and into the slit. Chayse whimpered and his cock flexed as she made ever-widening circles around him until she spiraled down to the base of shaft.

"Sweet Goddess!" Chayse's exclamation came with a jerk of his hips and she almost gagged on the long appendage.

She pulled back enough to savor the taste of him on her tongue. While he had undertones similiar to his brother's, Chayse's pre-cum was sweeter, more like the sweet and sour sauce found in Chinese restaurants. Her mouth watered with the tart sweetness and she drove back down on him, sucking his arousal to taste more.

While she tortured Chayse, Nik leaned forward over her hand stroking his shaft to run his palms down her back to her hem. He gathered the skirt of her dress and pulled it up to expose her ass to the cooler air of the room. One hand dipped lower and skimmed her nether lips. She gasped around Chayse's cock as Nik groaned in approval.

"Oh, fuck yeah. Our little succubus likes sucking cock. She's so fuckin' wet, I could drink from her pussy."

His words sent more cream to her core and she wiggled her hips as she swallowed around Chayse.

"Damn, you've got a mouth on you, Aislynn." Chayse moaned and his fist tightened in her hair. "Fuck, that feels so damn good."

His cock hardened in her mouth and she knew he was

close, so she pulled off him and switched back to his thicker brother. They both whimpered, Chayse from losing her mouth, Nik from gaining, and she hummed her pleasure as Chayse's hands took over where Nik's left off. Her blond wolf inserted two fingers into her slick slit and she keened around Nik's shaft.

"Fuck, what did you do, Chayse?" Nik growled as Aislynn tightened her lips around his cockhead. "She's sucking me so damn good."

"I'm teasing her pussy and she's so tight and wet." Chayse sighed as her grip on him tightened. "Damn, she knows what she's doing, but she's wearing too many clothes."

Aislynn couldn't see around Nik's thigh, but the laces of her corset loosened as Chayse pulled them open. He would've tugged the laces free if she hadn't sat up, releasing Nik from her mouth.

He stood before she could protest and moved around behind her.

"Ah, Nik, wait—"

"Don't worry, Kit. We need to get you undressed first. It's been too long since I've seen your naked body." He grinned as he reached around her belly to unhook the clasps of the corset. "Damn, this is so sexy on you. Maybe next time you can wear this and nothing else but heels."

"Just the corset?" She raised her eyebrows as she continued to massage Chayse's cock with her fingers.

"Oh hell yeah." Nik tossed the garment away before he returned to unzip her lace dress. "This dress is pretty hot, too. I think my favorite part of your outfit is that you're not wearing anything under it."

She had to let go of Chayse to allow them to peel the dress off her, and they both sighed when her breasts became visible. Nik dropped to his knees beside her, his cock bobbing against her hip as he latched onto her breast. Hot, tight pleasure unfurled in her belly as he sucked on her taut nipple. He held her close with one hand on her hip and rubbed his tip through the hair on her mound.

When he dropped his other hand to her pussy and slid his fingers between her slick lips, she whimpered and he swore.

"Fuck, she's so wet."

"But I want to suck cock." She'd never sounded so petulant in her life.

Nik growled, but a grin stretched his lips. "That's fine, kit. You suck Chayse's cock while I fuck your pussy."

"But I want to suck your cock, too, Nik. It's my fantasy."

"Aw, hell, Nik. You can't kill that." Chayse rubbed his cock with one hand to keep it beautifully stiff and she wanted to latch back on.

"I want you to suck my cock more, Aislynn, but not at the expense of your pleasure. This makes sure we all get some."

He shifted behind her as he pushed her back down into Chayse's lap. Chayse's cock brushed her cheek and she couldn't help but swipe at it with her tongue.

"Naughty minx." Chayse grinned down at her.

"You have no idea." She winked and he shivered before she looked over her shoulder at Nik. He stroked his thick shaft, his green gaze fixed on her weeping pussy. "I won't argue with a good fucking, Nik, but just be aware when fucking a succubus, their lovers are able to come more than once. It's simply the nature of a succubus's magic."

"Oh yeah?" Nik grinned. "I think we should test the theory."

Before she should protest, he thrust his cock deep in her pussy until his hips rested against her ass.

"Holy First Canid, you're better than I remember."

And better than she remembered. She closed her eyes briefly to savor the feeling of his hard shaft deep in her body. Goddess, she felt so full. But the memory of sweet and sour pre-cum lured her back to the long slender cock in front of her and she grasped Chayse's shaft before meeting his turquoise gaze.

"Now comes the fun part." She grinned before settling her lips around his cockhead and licked the flavorful juices off the shaft where they'd run.

He gasped as she hummed her delight, her pussy squeezing down on Nik's cock in approval.

"Oh, hell yeah, kit. Squeeze my dick." Nik gripped her hips and slowly pulled his shaft from her body, only to push back in just as slow. "I'm gonna fuck you slow until you can't take it anymore and come all over my balls."

His dirty words made her whimper and swallow hard around Chayse's shaft. His hands tightened in her hair again as he pulled out of her mouth then pushed back in.

"Holy shit, Aislynn. Your mouth feels so damn good. Suck me harder, sweetheart."

She was only too happy to oblige. His sweet tangy taste filled her mouth as she reveled in the texture of his skin. Hot and smooth, she slurped with happy abandon, so pleased to offer him pleasure.

Then Nik moved again.

Searing pleasure ricocheted through her from her pussy to her head and back, and she paused in her perusal of Chayse's cock to enjoy Nik's. *Goddess, it's been so long since I've enjoyed two men at once.* Millennia. She clamped her inner muscles down on her dark wolf and he groaned with pleasure. Chayse growled and pulled out of her mouth again, his blue eyes glowing with arousal.

"Don't forget to suck me, Aislynn. I know my brother is driving you crazy with that thick dick of his, but it's your chance to drive me crazy enough to come down your throat." He stroked her face with his fingers. "Do you want that?"

She moaned in assent and he smiled a feral grin.

"Then suck me while he fucks you."

She tightened her lips as Nik moved, rocking her onto Chayse's cock with each forward thrust. She tried to keep her attention on the hot shaft in her mouth, but the one in her pussy stole her attention. She drowned in the overwhelming pleasure of the thick shaft spearing her body, and her clit warned her she'd lose control each time Nik dragged past it.

To hold out just a little longer, Aislynn focused on the lovely flesh in her mouth and used one hand to caress the taut balls hanging beneath it. She swallowed each time Chayse pushed some pre-cum through the slit and reveled in the rich flavor of him. Skimming her tongue over the shaft, she tightened her lips and pulled back until her teeth scraped the edge of his cockhead.

"Oh, fuck, she's gonna make me...I can't hold back, Nik." Chayse threw his head back and thrust harder between her lips.

"It's time to come, kit." Nik's voice threw rough and he reached around her hip to strum her clit. "Come for me."

Her orgasm hit her with the suddenness of a freight train, barreling through her without her say-so. She warbled around Chayse's shaft as he shot down her throat, the hot, tangy cum filling her mouth with deliciousness. Nik roared behind her, thrusting harder as he poured his cum into her pussy, heating her from the inside out. She launched out among the stars, bright lights and bliss following her in a comet's trail of glittering ecstasy.

Nik gently extracted himself from her clenching slit and Chayse's spent cock slipped from her mouth as her dark wolf gathered her into his arms. But instead of relaxing her, their orgasms awakened the hungry sex demon within her, and she knew she needed more.

"Oh, sweet Goddess." Chayse's breathless voice made her open her eyes. He looked sated and content. "That's the best blow job I've ever had." He rubbed his cock, still hard and rosy from her mouth.

"Yeah?" Nik remarked from her other side. "It looks like you still want more, though."

"Yeah, that's what's weird. I'm satisfied, yet still fuckin' horny." Chayse met Aislynn's gaze. "And I think I'm not the only one. Do you want more of this cock, sweetheart?"

Her avarice must have shown on her face, because he laughed when she licked her lips and nodded. "Oh yes, my dear, golden wolf. I want to ride your cock into the Las Vegas sunset."

"Hot damn."

"What about my poor cock? I came hard, but I still want more." Nik's expression held a mixture of arousal and surprise.

"I told you you'd be able to come more than once. That's the nature of this beast right here." She grinned and the men in her bed shivered. "And I want more, so much more, Nik. I want you and your brother together, fucking me for all you're worth."

"Holy shit. Do you mean a double penetration?" Nik's eyes widened.

"I do."

She swore his eyes rolled back in his head as he shivered again, but he opened them and lust burned beneath the irises. "Where's the lube, kit?"

"On the table there."

She turned her attention to Chayse as Nik left the bed for a moment. His cock had risen to full mast and he watched her with desire tightening his nipples. She leaned forward and brushed one hand over his chest, enjoying the crisp hair against her palm as she rubbed the hard nub.

"You're so sexy like this, Chayse. My lovely golden wolf. And this." She dropped her hand down his belly to where his shaft rose, eager for petting. "I'm going to ride this until you howl my name. You're mine and I'm keeping you forever."

For a moment, Chayse's expression froze and she wished she could take the words back. *Are you stupid? Don't panic him.* But his cock jerked in her hand and the lust flared in his cerulean eyes, easing her concern.

"Master Kindle said you were the cure."

"What?"

Chayse sat up and took her face in his hands, staring down at her from inches away. "Master Kindle, my *Morukai* healer, said you were the cure for my addiction. I have no reason to doubt him, so being kept by you, Aislynn, is exactly what I want." He leaned forward and kissed her soundly, sending the flames of arousal roaring within her. "Now, when you're ready, I want you to ride me hard."

Relief, love, and erotic need mixed in a heady combination and she whimpered as she sucked on one of his nipples. *Goddess, I'm so lucky to have him. Thank you.*

Nik returned to the bed with the lube and growled with approval as he ran a hand between her legs. "Damn, kit, you're still so wet." When he tickled her clit, her pussy squeezed in pleasure and some of his cum slid down her thighs in a physical erotic memory.

Before she could do anything, Nik ducked his head between her thighs and licked her nether lips, cleaning her pussy with his dexterous tongue.

"Oh, sweet Goddess." She hadn't felt anything quite so luxurious in years.

Nik pleasured her pussy and clit with his tongue, working her arousal up to a screaming pitch as she laid her face against Chayse's belly. His own cock rubbed her lips and nose as Nik worked her close, only to back off at the last moment.

"Now, climb on Chayse's cock and show me that tight ass."

She whimpered at the sound of rough arousal in his voice and climbed over Chayse's prone form. He smiled at her and held his cock up for easy placement as she straddled his waist.

"Come ride my cock, Aislynn, and let me pleasure you."

She sank down on his long shaft and they both moaned their pleasure.

"Fuck, you're so damn tight."

"And about to get tighter." Nik crawled onto the bed and reached between her legs to caress her puckered hole.

The lube was cold as compared to her heated flesh and she squeaked a little when it hit her skin. The squeak turned into a purr as he massaged the space between her ass and her pussy, rubbing against Chayse's hard cock buried in her.

"It sounds like our little succubus likes this kind of treatment." Chayse's voice rumbled through her body.

"Let's give her more to enjoy." Nik pushed a finger into her ass and she lost the ability to breathe for a moment.

She'd done anal before, but it had been awhile and her body clamped down on his finger even as she tried to relax.

"Easy, kit. Push out against me now." He rubbed and pushed gently as she bore down on his finger.

Chayse groaned. "Damn. That's gonna make my eyes roll back in my head."

Nik snorted. "That's only one finger. What are you gonna do when my cock's in there, little brother?"

"Come, I 'spect." Chayse winked at Aislynn and she giggled, which made him groan again. "Oh, Goddess."

Nik chose that moment to insert a second finger and scissor them apart to stretch her ass. Pleasure and pain mixed, and she tightened her muscles despite Nik's coaxing words.

"Holy shit, Nik. She's got a helluva grip on my cock when you do that."

"How are you doing, kit?"

Aislynn whimpered and wiggled her hips, squeezing

her eyes tight. "It's...uncomfortable."

"Give it a moment and relax for me."

She tried, focusing on deep breaths and relaxing the muscles of her hips and pussy. The temptation to clamp down when Chayse's cock flexed inside her and Nik's fingers moved almost proved too much, but she forced herself not to respond.

"Good, kit. I think you're ready." Nik gently removed his fingers and she heard him smear more lube on his cock. "How about you, Chayse? You ready for this again?"

"Hell yeah. Aislynn, look at me."

She opened her eyes to meet his clear, blue gaze. "If it ever gets too much, say something, and we'll stop. We want to share you, but there are other ways, all right?"

She smiled. "You're very sweet, Chayse. I've done this before. It's just been a very long time."

"I don't think I want to know how long." He gave her a lopsided smile. "We'll still take it slow."

"Ready, kit?" Nik pressed the end of his lubed cock against her puckered hole.

Aislynn nodded. "Please, Nik."

"All right. Push back on me." He slowly inserted his thick head against her ass.

The stretch wasn't too bad until the flared edge of his cockhead hit the ring of muscle, and she couldn't hold back the mewl of pain. Nik stopped and Chayse rubbed the sides of her breasts with his palms. Nik waited, giving her a chance to get used to him then pushed in some more. With a subtle pop, the head of his cock slipped inside her ass.

"Oh, Goddess." Aislynn breathed deeply, trying to pass the point of pain to the pleasure. She didn't always reach the latter, but the discomfort finally eased into a pleasant burn, and she sighed.

"All right, kit?"

"Yes. More please."

"The lady asked for more." The strain in Nik's voice

accompanied the slow advance of his slick cock in her tight hole, and she squeaked as he pushed another inch in.

"Dear Goddess, you're big." She had never been so full and took a deep breath as if it would give her more space for his thick shaft.

"Almost there, kit. Do you want more?"

She sat on Chayse's cock as he stroked her breasts and tried to breathe around the tightness in her pussy and ass. *Good glory, how am I going to take them both?* She'd had double penetrations before, but the men had been smaller. *Lucky me, I get lovers who have no worry about their size.*

At last the burn settled again and she forced her muscles to relax once more. "Yes, I'm ready for more."

"Thank the Goddess." Nik's obvious relief made her chuckle, but it turned into a moan as he seated himself balls-deep in her ass.

Dear Goddess, I've never been so full. Somehow her body accommodated the two long cocks of her lovers, but she couldn't move. Everything had become hypersensitive—her pussy, her ass, her breasts, and her skin. Nik gripped her hips and bent over her back, his lips brushing her shoulder blades.

"Are you ready for us to move, sweetheart?" Chayse pressed a kiss to her forehead and his cock flexed in her core, setting off all sorts of erotic ripples.

"Yes, I think so. Just start slowly, please. It's been a long time since I've done this."

"Slowly, it is." Chayse nodded and flexed his hips, sliding his cock out of her tight grip.

With Nik's cock in her ass, her lips had stretched and her clit protruded enough to drag along Chayse's shaft as he moved. The pleasure jolting through her lit fires that had been smoldering after her last orgasm. When Chayse reversed his motion and pushed back in, Nik retreated from her ass until only his cockhead remained inside. Then he moved forward.

"Oh. Dear. Goddess."

They alternated thrusts in slow, careful slides, and Aislynn's mind filled with bliss. All she could do was ride out the pleasure they provided. Each thrust by Chayse wound the spring of her orgasm tighter matched only by Nik's retreat from her ass. When Nik slid back into her and Chayse pulled almost all the way out of her pussy, the burn from Nik's shaft stoked her erotic fires.

The alternating pattern seemed to go on and on, the advancing and retreating of their cocks pushing her higher and higher until the pleasure hit its apex and she clamped down hard on both of them.

"Oh, fuck, I'm gonna come. Holy shit!" Chayse arched and thrust hard into her pussy, his teeth bared as he filled her core with hot cum.

"Oh hell yeah. Come for us, Aislynn." Nik shouted his pleasure as he hit his release, pouring his cum into her ass.

The combination of their orgasms and explosion of sexual energy pushed her arousal higher until she shot into an excruciating release. Aislynn almost burst with the overwhelming pleasure, her inner sex demon gorging on the feast of their offerings. She reveled in the waves of bliss pouring through her until two sets of teeth hit her shoulders.

Nik and Chayse sank their canines into her shoulder muscles and she launched into another orgasm. The men's moans around her kept the pleasure going, fueling her ecstasy. Before she'd come down completely she dropped a swak Chayse's chest over his left nipple. Her golden wolf threw back his head and howled, making her shiver.

When Nik leaned his chest against her back, she turned her head and laid a swak on his nearest biceps. He let loose his own howl, the combination of their voices creating a beautiful chorus she'd remember forever. The swaks marked her mates as hers and hers alone, shimmering silver in the soft light. They couldn't be seen by humans, but the

Elder Races would know, and more importantly, any other succubae would know.

At last they all came down from their respective releases and lay in an exhausted, sweaty heap on her bed. None of them seemed inclined to move, and Aislynn reveled in being sandwiched between her two lovely wolves. *Light and dark, like the sides of the moon.*

Without a word, Nik pulled free from her body and retreated to her bathroom. She heard the water running, but couldn't bring herself to move off of Chayse's lovely body.

"Are you satisfied, Luna?" His voice rumbled under her ear.

"Oh, yes, Chayse. I've never been more so." She lifted herself off his cock and snuggled up to his side, wrapping one arm around his belly. "You're mine and I'm never giving you up."

Nik returned and smiled down at them before he used a warm wash cloth to clean her tenderly. He retreated to the bathroom once more to refresh the wash cloth before returning to the bed to hand it to Chayse.

"Allow me." She took it out of his hand and gently swiped it over his cock and balls, cleaning all the evidence of their mutual releases from his skin. "There. Better?"

"Yes, Luna."

She grinned and tossed the rag across the room into her dirty clothes hamper.

"Damn, sweetheart, nice shot." Nik laughed as he pulled the duvet off the bed so they could crawl under the covers.

"I've had a lot of practice from the bed. Sometimes I'm too lazy to get up. It meant I needed to be accurate."

Chayse lay back and opened his arms to her. "Come to bed, my sweet succubus. Rest your head on my chest."

Aislynn crawled in beside him and snuggled against his side, wrapping her right arm over his waist. Nik slid in behind her, tugging the covers up over them all. He tucked his right hand up between her and Chayse, grasping her left hand. She held it against her heart and smiled as she closed her eyes. This was where she wanted to be, always. Snuggled between her two wolves.

"I love you, Nik and Chayse. Stay with me, all night, every night."

"I'm yours, Luna." Chayse pressed a kiss to her forehead and tightened his hand on her arm.

"You're mine, kit." Nik kissed her cheek beside her ear. "We're not going anywhere."

"Good."

She smiled and closed her eyes, content for the first time in millennia. Everyone deserved a second chance at love, even the original succubus. She succumbed to her exhaustion, safe and cradled in the arms of her wolves.

THE END

AUTHOR'S NOTE
ABOUT SECOND CHANCE SUCCUBUS

You can find out how Aislynn helped the LVMPD the first time in BRONCO'S ROUGH RIDE, Book 0.5 in the Bad Boys of Beta Squad series.

Siobhan

BRONCO'S ROUGH RIDE
BAD BOYS OF BETA SQUAD, BOOK 0.5
SNEEK PEEK

What happens in Vegas, stays in the heart...

Chief Petty Officer John "Bronco" Andrews only meant to stay one night in Vegas for a little R&R before resuming his duties as a US Navy SEAL in Coronado. But someone slips him a mickey in the bar and he finds himself in Madame LeBeau's sex trade. As the product. Doped up on ketamine to keep him docile, Bronco has no choice but to let it ride.

Detective Lindsey Jarvis has been undercover in LeBeau's sex slave racket for two years and she almost has enough evidence to take it down. Between abduction, prostitution, and murder, she has LeBeau by the short hairs. All she needs is a "product". John is the perfect witness if she can get him out before the drugs shut down his heart. Then she'll be free to start a normal life.

Lindsey doesn't count on her overwhelming attraction for Bronco or her need to see him through detox. But she's a cop in Vegas and he's a Navy SEAL, two lifestyles with too much unpredictability to maintain a relationship. Neither have time for more than one wild rough ride, and what happens in Vegas, stays. Forever.

OTHER BOOKS BY SIOBHAN MUIR

Her Devoted Vampire (from Three Lakes Books)
Queen Bitch of the Callowwood Pack (Three Lakes Books)
Second Chance Succubus (from Three Lakes Books)
Darwin's Evolution (from Amazon)

Cloudburst Colorado Series
A Hell Hound's Fire (from Three Lakes Books)
The Beltane Witch (from Three Lakes Books)
Christmas I.C.E. Magic (from Three Lakes Books)
Cloudburst Ice Magic (from Three Lakes Books)

Rifts Series
Take the Reins (from Three Lakes Books)
A Centaur's Solstice Wish (from Three Lakes Books)
In Death's Shadow (from Three Lakes Books)

Bad Boys of Beta Squad Series
Bronco's Rough Ride (from Three Lakes Books)
The Navy's Ghost (from Three Lakes Books)
Rimshot's Hard Target (from Amazon)
Bam-Bam's Inked Hart (from Three Lakes Books)

Elemental Hearts Series

Wildfire's Heart (from Three Lakes Books)

The Ivory Road

A Walk in the Sand (from Three Lakes Books)

Outback Dreams (from Three Lakes Books)

Triple Star Ranch Series

Rope a Falling Star (from Three Lakes Books

Star Light, Star Bright (from Three Lakes Books)

Warbler Peninsula Series

Order of the Dragon (from Three Lakes Books)

The Valkyrie's Sword (from Three Lakes Books)

Coming Soon

Deli's Take Out (Bad Boys of Beta Squad #4)

Cloudburst Coffee & Spa (Cloudburst Colorado #5)

Loch'd Hearts (Elemental Hearts #2)

ABOUT THE AUTHOR

Siobhan Muir lives in Cheyenne, Wyoming, with her husband, two daughters, and a vegetarian cat she swears is a shape-shifter, though he's never shifted when she can see him. When not writing, she can be found looking down a microscope at fossil fox teeth, pursuing her other love, paleontology. An avid reader of science fiction/fantasy, her husband gave her a paranormal romance for Christmas one year, and she was hooked for good.

In previous lives, Siobhan has been an actor at the Colorado Renaissance Festival, a field geologist in the Aleutian Islands, and restored inter-planetary imagery at the USGS. She's hiked to the top of Mount St. Helens and to the bottom of Meteor Crater.

Siobhan writes kick-ass adventure with hot sex for men and women to enjoy. She believes in happily ever after, redemption, and communication, all of which you will find in her paranormal romance stories.

Connect with Siobhan online at:

http://siobhanmuir.com
http://www.facebook.com/siobhan.muir.35
http://twitter.com/SiobhanMuir
http://siobhanmuir.com/siobhans-blog
http://pinterest.com/siobhanmuir.35